RAVE REVIEWS FOR THE DEBUT OF AUDREY PETERSON'S

CLAIRE CAMDEN MYSTERY SERIES!

Books by Audrey Peterson

The Nocturne Murder
Death in Wessex
Murder in Burgundy
Elegy in a Country Graveyard
Lament for Christabel
Dartmoor Burial
Death Too Soon

Published by POCKET BOOKS

DEATH TOO SOON

AUDREY PETERSON

POCKET BOOKS

New York London Toronto Sydney Tokyo Singapore

An *Original* Publication of POCKET BOOKS

POCKET BOOKS, a division of Simon & Schuster Inc.
1230 Avenue of the Americas, New York, NY 10020

Copyright © 1994 by Audrey Peterson

ISBN: 0-671-79509-0

First Pocket Books printing July 1994

10 9 8 7 6 5 4 3 2 1

POCKET and colophon are registered trademarks of Simon & Schuster Inc.

Cover art by Kye Carbone

Printed in the U.S.A.

To Barbara and Phil Buckland

Thy brother Death came, and cried,
"Wouldst thou me?" . . .
Death will come when thou art dead,
Soon, too soon— . . .
—Percy Bysshe Shelley, "To Night"

DEATH TOO SOON

Chapter

1

THE KILLER LOOKED down at his victim, running his hand along the smooth skin of her arm. The heavy pounding of his heart had slowed, once he was sure she was dead. In the dim light, the marks around her throat were scarcely visible.

The day had begun like any other, except for a kind of tingling in his hands and those quick thumping beats in his chest. Then it was there: a wild, strange craving he couldn't drive away.

It had been easy enough to find his victim, and once he had decided where to hide the body, it would be all over.

But first, there was something important to do.

Slowly, he reached into his pocket and drew out the folded knife, opened its blade, and bent over the body.

Chapter

2

SPENDING A COUPLE OF MONTHS in Devon at the home of Bea Camden, her ex-mother-in-law, sounded fine to Claire Camden. While Bea was off with an old school friend on a cruise to sunnier climes, Claire could have her house in Morbridge, a village on the edge of Dartmoor, a few miles from Exeter.

In England for the year to work on her biography of a Victorian woman novelist, Claire had been holed up in London since her sabbatical began in the spring. Not that "holed up" was an accurate description. The spacious flat in Bedford Square that had come to her in the divorce settlement from her English husband wasn't exactly an atelier. The Camdens, while far from really rich, were equally far from poor, a consideration which hadn't been too significant during the twenty years of her marriage to Miles, but which now made things a lot easier all around. Claire herself was willing to live on her California professor's salary, but the Camden resources were a boon for her daughter Sally, now in her second year at the University of Exeter.

Staying in Morbridge would be great for seeing more of Sally, to say nothing of spending more time with Neil Padgett, the current man in her life. Detective superintendent of the CID, stationed in Devon, Neil had progressed in his relationship with Claire from casual acquaintance to friend to lover during the past year or so, and for the previous months they had spent time together when Claire came down to Morbridge or when Neil could get away to London. The good news was that from November to January, while Claire stayed at Bea Camden's home, they could forget those three- to four-hour drives.

Now, on a blustery mid-November day, Claire packed up her word processor and all the paraphernalia for her writing project, closed up the London flat, and set off on the motorway, taking the M4 west to Bristol and picking up the M5 south to Exeter.

At the outskirts of the city, she turned off the motorway and twisted through the knotted suburban traffic. Finally, she took a road that led out into the countryside, past tidy-looking farms and through rolling hills of lush green, graced with black-faced sheep, looking as if they'd been put there for somebody like Constable to paint rather than constituting one of the major industries of the country.

A few miles from Morbridge, she passed Newton Lane, the narrow road that led to the village of Bickford, where Sally shared a cottage with two housemates from the university. No point in stopping now. With many weeks ahead of her, she'd have plenty of time to spend with her daughter.

Coming into town, she threaded her way down the narrow high street. She passed a sixteenth-century inn and crossed the stone bridge, turning at the first roundabout and following the uphill curve of Abbey Road. At last she came to the comfortable old house that had been in Bea's family for several generations, the house where Bea had elected to stay on after her husband's death.

Flinching from the sleety rain that nipped her cheeks, Claire hurriedly carried her bags into the house, thinking fondly of Bea, who was an absolute darling. For years her friends had protested that it was unnatural to actually like your mother-in-law. One of her colleagues at the university in California declared that the best thing about her divorce was never having to see her husband's frightful mother again. Claire knew she was the fortunate exception.

In the early days after the divorce, Claire had found it painful to visit Morbridge, where she and Miles and Sally had spent some good times with his family. But after three years, the spooks were vanishing, and she looked around the house with pleasure. Neil Padgett would be coming at six o'clock. She phoned Sally to say she'd arrived, spent a couple of hours getting settled in, and just before six, lit the logs in the old-fashioned fireplace.

She was setting out the drinks trolley when the phone rang. Expecting to hear that Neil was held up at his office in Kings Abbey, ten miles or so from Morbridge—a policeman's lot is not a happy one for keeping to a time schedule—she was surprised to hear Sally's voice.

"Hi, Mums. Cheryl hasn't come home, and I'm worried." Cheryl was one of her housemates.

"Did she go in to the campus today?"

"Yes, I suppose so. Brenda and I drove in early, and Cheryl didn't want to leave then, so she said she would take the 9:20 bus."

"Did you see her later on?"

"No, but sometimes I don't. We're not in the same classes."

"Couldn't she have decided to stay on and have a meal with friends?"

Sally sounded doubtful. "She would have let me know. You see, it's Brenda's birthday tomorrow, and she has a date for that evening, so Cheryl and I were doing our thing tonight. We have a bottle of champagne, a cake and candles, and Cheryl was making a special card. There's no way she would miss it."

"Was she planning to take the bus home?"

"She didn't exactly say, but I assumed she would want a ride and I was surprised when she didn't show up at the library. But if she took the 4:40 bus, she'd be home by now."

Claire knew their arrangement. Since Sally was the one with the car—a gift from her grandmother Bea—they had agreed to meet at the university library at a stated time each day. Whoever turned up would go with Sally or, failing that, would take the bus.

Claire had met Cheryl a couple of times since the term began and agreed that Cheryl wasn't the type to forget her friends' plans. A serious and reliable young woman, she had come to Exeter with a group of students from Claire's own university at South Coast in California as a member of the "Third Year Abroad" program.

It was through Barry Nolan, one of Claire's colleagues in the English Department, that Cheryl had come to live at Sally's place. Barry was faculty adviser for this year's "TYAs," as they were dubbed, and he and his wife had come over in August to do some traveling and to look for housing before the term began in October. Stopping in London on their way to Devon, they had met Claire for dinner one evening.

"I don't intend to slave away at this job," Barry had said. "Herding the cattle—a prod here and a poke there is about what I plan. I do have to meet with the little dears every week and trot them around to Stratford and God-knows-where. But it's worth it to have a year in England."

Claire wondered if he would still think so at the end of the year, but that was his problem. Barry could be irritating but was always amusing company, and Claire liked his wife Frieda. Actually, she'd liked all of his wives. Frieda was the third, if her count was correct.

When the thirty-five students in this year's crop of TYAs had arrived and were being assigned to housing, Barry had phoned Claire with a problem.

"One of the girls, Cheryl Bailey, has asked not to share with another TYA, if possible. She doesn't exactly say they are below her standard, but she says she'd like to be with someone who has 'intellectual interests.' So what do you think, Claire, darling?"

Barry's voice oozed boyish charm. He was pushing fifty but his psyche was in delayed adolescence.

"What do I think about what?"

"Well, couldn't she bunk in with Sally and her friend? If ever there was a brainy kid, it's Sally. And gorgeous, too, like her mother."

Ignoring Barry's automatic flattery, Claire said she'd let him know.

Sally had found a congenial housemate the year before in Brenda Gilbert, whom she had met in a tutorial. Since their cottage had a third bedroom, they met with Cheryl, liked her, and invited her to share, and the arrangement had been a success.

Now, on the phone with Sally, Claire tried to sound reassuring, saying that Cheryl would surely turn up soon and promising to phone when she came back from dinner.

Neil arrived on time, and after a drink or two, they set off for one of their favorite spots, a pub in a village out on the moor where the food was good and the atmosphere casual. By now, their relationship was fairly settled and comfortable, barring minor flare-ups from time to time. It seemed to Claire that the best thing they had going for them—apart from the obvious sensual pleasures—was a genuine mutual interest in each other's work. She was fascinated by his stories of policing crimes, both large and small, and assumed everyone else would be too. Not so, evidently. His wife, with whom he was involved in a torturously slow English divorce, had found it all quite boring and tiresome, and had in fact left him when he took his present position in Devon. Too frightful, she had said, to be trapped in the country with a gaggle of police wives.

For his part, Neil, who had read English at the university before deciding to follow in his father's footsteps and become a policeman, actually enjoyed hearing about Claire's work on Mary Louise Talbot, the subject of her biography.

Talbot had been an enormously popular Victorian novelist whose works had faded into obscurity but who, as a woman, was an independent spirit in an age when Tennyson could write that "Woman is the lesser man" whose passions, matched with those of men, were "as water unto wine."

Quoting these lines one day, Claire had conceded, "To be fair, it was a dramatized character who said this, not Alfred, Lord T. in his own voice, but one can see his male readers nodding their heads and muttering 'Quite so.' "

Now, over dinner, she told Neil about the small parcel she'd received that day, just as she was leaving the London flat. "It contains a short note and some letters from a Mrs. Vickers, a collateral descendant of Talbot's, who found the letters while clearing up her attic."

Neil grinned. "Where would scholars be without those blessed attics?"

"Exactly. It seems a neighbor had clipped out my notice in the *Times Literary Supplement* ages ago and given it to Mrs. Vickers, who had just now got around to her cleaning task. She enclosed the first three letters in the bundle, asking me to reply if I wanted to see more."

"Sounds interesting. Will they be useful?"

"Yes, I think so. I'm really excited about this. I looked through them briefly this afternoon. The letters are not written *by* Mary Louise but were written *to* her by a cousin, a woman named Prudence Halley. The great thing is that there are some references in Mary Louise's other correspondence to a cousin named Prudence who was murdered, and I've never been able to track her down. This must be the one."

Neil's brown eyes flecked with the ironic humor she loved. "You want me to apply my professional skill to solving the crime, no doubt?"

"Of course. Why do you think I keep you around?"

"I rather thought I had other uses as well."

Claire patted his knee under the table. "A man of versatile talents is always in demand."

Neil refilled their wine glasses. "So, what does Cousin Prudence have to say?"

"Not a lot, so far, but she sounds like an interesting woman in her own right. She was an artist, and lived on her own, which was pretty rare for her day. Now, my question is this. I certainly want to see all of the letters. Do you think my lady is actually asking if the letters are valuable? I have some money left in my grant for buying such things at a modest price. But if I offer her money and that isn't what she meant at all, she may be offended."

"Mmm. I'd think you need to call on her in person and sound her out. Where does she live?"

"Somewhere here in Devon. A place called Sudbury. I haven't had a chance to look it up yet."

"Sudbury? It's along the seashore, perhaps half an hour's drive from here."

"Good. I'll give her a ring tomorrow. She still lives at The Laurels, the house where her ancestress Prudence lived in the 1860s."

But when tomorrow came, the letters of Prudence Halley had slipped to the back of Claire's mind.

For Cheryl Bailey had not come back to the cottage, and by morning, the police had begun an investigation into her disappearance.

Chapter

3

THAT EVENING, WHILE NEIL and Claire were at dinner, Sally Camden phoned a couple of the American students who had attended the Wednesday afternoon lecture with Cheryl and was told they hadn't seen her. Seriously alarmed, Sally and Brenda agreed that if Cheryl did not come home by morning, they would follow Neil's advice and report her absence to the local police. This they did, at eight o'clock in the morning, going in to the station at Morbridge, since the village of Bickford was too small for a station of its own.

At the same time, Claire called Barry Nolan to let him know what was happening.

"Bloody hell!" he groaned. Three months in England, she noticed, and he was already into the local profanity. "Look, Claire, I know Cheryl Bailey doesn't seem like the type, but you know these kids—away from home in another country, no one to really supervise them. Sure, they're supposed to be adults. Twenty, twenty-one years old, most of them. But what if she met some guy, and, you know—?"

Barry's voice trailed off as he clearly didn't find this scenario very convincing. "God," he added hoarsely, "I hope she's all right."

Claire asked him to try to find out if anyone had seen Cheryl at the university the day before, and in half an hour he called back to report that Cheryl hadn't been present at either her lecture or her tutorial, and no one had seen her elsewhere. "She does stand out, you know. The only African-American girl among the TYAs this year."

Barry was not noted for his sensitivity, but Claire had to admit he had a point.

When she phoned Neil to tell him what she had learned from Barry, he said it was time to have his officers ask a few questions. "Officially, you understand, where there's no actual evidence of foul play, we're skeptical of any adult disappearance. Our experience is that people whose families swear it was impossible for our Joe or our Betty to go off without notice often do turn up after a time. But in this instance, I'm afraid I'm not optimistic. I shall give a nudge to our usual procedures."

Claire suspected that a nudge from the detective superintendent of the district would be more like a clarion call to action, and it seemed she was right. An hour later, she had just arrived at the cottage at Bickford to offer moral support to Sally and her friend when a police constable from Neil's staff came to question them. At the same time, as she learned later, two officers had been dispatched to the university to talk with both faculty and students who knew Cheryl.

At the cottage, the young officer introduced himself as Police Constable Crofts. Taking out a notebook, he wrote down their names, looking with frank curiosity at Claire when she gave hers. "So this is the guv'nor's lady friend," his look seemed to say.

Asked if there was a photo of Cheryl the police

might have, Sally picked up her camera from a nearby table. "There are some snapshots in here, if you have the film developed. I took some when the three of us were walking up in the woods about a week ago. I was going to finish the roll last night at our birthday party for Brenda."

Her voice broke, and to hide her emotion, she bent over the camera, removing the rewound film.

As the constable took the roll, his eyes flicked over Sally in what could only be called the once-over. "Dishy as her mum" seemed to be his verdict. Claire, accustomed to the extreme courtesy of most British policemen, wondered if she was being unfair, and decided she wasn't. Crofts had the facile good looks and sexy swagger of a young man who fancied himself a Don Juan.

Putting the film in a small bag, the constable asked, "Will Miss Bailey have any pictures in her bedroom?"

Claire said, "What about her passport?"

Brenda started for the stairs. "Good point, Mrs. Camden. Come along, Sally. Let's have a look."

In a moment or two they returned, and Brenda handed Crofts a U.S. passport. "Not a good picture, but one can see it's Cheryl."

Sally held out a framed photo, showing Cheryl in cap and gown. "This looks like her graduation picture from high school, so it would be two years ago, but she hasn't changed all that much. She's very serious."

P.C. Crofts looked up in surprise. "Miss Bailey was—er—not Caucasian?"

Sally bristled. "No. Does that matter?"

He gave her an impudent stare. "It may help with identification, miss."

"Oh, I see." Sally rolled her eyes at her mother and subsided.

Asked to go over in detail the events of the morning before, Sally and Brenda stated they had left the cottage at about half-past seven. Sally said, "The parking places fill up early, and we often go at that time and then have coffee and rolls after we get there."

"And Miss Bailey did not go with you yesterday. Why was that?"

"Well, she had been up late working on an essay for her tutorial. That's another thing that makes this really frightening. It was for Professor Foley and she liked him very much and wanted to please him. She would never have decided to take the day off and not go. She only wanted to sleep in a little longer."

"And she would then take the bus?"

"Yes, there's one at 9:20. It's about a twenty-minute walk along the lane to the Exeter road."

Crofts nodded. "What is the approximate height and weight of Miss Bailey?"

Sally said, "We described her at the police station this morning, Constable."

"Yes, miss, but I need this for my notes as well."

"Oh. Well, she is taller than either of us. Probably about five feet eight. And very slim. She probably weighs about 120 pounds."

The officer glanced at Brenda, who translated. "About eight and a half stone."

"As to clothing, can you tell me what Miss Bailey might have been wearing yesterday?"

"Jeans, of course." Sally was in no doubt about that. "Probably a knit top and her black windbreaker."

"And how long have you known the young lady? Miss Gilbert?"

Brenda said, "Nearly two months. The American students came two weeks or so before the term began."

"And Miss Camden?"

"The same."

Now he turned to Claire, again with that glance that was just short of lascivious. "Mrs. Camden, were you acquainted with Miss Bailey before she came to England?"

"No, I wasn't. She is a student at the university in California where I teach, but it is a very large institution, and for the most part I know only those students who are in my classes or seminars."

"Then, had you met Miss Bailey here in Devon?"

"Yes, on two occasions when I came to visit my daughter."

"And what was your impression of her?"

"She is a lovely person, and a dedicated student. I agree that it's most unlikely she would go off like this without letting her housemates know where she is."

Sally explained about the planned birthday celebration for Brenda.

"And has Miss Bailey a boyfriend or a special male friend?"

Brenda shook her head. "She's been asked out, but she hasn't found anyone to her liking. The boys her age seem too young for her. I believe she'd like to meet someone like Dr. Foley, but unfortunately he's married."

The sergeant turned to a fresh page in his notebook. "Now, what can you tell me about the people who live hereabouts? Are you acquainted with any persons in the neighborhood?"

Sally replied first. "We know Adrian Abbott, up at the Priory, as he's our landlord, so to speak, and of course there's Jasper Martinelli."

Brenda added, "Technically he's Adrian's stepfather, although he's only a few years older. Adrian's mother died last year, and Jasper still lives there with Adrian."

"Was either Mr. Abbott or his stepfather acquainted with Miss Bailey?"

Brenda shrugged. "She knew Adrian, of course, and when we were asked to tea one day, Jasper sort of drifted into the room, drank some tea, and drifted away again. I expect one could say Cheryl had met him. He's an artist, you see, which appears to exempt him from ordinary conduct. You were there, too, were you not, Mrs. Camden?"

Claire nodded. "Yes. Jasper did seem to materialize and evaporate."

Sally said, "Cheryl mentioned having seen Jasper when she was out walking one day. He was up on the hillside, working in a section of the garden, and she said he actually conversed with her, but I've no idea what they talked about."

"Thank you. Now, I believe both of you young ladies occupied the cottage here last year. Are you acquainted with anyone else nearby?"

Brenda shook her head. "Actually, there isn't anyone nearby. There are a number of small cottages scattered along the road, but I've had no occasion to meet their occupants. Have you, Sally?"

"Not really. Sometimes someone will nod a greeting as we drive by and I wave back, but that's about it."

"So, as Miss Bailey walked along the road toward the bus stop, she would not be passing any acquaintances?"

Brenda frowned. "Probably not. Cheryl was rather reserved with strangers."

The constable closed his notebook and asked for directions to the Priory.

Sally said, "Just follow the drive up the hill. I'll show you."

As she started for the door, there was a knock, and she opened it to find Adrian Abbott on the doorstep, looking at her anxiously.

"Are you all right, Sally? I saw the police car—"

"Oh, Adrian, come in. Mums, you remember Adrian? And this is Police Constable Crofts. Adrian Abbott."

Brenda said, "Cheryl didn't come home last night, Adrian, and we're dreadfully worried."

"Cheryl? How odd. She isn't the sort to run off, I'd have thought."

Sally, obviously glad of this confirmation from another source, began to pour out the story when the constable broke in. "Excuse me, Miss Camden, but I'll speak with Mr. Abbott first, if you please."

He took Adrian by the arm. "If you will walk with me up to your house, sir, I shall also need to speak with Mr. Jasper Martinelli, if he is at home."

"Of course, Constable, come along. I expect Jasper's somewhere about."

With a solemn look at the others and a promise to return, Adrian followed the officer out of the door, and from the side window they could be seen walking slowly up the hill toward the Priory.

Chapter

4

P.C. CROFTS, ACCOMPANYING Adrian up the drive
from the cottage to the Priory, decided it was no good
trying to ask questions till they reached the top. He
puffed slightly as they zigzagged up the sharp rise of
the heavily wooded hill, where he caught glimpses of
stone walls and chimneys through the trees. Presently
they came to some fragments of ancient ruins, and
beyond these, an imposing house of gray stone.

The constable stopped, staring at the remains of two
walls. Attached to one was a staircase, running halfway up the wall until it broke off abruptly. Fragments
of a third wall clung to one side, the stone crumbling
in places, the suggestion of what may have been a bell
tower rising at the corner.

"And what is this, sir?"

"It's all that's left of a medieval priory, Constable.
It was destroyed after the Reformation, of course."

As they approached the house, standing where the
hill leveled before rising again, Crofts remarked, "A
fine place, sir. Is it very old?"

Adrian smiled. "No, I'm afraid it dates only from the late eighteenth century. It was built over the original site of the old priory and has kept the name. You're not a local lad, then?"

"No, sir. I was sent up from Plymouth a few months back."

"I see."

Crofts gestured to a bench, adroitly placed along the path to give a view of the small valley below. "If you'll stop here, sir?"

It was more a statement than a question, and Adrian sat down at one end of the bench while the constable took the other and opened his notebook.

"Now, sir, how long have you known Miss Bailey, the young lady as may be missing?"

"Since October, when the new term began at the university."

"And the other young ladies?"

"I had met Miss Sally Camden and Miss Brenda Gilbert a few times last year, when they occupied the cottage, although I was away much of that time."

"I believe you are the owner of the cottage, sir?"

"Yes, it is a part of the estate."

"You didn't object to a tenant of what is known as the black race?"

Adrian looked at the officer curiously. "No, certainly not."

The constable grinned. "All good-looking young ladies, are they not?"

Adrian stiffened. "Yes. If that is relevant to your inquiries."

"It may be that, sir. Are there many young men coming or going from the cottage?"

Tight-lipped, Adrian said, "I have no idea."

"You can see the cottage from here, sir."

"I can see the roof of the cottage, yes. I have no inclination to study the movements of its visitors."

Crofts smiled inwardly. All these toffs were the same. Wouldn't dream of having any curiosity about other people's doings. Not half. Didn't he see the way Abbott had looked at that blond one, the daughter of the guv'nor's bird?

Back to business. "And have you yourself formed a special friendship with any of the young ladies, sir?"

"No, I have not."

"You seemed to be on friendly terms just now at the cottage."

"That is not the question you asked me."

"Then you would say you are equally friendly with all three of the ladies?"

"Yes."

"Now, may I ask where you were yesterday from morning to evening?"

"Yesterday? Let me recall. I was here at the house in the morning. After luncheon, I drove into the city to attend a lecture, went into Morbridge to meet a friend for dinner, and returned about ten o'clock last evening."

"Did you see the dark young lady at any time yesterday?"

"I did not see Miss Bailey, no."

"Did you see anyone at or near the cottage as you drove past, either coming or going?"

"No."

"Right, then." Crofts stood up. "If I may speak with Mr. Jasper Martinelli—your stepfather, I believe?"

Adrian made no reply, but led the way toward the house, passing along well-tended paths where a few last yellow leaves of autumn clung to barren branches.

Crofts looked curiously at a structure that measured about six feet by four, whose sides were blocks of straw standing shoulder-high, topped by a canvas roof supported by poles at the four corners. Peering over the side, he saw a mass of leaves and cuttings which, little as he knew about gardening, he thought must be a compost heap.

Looking up, he saw a bearded man with a wheelbarrow coming down the path. The gardener, he thought, till he heard Adrian's voice. "Jasper, this is Constable Crofts. He'd like to ask you some questions."

Crofts looked at Adrian's departing back, then turned to the bearded man. An artist, the girl Sally had said, and not many years older than his stepson. Thick black hair, falling to the shoulders in the back, dark eyes looking at him with mild curiosity.

"Mr. Martinelli?"

"Yes."

"You were the husband of Mr. Adrian Abbott's mother?"

"Yes. She died last year."

"What is your age, Mr. Martinelli?"

"I am thirty-three."

"Your wife must have been considerably your senior?"

"Cynthia? Yes, she was. Is that what you came to ask me?"

Crofts swallowed and took out his notebook. "No, sir, I came to ask you to describe your movements of yesterday."

"Has something happened, Constable?"

"That has not been determined as yet."

Jasper looked puzzled but answered in a soft voice. "Yesterday? I believe I worked here in the garden for a while in the morning. Then, what did I do? Oh, I went into Kings Abbey for some supplies. I stopped in Morbridge for lunch and drove out onto the moor to do some sketching."

Jasper paused.

"And after that?"

Jasper blinked. "After that? Let me see. I dropped

20

in at the Crown for a pint. Then I presume I came back here."

"At what time was that, please?"

"Time? I can't say."

"Was it still daylight?"

"No, no. It was dark. I remember that."

Glad he remembers *something*, Crofts thought. "And did you go out again in the evening?"

"No, not that I recall."

"I believe you are acquainted with the young ladies in the cottage below?"

Again Crofts saw that puzzled look, as if Jasper couldn't quite place the cottage and its occupants. Then his face cleared. "Do you mean the students who attend the university?"

"Yes, sir. How well do you know the young ladies?"

"Not well at all, I'm afraid. They came to tea with Adrian one afternoon. He knows them better than I. Is this to do with them, Constable?"

"It may do, sir. I understand you had a conversation with Miss Bailey, the dark one, here in the garden on one occasion. Can you tell me what you spoke about?"

Jasper thought for a moment. "Reynolds."

"And who is Reynolds?"

"Sir Joshua. The painter."

"And what was the substance of your conversation?"

"She admires his work."

"Did you speak of any other matters?"

Jasper blinked. "Possibly Romney."

Crofts repressed a groan. "And did you speak with Miss Bailey on other occasions?"

"Other occasions? No. Has something happened, Constable?"

"Miss Bailey did not return to the cottage last night and has been reported as gone missing."

"Oh, I see. I do hope she's found safe."

"Did you see any of the ladies at any time yesterday, or notice any visitors at the cottage?"

Jasper blinked again. "No, I'm afraid not."

"Right. Well, thank you, sir, and if you remember anything at all, will you please notify us?"

As Crofts stumped down the hill, he snorted to himself. Talk of dim, I'm surprised he can find his way home. The mother must have been desperate to take up with that one.

Chapter

5

WHILE P.C. CROFTS WAS QUESTIONING Jasper, Adrian Abbott had gone back to the cottage to offer what comfort he might.

Claire knew something of Adrian's story from Sally. Now twenty-three, Adrian had been in his first year at Cambridge when his father had died of a heart attack. His mother, with what Hamlet would have called unseemly haste, had married a man fifteen years her junior. Jasper Martinelli—Italian father, English mother—had been a sort of protégé of the senior Abbotts, who took an interest in art but weren't rich enough to be significant patrons.

Adrian had spent little time at home during the three years of his mother's second marriage. "I felt jolly uncomfortable," he had told Sally one day. "Nothing against Jasper, actually. He's a bit vague but a decent enough sort. It was Mother: she was besotted with the fellow. What the psychology chaps call mid-life crisis, I expect."

At his mother's death, the house naturally came to

Adrian, but according to her will, the income from the estate was divided between Adrian and Jasper. She also left a strongly worded request that Jasper be allowed to live at the Priory if he wished to do so.

"He'd go if I asked him to," Adrian had told Sally, "but he's no bother and he's good with the garden—even still carries on with Mother's spring garden show for charity. We've more or less staked out our own quarters, and he pays his share of the expenses."

This was no small matter, Sally had surmised. Even in the father's day, the Abbotts were a classic example of old house, old family, but little money. After her husband's death, it appeared that Cynthia Abbott had fallen victim to some bad investments which reduced the income even more.

"We're not talking poverty," Sally had giggled, during a conversation with her mother one day. "Adrian isn't lining up for the dole. Just hasn't a lot to toss around."

"Couldn't he get a job?" Claire asked.

"He's planning to. He read history at Cambridge, which wasn't too practical. Now he's taking a course in accounting, and he's sure to find something once he's qualified."

During their first year at the cottage, Sally and Brenda had seen little of Adrian, as he had been off wandering around the Continent, living cheaply here and there. They paid their rent to an estate agent who managed the property, since Jasper was evidently incapable of such mundane actions as keeping records or calling in someone to do repairs. In the previous summer, Adrian had finally come back to settle, and when the term began in October, he and his young tenants had struck up a friendly acquaintance.

Now, as Brenda brought out a tray of coffee, Claire looked at Adrian's fine-boned face, with the lock of brown hair that he habitually pushed back off his forehead with a slender hand. Not handsome, but a nice face. Would he and Sally . . . ? *Come on, Claire,* she reproved herself. *What is this maternal reflex? Sally is quite capable of running her own life.*

Remembering that today was Brenda's twenty-first birthday, Sally brought out the cake they had intended for the evening before.

"We may as well have some now, I suppose. We'll save the champagne for—that is, for later."

They all knew she had wanted to say, "When Cheryl comes back," and they knew, too, that with each passing hour that prospect looked dimmer.

She and Sally discussed whether or not to go in for their afternoon lecture. They decided they'd be unable to concentrate and may as well stay at home. Since Brenda's boyfriend was coming at six to take her out, Claire suggested that Sally come in to Morbridge with her for the evening.

"Oh, Mums, I'll be okay here."

"I don't think you should be alone, Sally."

Adrian said, "Look, I'll come down, if I may, or you could come up to the Priory."

Sally gave him a grateful look. "Here, if you don't mind, Adrian. Then someone would be here if Cheryl should come back or phone."

On her way back to Morbridge, Claire remembered this was the evening she and Neil had been asked to dinner with Barry and Frieda Nolan. Claire thought surely they would want to put it off, but when she rang up to inquire, Frieda said absolutely not, they were to come anyhow.

"Of course we're terribly worried about the girl who's missing, but there's really nothing we can do, is there? Unless your handsome policeman can't make it?"

Neil said he could, unless the circumstances

changed, which Claire read grimly as meaning, "If Cheryl's body is found." He would leave the Nolans' number where he could be reached. As senior officer, he need not be out questioning people. Normally his job was to stay put, receiving the reports from his officers and only occasionally going into the field himself.

At seven o'clock, a cold, drenching rain pelted them as they climbed the steps to the house the Nolans had taken for their year's stay. Coming over in August to house-hunt, Barry and Frieda had found everything near the university in Exeter hideously expensive for a professor's salary. A country cottage that was cheaper was too isolated for their gregarious tastes, and they had finally settled for the modest rent of this modern bungalow on the hill not far off the high street in Morbridge.

Barry was pleased. "It's just a white stucco box, but the commute from here is shorter than the one I have at home to South Coast, and it's a heck of a lot prettier drive."

And Frieda had added, "We can use the extra money, that's for sure."

The white stucco box at least had cheery chintz on windows and furniture, and boasted central heating, supplemented with a fireplace that crackled alluringly as Barry led them into the living room.

Looking at Barry, with his little fringy beard and his red hair streaked with gray, Claire marveled, as she had for twenty years or more, that women seemed to find him irresistible. Here was Frieda, thirty-something, sexy figure, mop of curly hair, and impudent charm in her dark eyes, who, five years ago, had been more than willing to take on the job of wife number three.

The Nolans were notorious for uninhibited behavior, swinging from fawning mutual adoration to sizzling scenes of battle. This evening was no exception. Over drinks, they snatched nuzzles and kisses like honeymooners.

When the subject turned to Cheryl Bailey's disappearance, Barry took the line that they ought not to believe the worst until they were sure. "She may turn up yet, you know."

Frieda looked doubtful. "If Claire says she wasn't the type to run off, I must say it doesn't sound good."

Asked his opinion, Neil told them essentially what he had said to Claire about adult disappearances, adding that in this case, however, the police were already involved in an extensive search and questioning.

"We've notified the local news media and asked London television to run an item in the southwest spot tonight, with Cheryl's picture and a request for information. We've also alerted the Dartmoor Rangers."

Barry looked puzzled. "Do you mean, she might be hiding out on the moor somewhere?"

Neil paused. "Perhaps so."

"Oh, my God. You mean her body may have been hidden out there?"

"It's always a possibility."

Frieda broke the gloomy silence by heading for the kitchen and asking Claire to come along. Looking around at the bright modern appliances, Claire was glad she had advised Frieda, who was one of those women who actually liked to cook, that she would be wise to forego finding a house loaded with Olde English atmosphere in favor of one with modern conveniences.

Over Frieda's excellent dinner and a modest wine, they all chatted amiably, including, inevitably, the topic of the weather.

"It's simply awful," Frieda moaned. "You did warn us, Claire, but I guess I didn't really believe you. It's freezing already and this is only the middle of November."

Claire laughed. "It's mostly southern Californians who think the sun is supposed to shine all the time. I thought that at first, too, but I soon got the hang of it. After twenty years of commuting between California and London, I feel like a native."

Barry said, "At least I understand now why people here talk constantly about the weather. We never mention it at home except to complain when it's too hot."

"And when it rains, don't forget. I've told Neil how people cancel their plans in South Coast during the rain, as if it's some kind of social inconvenience."

The meal passed pleasantly, and when, over the dessert, Frieda asked Claire what was new with Mary Louise Talbot, she told the story of the letters from Prudence Halley. Barry, whose field was contemporary American literature, wasn't enthralled, but Frieda was. As a graduate student in Claire's Victorian seminar some years ago, Frieda had written a fine paper on George Eliot and early feminism.

"I'd like to know more about this Prudence," she said.

Claire smiled. "I'm going to Sudbury soon to look up Mrs. Vickers, the lady with the letters. Why don't you come with me, Frieda?"

"Great. I'd love to."

Barry snorted. "Good idea. You need something to keep you out of mischief."

Frieda glared. "What mischief? Who do I ever see in this place? Do you think I'm having an affair with the butcher?"

"How do I know? I haven't met him."

"You would if you ever did any of the shopping. Actually, he's not bad-looking. You just want me to be the little wifey in the kitchen with my apron on, I suppose?"

"Not a bad idea."

"Look who's talking. How are you making out with the barmaid at the Crown?"

Barry stood up, his hands curled, and shouted. "You don't say 'barmaid.' How many times have I told you that?"

Frieda lolled back in her chair, her voice sultry. "Enough times to make me wonder why you care so much *what* I call her."

With a glance at us, Barry sat down and poured himself the last of the wine, spilling it as he gulped it down. "Nora is a sweet girl. She's had a hard life, and she appreciates anyone who's kind to her."

Frieda snapped, "You're not supposed to say 'girl.' How many times have I told you *that*? And besides, I notice you don't take *me* along when you're being kind to her."

"That's not true. You were there with me just the other night."

"Right. And it seemed to me plenty of guys were being kind to poor Nora."

Barry looked sulky, evidently a sign that Frieda had won that round, for she got up, draped herself around his neck, and gave him a lengthy kiss.

All this was par for the course, and Claire was glad to see that Neil was mildly amused. On the first evening they had spent with the Nolans, when Claire had come down to Morbridge for a visit, they were out having drinks in a pub when an argument between Barry and Frieda had escalated to shouts of abuse, cut off when Barry mercifully stalked out.

Claire knew it was no use remonstrating with either of them. Their behavior was compulsive, although she'd noticed they could control it when they had to. She'd be willing to bet they would behave like angels with the English faculty members they were meeting at the university. They were having a party for that group soon, where she'd have the chance to test out her theory.

She and Neil left early, going back to Bea's place. Neil did a policemanlike check of the premises in case a killer was lurking somewhere—no small task, as the big old house sprawled from basement to attic.

Meanwhile, Claire rang up Sally. She knew there was no news, or Sally would have called at the Nolans' place, but she wanted to hear her voice.

"Oh, Mums, it's you! When the phone rang, I thought it was Cheryl!"

"I know, darling. I'm sorry, but I wanted to be sure you're all right."

"Yes, fine. Adrian's here. He brought his accounting books and I worked on my Renaissance essay. We actually managed to get some work done. So how are the Nolans?"

"Same as ever. Good fun, but on their emotional seesaw."

"How does Neil take it?"

"He seems to be unshockable."

"Good!"

I heard other voices, and Sally said, "Oh, Brenda and Garth just came in. Talk to you tomorrow!"

Chapter

6

ON FRIDAY MORNING there was still no sign of Cheryl. Sally and Brenda decided to go in for their tutorial, leaving a note for Cheryl at the cottage in the forlorn hope that she might return, and by eight o'clock, Claire was trying to get back to work on Mary Louise Talbot when the phone rang.

It was Barry, calling to ask her advice about notifying Cheryl's mother in California. "I don't know what to do, Claire. I was sure Cheryl would turn up by now, but when two nights have gone by, it's looking pretty bad. Cheryl's papers list only her mother's name, no father. Do you know anything about the family?"

"No, only that Sally said Cheryl spoke fondly of her mother and a younger brother and sister."

"I don't want to worry Mrs. Bailey unless we have to, but on the other hand, she ought to know what's happening. You're a mother. What do you think?"

"For myself, Barry, I'd want to know. There's another factor. If—well, if the worst has happened, it would be better for the mother to be prepared, I think. It's midnight in California. You'd better do it now."

"Oh, Christ. I'm sure you're right. Look, Claire, I don't suppose you'd call her, would you?"

"No, it's your job, Barry. You're the faculty adviser for the group. I'm on leave, and I have no official connection with the Third Year Abroad students anyway."

"Okay. I'll get onto it."

Claire knew she needed to hold firm with Barry, who was notoriously willing to shove responsibility onto anyone who was handy. She'd resolved not to get tied up with his TYAs just because she happened to be in Devon, although she hadn't bargained for this kind of trouble. But the truth was that she wasn't sure she'd be all that good on the phone to Mrs. Bailey, haunted as she was by the pain she feared was in store for Cheryl's mother. All of Sally's life Claire had been seized with panic at the thought of losing her. The high fevers of childhood illness, the report that she had been in an auto accident, the irrational nightmares that Sally was calling and Claire couldn't reach her, all overwhelmed her. Sally had been quite simply the delight of her life, as the lovely Cheryl must have been for her mother, and Claire didn't know if she could trust her voice on the phone at this point.

Claire remembered too well an occasion in her office at the university when her emotions overcame her professional manner. Unlike small private colleges where students and faculty might be personally acquainted, South Coast was an enormous commuter institution, with students driving in from all over southern California to take their courses. In addition to the undergraduates just out of high school, there were many mature students, women and men who for one reason or another had dropped out or perhaps had never attended college and who were now working on degree programs. And what fine students they were. Undistracted by the foibles of youth, they were for the most part reliable, bright, and altogether pleasant to have around.

It was one of these, a delightful woman in her fifties, who came to Claire's office on a day during the week before final exams to explain that she could not come to the final for the course, as her son had died quite suddenly. One look at the distraught face and Claire felt tears forcing themselves through her desperate blinking. Her throat closed with pain, and by the time she had choked out her sympathy and said to forget the final, they both sat weeping silently until the lady pressed Claire's hand and walked swiftly out the door.

Now, she wrenched her mind away from Mrs. Bailey in California, waiting through an endless night for further word of her daughter, and forced herself back to her desk.

Picking up the three Prudence Halley letters that Mrs. Vickers had sent from Sudbury, she started working out the chronology. The first letter was dated 10 October 1861, during the year that Talbot, at the age of twenty-four, had seen the publication of her first novel, *The Secret of Lady Caroline*.

Just as the Brontë sisters, two decades earlier, had submitted their work with the pseudonyms Currer, Acton, and Ellis Bell to disguise their sex, so Talbot had submitted her manuscript as "M. L. Talbot," and even her publisher believed her to be a man. When the novel was an overnight success, the public wondered who Mr. Talbot was, but no one cracked the secret for some time to come.

Thus, Prudence's first letter was addressed to "Mr. M. L. Talbot, Esq.," in care of the London publisher, and had been duly sent to the convenience address Mary used to conceal her whereabouts.

After expressing her pleasure and excitement in

reading Mr. Talbot's novel, Prudence went on with some diffidence:

"I hope you will forgive my presumption in putting this question to you. I should like to know if you are related to a lady named Mary Louise Talbot, whose father was my cousin. We are a Cornwall family."

The letter closed with apologies for having disturbed Mr. Talbot if his was an entirely unrelated family.

The second letter, dated only a week later, indicated that Mary must have responded warmly, judging by Prudence's reply.

> The Laurels
> Sudbury, Devonshire
> 15 October 1861

My dear Mary Louise,

I am delighted to learn that you are indeed my cousin and that you are yourself the author of that splendid story, which gave me such pleasure. I shall indeed keep the secret of your identity until such time as it may become generally known.

I am equally happy to hear of your family. Your infant son must give you great pleasure, and I marvel at your industry in writing each day with the added responsibility of your husband's four children. Although I have none of my own, I am exceedingly fond of children. How fortunate that you have your dear mother with you to be of assistance.

You have kindly asked me to tell you something of myself. There is little of interest to tell. I shall have my fifty-first birthday this year. I am a spinster, living alone in the world, a state which I have never desired to change. This modest house, left to me on the death of my parents, is sufficient for my needs, and I have supplemented my small income by taking in lodgers and through the sale of my sketches and watercolors. For my own pleasure, I paint in oils, but these do not suit the taste of the public and have rarely been purchased.

Thank you for inviting me to visit you in London. I fear it is a long and costly journey, but I shall hope that one day I may accept your very kind offer.

Please convey my regards to your family.

Faithfully yours,
Prudence Halley

What Mary did not say, and what Prudence learned only much later in their acquaintance, was that the man with whom Mary Louise Talbot lived was not in fact her husband but a man whose wife was tragically confined to a sanitarium with incurable mental illness, unable to recognize either him or their four children. The wife's family provided the best possible physical care for her but were unwilling to take on the responsibility of the children. That Mary was willing to live with the man she had come to love, and to care for his children as well as her own, was an act of courage in a period when social conformity reigned supreme.

It wasn't the first act of independence in Mary's life. There was good reason why she and her cousin Prudence had never met. Mary's father had been a gentleman, long on charm but short on money, who had brought his wife and small daughter to London when Mary was ten and promptly left them, wandering off and coming back at intervals to dole out some money, then disappearing again. Tired of living on the edge of genteel poverty, Mary decided at the age of nineteen to join a theatrical touring company as an actress. Although her mother accompanied her as chaperone, protecting her daughter from the scandalous implications of a life on the stage, the Cornwall relatives were so shocked at the impropriety that they ceased all communication with her. To Mary herself, their disapproval meant nothing compared with the pleasure of having an income, modest as it was.

Since the time of her father's death four years earlier, the rift with the Talbot family had remained intact. The value to the biographer of letters like those from Prudence was not merely in the fact of the acquaintance with her cousin but in the insights they offered about the subject herself. Receiving a letter from a Cornwall cousin, Mary would have had every justification for giving a stiff reply, or none at all. That she did not do so was testimony to her warm and generous nature.

After the arrival of the second letter from Prudence, it was easy enough to speculate that Mary's interest would be further kindled by her cousin's tone of independence. While Prudence would have no knowledge of Mary's unconventional "marriage," she would have heard through the family grapevine of Mary's shocking venture in the theater and had nevertheless written to inquire about her cousin. Mary would recognize, even through the formal prose of the letter, a kindred spirit in Prudence, and must have responded accordingly, as Prudence's third letter indicated:

> The Laurels
> Sudbury, Devonshire
> 30 October 1861
>
> My dear Mary Louise,
>
> How kind of you to reply so promptly and to speak so frankly of the coolness that has existed between you and the members of our family. I may say at once that when I heard, some years ago, of your decision to appear on the stage, accompanied with complete propriety by your estimable mother, I ventured, while on a visit to the ancestral home in Cornwall, to express my admiration for your courage and was met with the horror you can well imagine. It is in part my dislike of such intolerance that

keeps me content with my life here, away from the bigotry and narrowness of those who prize social convention above the real needs of people.

Now, to reply to your question about my painting, I prefer landscape to portraiture, although I do sketches of persons when I am commissioned to do so, and am glad of the small fees they bring. I am fortunate in living near the seaside, where I can do many studies of the coastal cliffs, of small boats, and of sailing ships, trying to convey the changes in the light upon the water at various hours of the day and in times of calm or storm.

The painter I most admire is Mr. Turner, whom I had the inestimable privilege of meeting on several occasions in the year 1847, when he was an elderly gentleman.

The letter concluded with other details of Prudence's life in Sudbury, leaving Claire eager to get her hands on the rest of the bundle. Calling Directory Assistance, she got Mrs. Vickers' phone number in Sudbury and dialed. What sounded like a teenage boy answered, saying his mum would be home about half-past five and to please ring back then.

Claire had gone back to her desk and worked on for close to an hour when the phone rang.

It was Neil.

What they most feared had happened. Cheryl Bailey's body had been found in a kistvaen, an ancient burial site on the moor.

Chapter
7

SCATTERED OVER THE VAST AREA of Dartmoor are a dozen or more ancient stone circles, remnants of the Bronze Age. Whether these were parts of religious ritual or were used as special meeting places is not known, but it is certain that some circles were connected with burial rites. Among these can be found cairns and kistvaens, where primitive people deposited their dead.

A few miles from Morbridge, beyond the cultivated farms that ring the moor, a narrow road runs out into the open moorland. It passes along the foot of a high ridge topped by a spectacular outcropping of granite known as Hound Tor, for its imagined resemblance to a pack of hounds. Down the rocky slope below the tor, perhaps fifty yards from the road, are the remnants of a circle. Its shardlike stones, which may at one time have been roofed over with thatch, enclose a small rectangle of other flat, oblong stones known as a kistvaen, from the Celtic for "stone chest."

In the shape of a grave, but too small for even a

short-statured adult to lie full length, the kistvaen looks like nothing so much as a child's grave. The body was fitted in by being placed in the fetal position, with updrawn knees, and was often cremated, the remaining bones eventually consumed by the intensely acidic moisture of the Dartmoor peat.

It was here that Cheryl Bailey's nude body was found. Two officers of the Dartmoor National Park Rangers, alerted by Neil's office to look for evidence of a recently concealed body, had made the find more or less by chance. Sent to the aid of a hiker who had fallen from the tor and was injured, they were bringing their stretcher up the hill past the stone circle when one of them noticed that the turf in the kistvaen had been disturbed.

Once they had carried the injured man to their Land Rover, one drove away while the other took a shovel and went back to the rectangular area of the ancient gravesite. In most areas of the moor, the ranger reflected, it would be too difficult to dig deeply enough into the rocky soil to bury a body, but many kistvaens had been robbed for artifacts in recent times, their soil loosened sufficiently to permit some removal.

Now he noticed the clumps of earth scattered about the perimeter of the kistvaen, making it more than likely that a fair amount of soil had been displaced. And indeed, only inches below the surface of the mound, where the turf had been tamped down in an obvious but futile attempt to make it appear undisturbed, lay Cheryl's body, wrapped in a quilt, her knees drawn up to her chin.

The ranger's finding of the body was relayed directly to Neil, as senior officer. After putting into motion the requests for the technicians who would work at the scene of the crime, he had phoned Barry Nolan, as the person officially responsible for Cheryl Bailey during her residence in England.

Then he phoned Claire. "I know you'll hear this soon enough, darling, but I wanted to tell you myself, before I go out to take a look at the scene. It's going to be rough on Sally, I'm afraid."

No matter how much it's expected, the blow that dispels that last fragment of hope is hard to take. Claire knew that Neil himself, for all his professionalism, was never immune to tragedies like this one. Wondering if Sally and Brenda would hear the news on the campus, she got the answer to that question when, minutes later, Barry called, his voice thick.

"I know you've heard from Neil, Claire. Oh, God, it's awful. I just called Mrs. Bailey again, and when I said I had very bad news for her, she was completely silent at first. It's three o'clock in the morning there, and I thought maybe she'd been asleep and didn't catch what I said, so I repeated it. Then she said, 'Yes. Please tell me about it.' I told her all I knew, that Cheryl's body had been found buried out on the moor, and again there was this awful silence. Then she said, 'Thank you, Dr. Nolan. Please keep me informed of what the police find out. I must hang up now.' "

Claire understood that silence, felt the pain of it in the pit of her stomach. "Are you announcing the news on the campus, Barry?"

"Yes, your friend Padgett suggested I do that, and that I ask again for people to report anything at all they might remember that would help the police."

"So Sally and Brenda will hear it there?"

"Yes. I'm informing the faculty and also posting a statement on the notice board in the lobby of our building. The word will travel like lightning, that's for sure."

The next twenty-four hours were a nightmare of grief and pain. Sally, cradled in Claire's arms, wept as she hadn't done since childhood. She consented to spend the night with her mother, as Brenda's friend Garth had taken her to her home in Kent for the weekend.

Claire was seized with panic the next day when Sally wanted to go back to the cottage. "You can't be alone, darling. Let me come and stay with you."

"No, it's okay, Mums. Adrian said he'd be there for me."

"But overnight?"

"Sure. He'll sleep in Brenda's room if I ask him to."

Claire could see that Sally still hadn't thought in terms of a killer on the loose, assuming her mother didn't want her to be lonely or depressed. Claire decided to lay it on the line. "Look, dear, there doesn't seem to be any motive for Cheryl's murder. It must be a stranger, a deranged person, and he's still out there somewhere. You simply can't be alone in the house until he's caught."

Sally, too sensible to protest, said slowly, "Yes, I see. Still, it isn't likely he'd come back to the same place, is it?"

"Perhaps. Perhaps not. We don't know where she was when—when it happened. She may have been walking toward the bus stop, and he would have no idea where she lived. It's even possible she arrived in Exeter and was abducted after she got off the bus."

"Oh, God, Mums, it's so awful. We don't know anything about what happened. But I think you're right. Brenda and I will make sure we stay together or have someone with us all the time. Or I'll come and stay with you if I need to."

At noon, Sally went back to the cottage, having confirmed that Adrian would be with her. Claire knew she needed to study, and it appeared that Adrian's presence was no distraction. Doesn't look like *la grande passion,* she noted with a shrug, but maybe it's too soon to tell.

When Sally had gone, Claire remembered she hadn't phoned back the day before to Mrs. Vickers in Sudbury. Today was Saturday. May as well give her a try now.

The same teenage boy answered the phone, and Claire heard "Mum!" in a piercing shout, then some murmurs before she picked up the phone.

"Mrs. Vickers here." The voice was timid.

"This is Dr. Camden." Claire used the title in all the dealings with the book, reverting to Mrs. Camden socially.

Thanking Mrs. Vickers for the three letters, Claire assured her she would like to see the rest, and heard a hesitation so marked that she decided maybe the lady really did want money.

Claire said, "I'd be happy to talk over the matter with you. Can you suggest a convenient time for me to come to you?"

A sigh of relief. "Yes, if you will, please. I'm at work during the week. Would you—that is, if tomorrow would do—?"

Claire thought quickly. The next day was Sunday. Brenda would be back with Sally by the afternoon. She may as well go.

They agreed on four o'clock, "in time for a cup of tea," and Claire jotted down the directions for finding the house.

Claire was glad Neil could spend the evening with her. More shaken than she cared to admit, she had been afraid he wouldn't be able to get away, but he had put his detective chief inspector in hourly charge of the case. A massive investigation was now under way, with officers conducting door-to-door inquiries and covering a large area on the lookout for suspicious persons. Neil had only to remain available by phone in case of a major breakthrough.

They sat for a long time before the fire with their drinks, talking gloomily about the murder. The report from the pathologist had come in that day, bringing with it some disturbing questions.

Neil said, "There's no doubt she was strangled. Bruises around the neck and throat, pinpoint hemorrhages in the eyes. The pathologist can't place the time of death with any certainty, as the body temperature had already reached equality with the surrounding air and is therefore no longer a valid measure."

"She must have been abducted some time on Wednesday morning," said Claire. "Sally saw her at seven when she came out of her room to say she was going back to sleep and would take the 9:20 bus. Even if she overslept and planned to take a later bus, we can be pretty sure she was gone before her one o'clock tutorial with Dr. Foley."

"Evidently she had taken—or was given—a heavy dose of barbiturates, but we have to wait for the test results from the laboratory to confirm that."

"Then she might have been kept alive for a time before—"

"Yes, it would appear so."

"Was she still clothed?"

"No. The body was nude but wrapped in a quilt. If we can find her clothing, we hope it will give us a clue to the killer."

"Neil, had she been—that is, was she sexually assaulted?"

"Yes, probably so. There was slight bruising at the entrance to the vagina, and seminal fluid was present."

Claire stared into the fire, where a green flare shot up from the burning logs. Remembering a notorious case in California the previous year, she hesitated, then asked, "She hadn't been otherwise tortured, had she?"

Neil took her hand. "No, darling, thank God for

that. No sign of physical violence, except at the throat, of course. Not even signs of a struggle. No flesh under the fingernails, for example, or bruises on the arms. We can hope that she was sufficiently sedated not to have suffered too much."

After a while, Claire served up some Chinese take-away and a bottle of wine at the small table in Bea's kitchen. This was no time for a candlelight dinner. Neil's troubled silences were not unexpected, but it occurred to her that he wanted to say something else, and hadn't made up his mind whether or not to do it.

She looked into his eyes, their warm brown dulled with anxiety. "There's something else, isn't there?"

"Yes. This is utterly confidential, Claire."

She was surprised at his reiteration of caution, as he had long ago learned that he could trust her without question. It had, in fact, been good for him to be able to talk freely to her about his cases, a solace he hadn't got from his wife.

"You see, there was a mark on the body which may be a 'signature' for this particular killer. It looks like the letter 'C,' about an inch high, carved into the flesh between the breasts. From the minimum of bleeding, it appears to have been done after death, but probably quite soon after. Obviously, this mustn't be made known. We might get a copycat murder, and more important, we want to be sure it's the same bloke if we find another one."

"Then you do expect he will kill again?"

"I'm afraid so, although we can hope to catch him before he does."

"Have there been others in the past with this mark?"

"Apparently not. We've had the HOLMES office in London checking the computer records throughout the United Kingdom and they've not come up with anything similar."

"I wonder what the 'C' could mean. If it's the initial of a person, it may be someone the killer loves."

"Or someone he hates."

At ten o'clock, Neil said he should be getting back to the station.

"I'll stop by the Incident Room on the way home, but let's be sure you're thoroughly locked up before I go."

Having lived in the days when people in the country seldom locked their doors, Bea had been persuaded in recent years to install double locks front and back and security catches on the ground-floor windows.

When Neil had checked these out again, as he had done the night before, Claire smiled grimly. "Don't worry, darling. The repeat killers usually follow patterns in their victims, don't they? This one appears to go for young women. I don't think this lady of forty-five will appeal to him."

Holding her close, Neil said, "She appeals to *me*. I'd like to stay and show her how much, but not tonight."

Chapter

8

Frieda Nolan opened her eyes and looked fuzzily at the bedside clock. Seven-thirty. Pretty early for a Sunday morning. Turning lazily on her side, she studied her sleeping husband. Not exactly a prepossessing sight. Mouth slightly open, little gaspy snorts on every third or fourth breath. His wispy beard was more red than gray, but you couldn't say the same for his hair, which sprouted only a few strands of its original color.

So what did she see in him? It was the old Irish charm, no doubt about it. He wasn't even the world's greatest lover, although last night had been more than satisfactory. She stretched and smiled to herself, holding up an arm to check for bruises. A couple of green spots, but nothing a sleeve wouldn't cover. She didn't really mind that Barry needed a little rough stuff before he got turned on. At least it wasn't boring. But she sometimes wondered about his chronic philandering. Was it all talk and no action? Hard to say.

Anyhow, it was no problem for her at the moment. Again, she stretched luxuriously. Off and on for a couple of months now, she'd had her own consolation prize. When Barry took the TYA assignment, she had thought vaguely that she might find an English lover during the course of the year, but that it happened so soon was pure luck. At their first meeting, what the French called "the language of the eyes" had gone into full operation, but only between the two of them. To the others present, they were propriety itself. Then she had made all the right moves, and the rest was easy.

What a contrast to Barry he was. Undemanding, grateful, as if she were a princess granting royal favors. And Barry hadn't a clue. She smiled to herself.

At last, the thought of coffee lured her out of bed and into her bright, modern kitchen. Claire was right, she thought. She'd have hated an antiquated place to cook. This little house was just right for the year. She loved being in England, in spite of the weather, its green countryside welcome after dry southern California, and its literary associations enticing. She'd enjoyed going with Barry and the students on their tour of Dartmoor, and on the excursion to the Thomas Hardy country in nearby Dorset.

She caught her breath, remembering Cheryl Bailey on the tours. A lovely, slim girl, quiet and intelligent.

Poor old Barry. When he'd had to go to the morgue to identify the body, she'd never seen him so shaken.

Think about something else.

This afternoon she was going with Claire to check out the rest of the letters written by the artist cousin to Mary Louise Talbot. Claire had given her copies of the first three, and they were fascinating. Frieda loved everything to do with research: looking things up in the library, reading all the preceding critical writing on a given topic, putting together a thesis that gave a new interpretation of a work or related it to an incident in the author's life or to contemporary society. What she didn't like was the writing. That was slavery.

In the Victorian seminar, Claire had urged her to turn her term paper into publishable form and send it out to a journal in the field, but Frieda had laughed and said she was too lazy. She admired Claire's energy, but all that work wasn't for her.

And there was Sally, no doubt following in her mother's footsteps. What a great kid she was. Bright and pretty, with a mind of her own but with a loving nature. In the five years Frieda had known her, she had sometimes looked at Sally and thought maybe she missed something, not having a child. Her ex-husband hadn't wanted children, and to be honest, she had to admit she hadn't tried to change his mind. Then the marriage broke up and she was glad there were none. She'd never been keen on the diapers-and-bottles bit. What she might have liked was to be presented with a Sally about the age of ten.

But was it really too late? She was only thirty-three and feeling great. True, Barry had two grown sons living on the east coast, and he'd never wanted more kids. He'd taken care of that problem long ago. But maybe he would change his mind, if she asked him sweetly. He was crazy about her, after all. They could always reverse the surgery.

No harm in trying.

But when they were sitting over their breakfast and she casually dropped the question, he stared at her. "Listen, sweetie, you have to be kidding. No way."

At three o'clock that afternoon, Claire set off with Frieda for Sudbury, with Frieda holding the map as navigator. Neil had said it was no more than half an hour's drive, but that's if you knew where you were going. Experience, as Claire told Frieda, had taught her to allow plenty of time for the vagaries of English topography.

"Miles could usually zip around London with ease, but even he had trouble finding places he wasn't familiar with."

Frieda said quietly, "I know the divorce was rough for you, Claire. Is it easier now?"

"Yes. Time the healer, and all that."

"And having Neil?"

"Sure, but it was getting better before."

"I wonder if living in two countries was too much pressure?"

Claire shook her head. "Actually, no. I took several leaves, when Sally and I stayed in London. She went to school here twice and loved it. We always had summers and long holidays together, and Miles took two leaves and stayed with us in South Coast. No, it wasn't that, Frieda. I think he knew for a long time that he wanted to acknowledge his sexual preference, and when he met Pierre, that was the deciding factor."

"Are they still together?"

"Yes, and evidently it's a good relationship. Sally has handled it very well and enjoys her visits with them."

"I'd say you've handled it well, too, Claire."

"Not at first, I'm afraid, but later on I accepted it."

As they approached the A38, they concentrated on getting onto the correct on ramp. From there, finding Sudbury proved easy enough. A few miles on the A38, then the turnoff, and some perfectly clear signposts to the town. In the summer, any approach to the seaside would be clogged with cars, especially on a Sunday, but on a miserable day in November, the traffic was light.

Finding "The Laurels" was another story. Sudbury may have been a tiny village in the 1860s, when Prudence Halley was writing her letters to Mary Louise

Talbot, but not now. A large town, it bristled with traffic lights, one-way streets, and the inevitable rows of bed-and-breakfast hotels. Threading their way through the town center, they made a wrong turn and found themselves in a bewildering network of angled streets from which they escaped by sheer good luck, emerging onto a main road that eventually led to the seaside esplanade. Here, through thickened traffic, they moved slowly along, the sea at their left gray and sullen under glowering clouds.

Ahead of them towered the sheer cliff of a headland, dotted with houses along its rim. Frieda, studying the directions, said, "It must be up there. What a view she must have."

But when the road climbed and leveled at the top of the hill, and they had turned onto Cudworth Way, they went along inland for a quarter of a mile or so before finding The Laurels. Smaller than most of its neighbors in the street, the house would have been described as modest even in Prudence Halley's day. Now, its peeling paint and neglected front garden suggested its owner was less affluent than her neighbors.

Pausing in front of the house, Claire looked at her watch. Quarter to four. As she hesitated, a thin woman came out the door and down the walk, approaching the car with a tentative smile. "Dr. Camden?"

"Yes. I'm afraid we're rather early."

"No, it's quite all right. I'm Mrs. Vickers. Won't you come in, please?"

Claire introduced Frieda and they followed their hostess up the walk.

"I'm afraid the garden is in a dreadful state. Since my husband died, I have been quite unable to manage it."

Beyond the small entry hall, they were ushered into

a room at the left which was surely the parlor, used only for guests.

Mrs. Vickers' pale face looked chronically anxious. "Please sit down. I'll just bring the tea. I won't be a moment."

Delighted with the classic Victorian charm of the room where they sat, Claire exchanged a smile with Frieda. "This must be exactly as it was in Prudence's day."

"It's marvelous."

The dark wood of tables and cabinets, the green plush of the chairs, the curio cabinet with china shepherdesses and ruby crystal were characteristic of the period but reflected a personal taste beyond the ordinary. Only the oil painting hanging over the mantel seemed out of keeping with the mid-nineteenth-century decor. Its swirls of reds and yellows, blues and grays, looked more like something in today's contemporary art, yet with a thickness of paint and a finish that reminded Claire of something else.

Stepping up for a closer look, she saw on the simple gold frame the title in black letters: *Sunrise at Sea,* and in the lower right corner of the painting the initials "P. H." She moved back until the paint strokes began to blend and take form, and now she could identify the white tips of gray waves and the fragments of blue sky suggestively emerging from the overwhelming blaze of sunrise colors.

"Look, Frieda. This is done by Prudence herself. I'm no art critic, but I think this is rather good. She mentions admiring Turner. It looks something like his late style, don't you think?"

Frieda looked up. "Now you mention it, it does look like some of those we saw at the Tate in London, especially the ones that look so modern you can't tell what they are. I like the colors. They really glow."

Mrs. Vickers, coming in with the tea trolley, looked

pleased when Claire expressed admiration for the painting.

"Yes, Prudence was truly gifted, was she not? She evidently earned a good part of her income with the sale of her sketches and watercolors, most unusual for a lady in her day."

When the tea had been poured and the cakes handed round, Mrs. Vickers' face lighted with her timid smile. "I do a little drawing but I'm afraid I haven't inherited the family talent. I was rather hoping Toby would show some aptitude, but he has not."

The roar of a motorbike coming up the drive brought a glow to the pale face of their hostess. "Oh, here is Toby now!"

A boy of sixteen or so stood in the parlor door, looking with frank curiosity at Claire and Frieda.

Introduced, he turned to Claire. "You're the lady as wants to see the other letters, right?"

Chapter

CLAIRE WONDERED if Mrs. Vickers, that model of gentle propriety, would be embarrassed by Toby's crass question, but she saw only the glow of maternal pride as the mother watched her son help himself to a mammoth slice of cake and sit down on a tufted chair, his legs stretched to the limit.

"Was there anything available at the garage, dear?"

Toby, mouth full of cake, said "Rrhh," to which his mother smiled sadly. "Since he left school, Toby has been seeking employment, but in these times there is so little one can find."

Claire murmured sympathetically, repressing a desire to suggest that Toby might help his mother with the garden, for a start, if he had been lolling around since the end of the term in the summer.

"The ladies have been admiring the painting of our ancestress," Mrs. Vickers went on.

Toby glanced toward the mantel. "Looks like a blob, dunnit! But I asked the bloke at the antique shop to have a look and he said it would fetch something, only Mum didn't want to sell."

"It wasn't very much, dear. Truth to tell, I believe he wanted it for the frame."

Frieda asked, "Is this the only Prudence Halley painting you have, Mrs. Vickers?"

"No, there are a few canvases in the attic. This is the only one that is framed, and I've never got round to doing anything with the others."

Claire decided it was time to get down to the business of the day. "As for the letters, Mrs. Vickers, I wondered how they came to be in your possession? Often letters remain among the effects of the person to whom they were written."

"Oh, yes, I see. After Mary Louise Talbot died, her son sent the letters back here to The Laurels, where Prudence's nephew still resided. He enclosed a note saying that Prudence Halley's descendants might wish to have them. Evidently he was going through his mother's things and kindly returned many such items to the families concerned."

The ring of the doorbell brought Mrs. Vickers to her feet with a flutter. "Oh, that will be my neighbor, Rodney Simms. He is the person who called my attention to your request for information relating to Mary Louise Talbot. I asked him to step in while you were here."

A plump young man in his twenties came into the parlor, smiling broadly. When introductions had been made, he turned to Claire.

"It's such a pleasure to meet you, Dr. Camden. I'm terribly excited about your book on Talbot. High time someone did her life, I must say. Such a popular writer in her day, and quite the equal of Wilkie Collins in novels like *The Secret of Lady Caroline* and *The Specimen,* wouldn't you say?"

Claire smiled. "Yes, I agree. It's always a pleasure to know people still read Talbot today."

"Actually, I began reading her novels on the recommendation of a friend. Oh, thank you, Mary. Yes, the cherry cake, if you please." Rodney Simms took the teacup proffered by his hostess and went on. "Mary had told me that she had some letters from Prudence Halley to her cousin, and when I saw your notice in the *TLS*, I snipped it out and suggested she write to you."

"I'm most grateful, Mr. Simms."

"Rodney, please!"

Claire smiled again. "Rodney, then. Have you seen the letters?"

Rodney swallowed a forkful of cake before answering. "Oh, I looked through them rather hastily. Can't say I read them all. You know how difficult it is to decipher that Victorian handwriting."

Mrs. Vickers said shyly, "I tried, too, but I'm afraid I gave it up after a bit."

Rodney looked at Claire curiously. "You're from the States, Dr. Camden?"

"Yes, from California."

"I must confess I'm surprised that you are an American lady, as I believe you gave a London address. Do you live in England, then?"

"I'm here on leave for the year. At the moment I'm staying in Morbridge until January."

Young Toby's head shot up. "Morbridge? That's near where the American student's body was found—out on the moor, wasn't it? It's been on the telly."

Rodney Simms' eyes glinted with curiosity. "Did you know her?"

On the drive down, Claire and Frieda had agreed that if that question arose, as well it might only a few miles from Dartmoor, they would deny any acquaintance with Cheryl Bailey. Both were too shaken by the girl's death to be willing to discuss it with strangers.

Accordingly, both murmured negations, and Frieda briskly switched the conversation to the purpose of their visit. "How many of Prudence Halley's letters are there, Mrs. Vickers? May we see them?"

With a nervous glance at her son, Mary Vickers stepped over to a handsome escritoire, opened the desk top, and removed from a pigeonhole a small bundle, tied with a pale blue ribbon. "There are ten here, in addition to the three I sent to you. Toby said I ought to have sent only photocopies, but I'd already posted them before I mentioned it to him. These go up to the time of her death in 1863."

Claire's heart gave a leap as the letters were placed in her hands. No lover, on seeing letters from the beloved, could be more inflamed than a literary scholar at the sight of correspondence that may prove vital to the work in hand.

She untied the ribbon. Yes, there on the top was the note from Talbot's son. Laying it carefully aside, she opened the first letter, noting the date a few weeks following the last one she had read.

Toby wasted no time. "I expect these ought to fetch a good price, Dr. Camden?"

Claire smiled. "Well, Toby, as 'autographs,' the letters have little value, since Prudence Halley was not herself a person of renown. Their references to Mary Louise Talbot, however, might be of interest to a university library, but the value would be relatively small."

"How about for yourself, then? Would you give fifty quid to have a look at 'em?"

"Toby!" Mrs. Vickers looked distractedly at Rodney Simms, as if for support, but Rodney deserted the ship. "Why not, Mary?" he asked. "If you can make something from them, you may as well."

"But Dr. Camden needs only to look at them, not to own them, isn't that correct?"

Claire nodded. "Yes. I can work from photocopies if need be, although having the originals is sometimes better. They would be returned to you promptly, of course. I might point out that after my book is published, there may be some slight revival of interest in Talbot. You would no doubt get a better price for them then than now."

Toby's eyes narrowed. "But you'll need to see them now, before you finish writing the book, won't you?"

He's got me there, Claire thought. I wonder if the little creep worked that out for himself or had some help from friend Rodney.

Curbing her longing to snatch the letters and run for the car, Claire said coolly, "I believe they may be of interest, yes. I can't be sure till I've read them, of course."

Mrs. Vickers opened her mouth and closed it again, obviously wanting to offer the letters but terrified of crossing her son.

Rodney gave Claire a shrewd look. "I do believe you will find them helpful, from what I've read."

Claire decided to throw in the towel. After all, it would be worth fifty pounds—roughly a hundred dollars—out of her grant to see them. She took out her checkbook and wrote the amount to Mary Vickers, whose embarrassment, mixed with pleasure at the sight of the money, was painful to see.

Frieda broke into the lady's protestations of apology and thanks by asking if they might see the other paintings of Prudence Halley.

"Yes, indeed! If you'll just step this way."

Like a line of ducks, they followed her up the staircase to the floor above, where they saw the doors of four bedrooms, two on each side of the stairs. Mrs. Vickers explained that she took lodgers in the summer but was too far from the town center to keep the rooms occupied the year round.

At the back of the house, a steep flight of uncarpeted stairs led to the attic, where the clutter of objects had obviously been set in order by the recent cleanup. Against a wall, resting face down on an old trunk, were three canvases on stretchers.

Lifting the top painting, Mrs. Vickers picked up a cloth and flicked over its surface before setting it out to view. "These are all that are left now. I remember my grandmother Halley saying there had been some watercolors and etchings in her day until her father sold them off, but no one ever wanted the oils, it seems."

Reaching for the other pictures, Rodney Simms stepped forward. "Here, let me help you, Mary." With his plump hands, he set the other canvases out where they could be seen.

All three were similar in style to the framed oil in the sitting room, although the subjects differed. One appeared to be a view of the headland from below, suggesting the sweep of the shore and the cliff towering in an ominous gloom of blacks, browns, and grays. Another was a particularly Turneresque study, with fragments of what might be sailing ships tossed wildly in a murky sea. The third was serene, suggesting light on water, Claire thought, but difficult to identify.

Rodney's round face was solemn. "Of course it's obvious that J.M.W. Turner was her god. Even if we didn't know that from her letters, we can see it in these."

Claire nodded. "It's fascinating that her paintings are so nearly nonrepresentational, yet there *is* a discernible subject in all but this one. Or have I just missed it?"

Rodney thought he detected a small boat; Frieda asked if a white bit might be a bird; Mrs. Vickers timidly wondered whether certain blues were sky or water.

This was too esoteric for Toby, who announced, "I'll be off then, Mum," and clattered down the stairs.

When they had returned for a last cup of tea and bade their farewells, Claire and Frieda drove back through the town with no problem. "Easier when you know where you are," Frieda remarked.

When they had turned onto the A38, Claire said with a frown, "I'd like to think my fifty pounds would help Mrs. Vickers, but I'm afraid that lout Toby will have it out of her by the time the banks open tomorrow."

"It's known as mother love, I guess. With her husband gone, Toby is all she has. Unless neighbor Rodney is more than just a friend."

"I doubt it. She must be at least ten years older than Rodney. Besides, it didn't look like it to me."

Frieda smiled to herself. "You never know about things like that."

As they drove into Morbridge, approaching the car park next to the Crown, Claire heard a triumphant hiss from Frieda.

"Look! There's our car. Barry's visiting his poor little Nora. Let's go in. You can use a drink, can't you?"

Claire hesitated, then decided she may as well leave Frieda at the Crown, where Barry could take her home. If the two of them erupted into fireworks, she could slip away.

She needn't have worried. Too early for the Sunday evening crowd, customers in the pub were scarce, and Frieda oozed charm as they walked in and found Barry perched on a stool, engaged in conversation with an extremely pretty young woman on the other side of the bar.

"Hello, darling, we saw the car and decided to join you for a drink."

Barry beamed. With an arm around each, he kissed Frieda, then leaned toward Claire, who adroitly turned to catch the kiss on her cheek. "So, did you find Sudbury all right? And the letters?"

"Right. No problem. Claire's got them." Frieda smiled angelically. "Hello, Nora. How are you?"

"I'm fine, thank you, Mrs. Nolan."

Claire studied Nora as she took their orders and prepared the drinks. Claire had been in the Crown off and on in the past, but not since Nora had come to work there, and she saw why men would be enamored. Nora was young, about Sally's age probably, with an enchanting smile, masses of black silky curls halfway down her back, fair skin, deep blue eyes, and a body to die for. She certainly didn't fit the picture Barry had sketched of someone who'd had a hard life and needed kindness, but who knows from looking?

Frieda was talking brightly to Barry, leaning on his arm, her attractive face close to his, claiming possession. No doubt wasted on Nora, Claire thought. To Nora, Frieda probably looks too old to matter and Barry could stand in for the Ancient Mariner.

Claire was sipping her drink when a bearded face appeared at her side and a low voice said, "A pint, please, Nora."

Nora turned her miraculous blue gaze toward the man. "Hello, Jasper. What's up?"

"Nothing new. How's the nipper?"

Nora's glow turned up a few gamma rays. "Never better. He'll be five tomorrow."

Must be older than I guessed, Claire thought, if she has a child of five.

Now she turned to the man at her right. Deciding "stepfather" sounded too absurd, she said, "You're Jasper Martinelli, aren't you? Adrian's—er—friend? I'm Claire Camden. I believe we met one day at the Priory."

Jasper looked into Claire's face, then past her to

the Nolans, and recollection seemed to seep slowly in. "Oh, yes, you came to tea."

"Frieda, Barry, you remember Jasper? At the Priory?"

Both Nolans smiled politely and Barry said, "Of course. Good to see you."

They covered the weather and moved inevitably to the topic of the murder, joined by Nora, who gave Barry a look of melting pity. "Poor Dr. Nolan had to go to identify the body. It must have been dreadful."

Frieda dripped molasses. "Yes, poor darling." She gave him a wifely kiss on the cheek and patted his arm consolingly.

Nora's voice was solemn. "Did you know her, Jasper?"

"Scarcely at all. I spoke with her once or twice, I believe."

Nora shivered. "The police say we must all be careful till the man's caught. I'm having someone walk me home at night, I can tell you."

Plenty of willing candidates for that job, Claire thought, as she finished her drink, thanked Frieda for going to Sudbury, and made her farewells.

Chapter

10

ONCE SHE HAD CHECKED that Sally was all right, Claire changed into sweats and warmed some leftovers in Bea's microwave, watching the news as she ate. She was just in time to catch Neil, being interviewed as senior officer for the area, looking grave, reviewing the steps being taken by the police to search for the killer, acknowledging that there were no leads at the moment.

At seven o'clock, Claire decided this might be an appropriate time to phone Mrs. Bailey in California, where it would be eleven o'clock on a Sunday morning. Hearing Cheryl's mother's voice, she swallowed hard, then expressed her sorrow as briefly but poignantly as she could. Asking if Sally and Brenda might call, she was touched by the quiet dignity of the response. "Cheryl was very happy with your daughter and her friend, Mrs. Camden. I would be glad to speak with them."

With an effort, Claire tore her mind away from the pain of the tragedy. Since Neil was spending the evening at the station, she would take a look at the new Prudence Halley letters. She had transcribed the first three onto a disk, and now she settled at the word processor to go on with the task.

In the fourth letter, after various salutations and replies to Mary's last, Prudence described her first meeting with the painter Turner.

I am delighted to learn of your admiration for Mr. Turner's work and will be happy to tell you how it came about that we met. There is a shop here in Sudbury where summer visitors sometimes buy my sketches and watercolors. It was one day in early June, at the beginning of the season, in the year 1847. I had brought my portfolio into the shop and was giving the proprietor some selections of my work to be offered for sale. One of my oils on a stretcher was in the folder, and I had propped it against a wall to be out of the way. It was a seascape, showing a fishing boat barely visible through the mist. We had just finished our transactions when I heard a voice behind me.

"Excuse me, madam, is that yours?"

I turned and saw an elderly gentleman, small in stature, and not at all well dressed, looking at my painting from a distance of ten feet or so.

I said, "Yes, sir, it is mine."

He gave a kind of snort and stared at me most rudely. At that, the shopkeeper dropped my sketches and gave a deep bow. "Good afternoon, Mr. Turner. It is an honor to have you here, sir. How may I serve you?"

Mary, you may well imagine my astonishment. From the shopkeeper's manner, there was little doubt that this was the great painter himself. I kept my eyes lowered, as I did not wish to stare, while he purchased a large sketch pad and some pencils, which were wrapped in brown paper for him. The shopkeeper asked where he should send the parcel and was told The Bull, an inn on the waterfront. I stole a quick glance at Mr. Turner and saw that he was studying my watercolors and sketches. "Very pretty, very ladylike," he said to me, "but why do you do these and paint like that?" and he pointed to my oil.

Incensed at his lack of courtesy, I looked him straight in the eye. "I sell these, sir. I paint my oils as I must, for myself alone." And with that, I picked up my things and walked out of the shop without so much as a backward glance.

At this date, I had of course seen many reproductions of Mr. Turner's work in engravings, done by himself as well as by others, but only once had I seen his paintings in the original. This was on a memorable visit to London with my parents in the summer of 1828. We went first to the National Gallery, which had been opened four years earlier so that the public might have the opportunity to view many great works of art. At that time, the pictures were still in the Pall Mall at the former home of Mr. Angerstein, who had given his collection to the nation.

I was overcome by seeing works by such masters of the past as Correggio, Titian, and Claude Lorrain, to name but a few. I also enjoyed the more recent works of Mr. Reynolds and Mr. Gainsborough, combining as they do the arts of landscape and portrait, with aristocratic ladies in their dazzling gowns against a background of trees and sky.

On the following day, my father took us to the Royal Academy, where the works of today's artists are hung at this time each year. It was here I saw several magnificent paintings that Mr. Turner had done within the past year. There were two works on themes of antiquity, and most enchanting to me, two paintings done of the regatta at East Cowes, magical in their treatment of light on the water.

Having formed such admiration for his artistry, it was therefore a great sorrow to me, as you can well imagine, that my meeting with Mr. Turner had produced such an unpleasant impression. His scorn for my work was surely understandable, but I saw no necessity for him to express it so openly. It was therefore the more surprising when, on the following day, we met again. I was sitting on the headland, sketching a view of the town and the harbor, when I heard a voice behind me. "Miss Halley?"

I glanced round and saw that it was he. I said, "Good afternoon, Mr. Turner," and went on with my sketch as if he were not there. He must have obtained my name from the shopkeeper, but he made no explanation. At last, he said, "Come, show me what else you have done."

At that, I looked up at him and saw that there was no malice in his eye, only a kindled interest.

"Very well," I replied. Without haste, I gathered up my things and began to walk back on the road toward my house. He came along at my side, saying nothing. It is a walk of perhaps a quarter of a mile, and in that time we exchanged not a word, yet I felt a curious calm in his presence. I have always found it tiresome to be forced to express the usual pleasantries required by social intercourse, and clearly Mr. Turner was of the same mind.

When we reached The Laurels, I laid down my things and led the way up one flight to my studio, where I displayed some of the oils I had done within the past year. He studied them for a time, then gave me a piercing look. "What have you seen of my work, Miss Halley?"

I named those I had seen in London.

"Nothing since?"

"No, sir."

"Very well. When next you visit London, come to see me here." He handed me a card. "I have something to show you."

I believe he saw my hesitation, for before I could protest against the cost of the journey, he said quickly, "I should like to have this one, if I may." He held up an unframed canvas, a view of the harbor with the light emerging through heavy clouds, the colors swirled so that the subject was not clearly delineated.

And the next moment he had laid some guineas on the table, seized the painting, and vanished down the stairs.

I must tell you, my dear Mary, that I have never spoken of this to anyone until now. Although you and I have not met, I am confident that you will understand the nature of this encounter. At that date, I was thirty-seven years of age and Mr. Turner was past seventy. Nevertheless, you may well imagine the horror with which our Cornwall relations would regard the impropriety of my taking a strange man into my house without a chaperone and without a proper introduction. I can only say that never for a moment had I the least doubt of his integrity. His manner was far from polished, his language had none of the Cambridge affectations of my brothers' speech but did rather reflect his more humble origins, yet Mr. Turner was a true gentleman. That he did not engage in the outward amenities of polite conversation was, in my view, greatly to his credit.

The letter closed with the usual greetings to Mary's extended family, and Claire sat with it in her hand, her heart doing little flip-ups. The episode she had just read, describing the meeting on the cliff, was reproduced in Mary Louise Talbot's novel, *Eleanor*, published in 1865, three years after the date of the letter from Prudence Halley.

In the novel, the heroine, Eleanor, falls in love with an artist of humble origins and unpolished manners, to the horror of her parents, who consider the man totally unsuitable for their daughter. Critics at the time the novel appeared had noted certain parallels to J.M.W. Turner in the character of the painter. Now, Prudence's letter provided new material, hitherto unknown to scholarship, establishing a source for the incident in the novel. No doubt, subsequent letters would add more to the story.

Claire laid the letter on the desk and was eagerly reaching for the next one when the phone rang. It was Neil, calling from the flat where he lived in Kings Abbey, not far from the police headquarters.

"I walked here to fix a meal and relax for a bit. What happened this afternoon, love? Did you get the letters?"

Claire gave him a summary of the visit to Sudbury, describing young Toby conning her into the fifty pounds. "It's worth it, though, to get the letters. By the way, darling, I caught you on the telly. You looked marvelous, to my prejudiced eye."

"Thanks, but I'm not reading for a part on the stage, you know."

"Don't be silly. You know what I mean. Is there anything new on the case?"

"Nothing I can mention on the telephone. I'll see you tomorrow evening, shall I?"

That same afternoon, while Claire and Frieda were in Sudbury, a sergeant was assigned to call on George Foley, the professor Cheryl Bailey had been said to admire. Once the young woman's body was found, officers had been sent out to talk again with everyone who had known Cheryl. This was the third interview with the professor. The constable who had spoken with him on the campus on Thursday, and again on Friday, had been assured that Foley had not seen Cheryl at any time since her last attendance at his tutorial, but the constable mentioned in his notes that the professor had seemed unduly nervous.

Now, one of the TYA students, questioned again on Saturday, had stated that she had seen Cheryl sitting with Dr. Foley in his car in a campus car park, about a week before her disappearance. Desperate for leads, Neil and his detective chief inspector, deciding that another interview was in order, dispatched James Barnes, a uniformed sergeant known for his skill at low-keyed questioning. "One look at that wholesome country-bred face," Neil had once remarked, "and hardened types are beguiled."

As it was a Sunday, the sergeant went to Foley's home, a pleasant house with a generous garden, set back under trees on a lane a mile or so beyond the village of Bickford, in the direction of Exeter.

The door was answered by a woman of thirty or so, wearing jeans and a sweatshirt, her brown hair drawn back in a ponytail. The fine bones of her pale face reminded the sergeant of one of those Gainsborough ladies they had studied in school, so classic was its look of the well-bred Englishwoman.

"Yes?" The tone was icy.

"Mrs. Foley?"

"Yes."

"I should like to speak with your husband, if I may."

"Wait here, please."

The sergeant heard the murmur of voices beyond the hall. Then a thin man came to the doorway, his high forehead creased.

"I am Dr. Foley. How may I help you?"

"I am Sergeant James Barnes. I should like to ask you some questions, sir."

"Is this concerning Miss Bailey?"

"Yes, sir."

"Really, Sergeant, I have nothing to add to what I have already told the police."

"I understand, sir. However, we have had a report which occasions further questions. If I may come in, please?"

Foley shrugged and led the way to a spacious sitting room, its walls lined with books. "Have a seat."

He walked over to a table lined with bottles and glasses. "Will you have a whiskey, Sergeant?"

"Thank you, no, sir."

"Caroline?"

"Yes, please."

Foley poured two sizable drinks, splashed them with soda, handed one to his wife, and took the other to a chair opposite the sergeant, where he assumed a negligent pose, long legs extended and crossed at the ankles.

"So, what is this new report, may I ask?"

The sergeant heard the casual tone but noticed the trembling of the professor's hand as he took a deep drink and set the glass down on a table at his side.

Taking out his notebook, Barnes made a show of consulting his notes. "One of the students at the university has reported seeing you and Miss Bailey, seated in your automobile, engaged in conversation."

Caroline Foley glanced sharply at her husband. It was she who asked, "When was this?"

"The young lady believes it was a week or so before Miss Bailey's disappearance. Can you tell me about this, sir?"

Foley made a show of trying to recall. "Yes, I believe I did offer her a ride one day. It was of no consequence."

"And where did this occur, sir?"

"Let me think. Miss Bailey was waiting for the bus to Exeter. I simply stopped and said, 'Hop in,' and we drove on to the campus."

"On what date did this take place, sir?"

"I've no idea. It may well have been the week before last."

"At what time of day, please?"

"Oh, it would have been in the morning, would it not?"

"That is for you to say, sir."

"Yes, I'm sure it was in the morning. Perhaps nine o'clock or so."

Then Caroline Foley spoke again. "I believe I saw in the news that Miss Bailey lived with her housemates in Bickford. Is that correct, Sergeant?"

"Yes, madam. Below the Priory, between the village and the Exeter road."

"I see."

The sergeant wrote slowly in his notebook, letting the silence lengthen. Foley was clearly squirming, as all three fully understood that his normal route from his home to the university would have taken him in the opposite direction. To reach the spot where Cheryl waited, he would have had to go back through the village, turn onto Newton Lane, drive past the cottage where the young women lived, and follow the lane for a quarter of a mile to the bus stop.

Now Foley ran a bony hand through his hair. "I believe I went into the village for something and decided to go along Newton Lane to the Exeter road."

Caroline Foley's lips tightened but she said nothing.

Can't wait for me to leave, thought the sergeant. By then, her husband will have had time to think of a reason for stopping in the village. Cigarettes? No, they obviously didn't smoke. He'll have to come up with something.

Now it was time for him to drop his small grenade. "Thank you, sir. That must have been on a separate occasion, then, as the young lady described seeing you with Miss Bailey in the afternoon."

"Oh, I see. Well, then, I seem to recall an occasion when we came out of the tutorial together. She walked along with me to the car park. We were speaking of her essay, and I suggested she sit in the car while we finished our discussion."

"At what time would this have been, sir?"

Caroline Foley spoke sharply. "The tutorial meets from one to three o'clock, does it not?"

The professor looked uneasy. "Yes, yes, so it does."

His wife went on. "Then it would have been shortly after three. Is that correct, Sergeant?"

Barnes again studied his notes. "The report names half-past four o'clock."

Foley made a try. "We may have gone to my office first. I really don't recall."

Again the sergeant let some moments of silence pass. Then he asked, "Now, Dr. Foley, will you please describe in detail your movements on Wednesday last?"

"Look, I've been over this ground twice already. I really have nothing to add. I went to the university, arriving about half-past nine, met with students in my office, attended a meeting with other faculty, met my tutorial from one to three, and returned home about four o'clock."

"And you were at home all evening and through the night?"

"Yes, certainly."

"And Mrs. Foley? You were also at home?"

Caroline's eyes flicked up in surprise, then she said smoothly, "On Wednesday? Yes, I was at home."

The sergeant rose. "Thank you very much, sir. You may be asked to come into the station and sign a statement."

At this, Caroline Foley flashed out in anger. "Really, Sergeant, this is absurd. My husband has answered all of your questions. Anything more may constitute harassment."

She turned to her husband. "George, perhaps we should consult Daddy. Who is your superior, Sergeant?"

"Detective Superintendent Padgett, madam."

"My father, Alastair Dutworth, is a member from Hampshire. There have been questions in the House on the activities of the police. Will you please inform your superior accordingly?"

Barnes had been around long enough to guess at the reception this statement would receive from the superintendent, but he kept his face solemn as he promised to deliver her message.

Driving back to the station, Barnes mused. Something fishy there, the way the lady looked when I asked if she was at home that night.

The sergeant's shrewd guess wasn't far wrong, for when he had gone, Caroline Foley turned to her husband.

"Wednesday night, George? Wasn't that the night I was in Hampshire with Mummy and Daddy?"

Chapter

11

By TEN O'CLOCK THAT EVENING, the last drinks had been ordered at the Crown, the proprietor had dimmed the lights to signal the early Sunday closing time, and the last of the customers had straggled out the door. Only Barry Nolan still sat at the end of the bar, watching Nora McBain as she washed up the last of the glasses and wiped the surface of the bar.

She looked up, her soft cheeks dimpling as she smiled. "It's kind of you to wait, Dr. Nolan."

"I'm not having you walk home alone, Nora."

"Thanks, then. I won't be a minute."

She disappeared into the ladies' room, while Barry watched the proprietor make his rounds, locking up for the night.

Barry still couldn't believe his luck. When he and Frieda had left the Crown earlier that evening, she had been sweet as an angel, saying not a word about Nora and preparing a scrumptious meal. Then she announced that a neighbor had invited her to go into Kings Abbey to see a film, and would he mind?

No, go ahead, he had said. He'd work on his lecture notes.

And for a while, he did. The TYAs weren't so bad after all, he'd decided. A good bunch of kids, and all really shaken up by what had happened to Cheryl Bailey.

Thinking of Cheryl made his head throb. What he needed was a beer—or a pint, as they said over here. He'd drop into the Crown and offer to see Nora home.

Good thing he'd asked her soon after he arrived. Later, she'd had two other offers of safe conduct, which she had declined with that enchanting smile.

Now, bundled into coat and muffler against the November cold, she stepped into his car, settled back in the seat, and directed him through a network of narrow streets and down a lane that ran between the back gardens of small row houses.

"Just here," she said. "We can go through the gate. I live in the caravan."

Barry's heart did a flip as he saw that he was being invited in.

He smiled at her. "This is what we call a trailer or a mobile home in the States."

Nora fastened the gate behind them and unlocked the door of her small abode. "Would you like a coffee?"

"Yes, that would be great."

Half expecting to see a sleeping child, he asked, "Where is your little boy?"

"Willie? He's at my mum's. Just there." She pointed to the house beyond the back garden.

Nora tossed their coats onto the bed that filled one end of the caravan and gestured to a tiny built-in table with a bench on either side. "Have a seat."

While she plugged in the kettle, Barry looked around. Along the center wall was a small sink and counter top, a cabinet which probably held the W.C.,

and at his left a row of cupboards and the open door
of a closet, crammed with clothing, shoes, and odds
and ends that spilled out onto the floor. A pile of
magazines littered the table where he sat, and Nora
impatiently pushed aside some unwashed dishes as she
set out two mugs and spoons.

From conversations in the pub, Barry knew in a
general way that Nora's husband had taken off when
the child was an infant and that she had had to manage as best she could. He also knew she didn't welcome pity.

Now he asked, "Have you always lived with your
mother, then?"

"No, it's been off and on. We was in London when
Mick left, and I come back here to Mum then. I was
only sixteen, and Mum said I ought to give up Willie
to adoption, but I wouldn't hear of it. I stayed for a
year, but after that I had to leave."

Barry said, "What happened?"

Nora shrugged. "Mum's friend, as lived with us,
wanted me out. I didn't earn much, see, and he said
we was costing too much, and he didn't want a crying
brat around anyhow. Willie was ever so good, really,
but I didn't like to stay where I wasn't wanted."

"So, where did you go?"

At a whistle from the kettle, Nora made their powdered coffee and brought out a carton of milk from
the little fridge. "Milk or sugar?"

"No, nothing, thanks."

She splashed some milk into her coffee and sat
down across the table.

"Do you really want to know all this?"

"Not if you don't want to talk about it."

She put her hand on his arm. "You seem kind, Dr.
Nolan. I like you."

Barry swallowed. Frieda would think his only design

was to get Nora into the sack, but he did have his nobler side, didn't he?

He gave Nora the crinkly smile that endeared him to women of all ages, and she went on with her story.

"Well, then, I went up to Exeter and worked as housemaid and nanny for a lady who had a little one Willie's age and let us both live in. That was the best time I ever had. They lived in a beautiful house up on a hill and were very rich. The woman was a real love, and the babies were that adorable together. We was more like friends than mistress and servant, even though she was so much older. Twenty-eight or so. I was there for almost a year."

"Why did you leave?"

Nora sighed. "It was *him*."

"Her husband?"

"Right. For a long time, he didn't pay me much notice. He was always occupied with his business, on the phone and all, and away on journeys. Then, out of the blue, so to speak, he began pestering me. First, it was just pats on the bum or putting an arm on my shoulder, sort of innocent like. Nothing I could complain about. But soon, he started really coming on to me. If his wife went out for the evening, he would kiss me and run his hands down my back and that. I told him to stop, and he'd laugh and say all right, but the next time he would be after me again. Then, she took the baby and went to visit her mother, and that's when it happened."

The deep blue of Nora's eyes misted with tears, and Barry said softly, "I think I understand."

"You see, he was ever so handsome, and I hadn't been with anyone since Mick went away. I knew it was wrong, and I didn't want to hurt my lady, but I couldn't help myself."

"Of course you couldn't. It was only natural."

"You *do* understand, don't you? He was so gentle,

and he made me feel so—so happy. With Mick, we had been kids, and it was all quick and sort of rough. But with this man, it was different. It was not just sex. I saw what was meant by making love. When his wife came back, we acted as if nothing had happened, but whenever she went out in the evening, he came to my room and it was the same as before. I felt so guilty, and I tried to stop, but it was no good. Of course, in the end, she found out and I had to go."

"Was she very angry with you?"

"No, the odd thing was, she blamed *him*. She and I both cried, and she said he ought to have left me alone, that I was only a child and she pitied me. She even said she ought not to have hired me and put temptation in his path, and her next nanny would be old and gray. But still, there was no way I could stay on."

"What did you do then?"

"It's hard to find lodging where they'll have a young child, I can tell you. I lived in some seedy places. First, I worked in a laundry and found a neighbor to look after Willie. Then they cut back on staff at the laundry and I took different jobs as time went on. I put Willie in day care wherever I could. Once I found out the woman was beating the kids she looked after, and I took him away from there."

Nora stopped to drink more coffee, and Barry sat quietly, not wanting to break the spell. Obviously, she was in a mood to talk, but there was no hint of playing for sympathy in her artless recital. Her tone was matter-of-fact.

"Did you ever find a young man you could—er—be happy with?"

"There were plenty as wanted what they all want, and I didn't mind if I liked the chap. Sometimes they gave me presents or brought in food, and that was the best, as I had to feed Willie as well as meself. You wouldn't believe what he eats. He's a sturdy lad, like his dad."

"Do you ever hear from your husband?"

"Mick? Not a word, going on five years."

"Wouldn't you like to marry again, Nora?"

"I'd have to be divorced first, wouldn't I? Don't even know where to find Mick, if I did."

"Yes, I see."

Nora refilled their cups. "Last year, there was a bloke as wanted to marry me. Hubert Hart, his name is. Lives over to Kings Abbey. I was working there in a cafe. He was ever so kind. Lived with his mum, went to church, or chapel rather. Very strict and all. He wanted to find Mick and have me get free. I said, Why didn't we just live together, and he was that shocked, said it was against his beliefs. He was an odd one. We'd kiss and fondle and all, but he never went the whole way. In the end, he found out I'd been with other chaps and he broke it off. Poor fish thought he'd been the only one since Mick. He turned up here not long ago. Wanted me to go about with him again."

"Will you do that?"

The dimples flashed. "I dunno. I told him I'd think it over."

"How did you happen to come back here to Morbridge?"

"I had a bad cough, and I couldn't shake it off. In the end, I collapsed at work and they said it was pneumonia. Mum came and took Willie, and when I came out of hospital, she had the caravan moved here. At first, Mum was none too pleased, but she's grown that fond of Willie, and she said I could stay on if I could work at night. Now, I'm with him days while she works, and she keeps him while I'm at the Crown. I pay her for the caravan and something toward Willie's keep, and he sleeps in the house at night."

"Her friend no longer objects to your being here?"

"Him? Oh, he's long gone. She has another bloke now, and he doesn't take no notice. Just sits in front of the telly most evenings with his beer."

Nora drew a deep breath that turned into a lengthy yawn, and Barry stood up. "You must be tired."

"I am, a bit. Thank you for the lift, Dr. Nolan."

Barry bent over and touched his lips to the petal softness of her cheek.

"Goodnight, Nora. I've enjoyed getting to know you. Lock this door after me."

And he went back through the gate to his waiting car.

Chapter

12

By the time she was ready to quit for the night, Claire had transcribed four more of the Prudence Halley letters, and as she had hoped, she had found more material Talbot had used in the novel *Eleanor*. In the interests of romance, Talbot had made Eleanor a young woman of twenty-two and the painter in his early forties, but some incidents were taken freely from the letters.

Reading Victorian handwriting was always a minor agony, although she was pleased that Prudence's script was somewhat more legible than many others she had dealt with over the years of her research. Readers today were often amazed at the lengthy correspondence that went on in earlier times, forgetting that there were no telephones and no typewriters. If people wanted to communicate at any distance, it had to be by hand, and letter-writing was a daily occupation for those who had had the advantage of education.

After the fourth letter, in which Prudence described her first meeting with the painter Turner, the next one contained little of special interest, except for some amusingly tart comments on the eccentricities of her lodgers.

It was in letter number six that Claire found a startling statement. Evidently J.M.W. Turner had painted a portrait of Prudence Halley and given it to her. In the novel, the artist had painted several portraits of his lady, but to learn that the real Turner had done one of Prudence was another story altogether.

For many artists, this might not be front-page news, but for Turner, whose enormous output was devoted almost entirely to subjects of landscape, history, and architecture, it was surprising, to say the least. Claire was no Turner expert, but it was her general impression that he rarely did portraits. Certainly, she didn't remember seeing more than one in a fairly recent visit to the Turner wing at the Tate Gallery in London, although she might have missed something.

In the letter, Prudence gave an account of her second meeting with the painter:

I need hardly say how much I longed to accept Mr. Turner's invitation to come to his studio in London. The guineas he left were more than adequate to pay for the journey and a stay of several days in the metropolis, but in the beginning, I could not bring myself to accept, as it seemed to me his generosity arose from a momentary impulse and I might arrive and find that he regretted his invitation. I had wrapped the guineas and prepared to return them to him when I received a note, hastily scrawled on a scrap of drawing paper. It said simply, "Come on Wednesday next" and was signed, J. M. W. T.

Now I no longer hesitated. I informed my lodgers that I should be away for a few days, and on the following Monday, I set off for the town of Exeter, where I boarded a train which took me to London. The Great Western Railway had only recently extended its service into Devon and Cornwall, and what has become a commonplace mode of travel today was at that time a true miracle. You may well imagine my excitement, Mary. The speed of the train was frightening but at the same time exhilarating, and my fellow passengers exclaimed at the remarkable advances we are witnessing in our century.

When I arrived in town on the Tuesday evening, I went directly to the small hotel where I had once stopped with my parents on a visit to London. Recalling how restricted my movements had been at that time, although I was eighteen years of age—never being permitted to go out without a chaperone, and then only to the approved sites of historic interest—I experienced again the rush of joy I had felt when, after the sorrow of my parents' death, I learned that The Laurels had been left to me. It was not, of course, our family home, but merely a small house in the possession of the Halley family, and I believe now that my dear father understood my need for independence when he made the bequest to me in his will.

At the hotel in London, located in a small street leading off the Strand, I sent a note by messenger to Mr. Turner announcing my arrival and inquiring at what time he wished to receive me on the following day. The reply, another scrawl, said, "Come early." Having no idea what was meant by early, I decided upon ten o'clock in the morning. From his manner at our first meeting, I surmised that he preferred that I be informally attired, and accordingly, I rejected the one silk gown I had brought with me, and wore instead the plain mauve I had been wearing on the day we met in Sudbury, putting on my feet the stout shoes, comfortable but unfashionable, that were my daily custom.

I gave the address in Queen Anne Street to the driver of the fly, who took me along the Strand to Trafalgar Square, where I recognized the church of St. Martin-in-the-Field and the grand facade of the building which now housed the National Gallery, then up Regent Street with its elegant shops, into Oxford Street, and at last to my destination.

Mr. Turner's townhouse, although spacious, had a dreadfully neglected appearance, and the interior, as I soon saw, was the same. A sour-looking old woman opened the door to me, took my card, and asked me to wait in the hall, as if I were a visitor of no importance. However, a moment later, Mr. Turner himself appeared, looking extremely pleased to see me.

"Here you are! Splendid! Hannah, take Miss Halley's things, if you please."

He led the way through a drawing room which had once been fine but whose faded furnishings and a fine line of dust on the surfaces bespoke a lack of care. Down a long corridor, past closed doors, and up a flight of stairs, we came at last to an immense gallery, where paintings hung in masses on the walls, while others stood about on easels. I had read enough about Mr. Turner to know that this was the gallery where patrons came to view his work and to buy, although in recent years it was said that he no longer welcomed visitors. Many years earlier, he had been one of the first painters of his generation to take the bold step of opening his own gallery—first in Harley Street, as I recalled, then here—in addition to exhibiting at the Royal Academy and selling his work through dealers. That he had made a great deal of money was common knowledge, giving rise to some resentment amongst his rivals, although his genius was universally acknowledged.

Slowly, very slowly, I made the circuit of the room, studying each of the paintings, overwhelmed by the technical skill and the sheer beauty that burst with such exuberance onto the canvas. There were magnificent landscapes and scenes from mythology showing the influence of Claude, the great master who had been his first idol. There were seascapes, scenes of the English countryside, of great houses and churches, of Alpine views, of Rome, and perhaps most superb in their shimmering unreality, the incomparable scenes of Venice.

Neither of us spoke, until at last I turned and asked how it came about that so many paintings were still in his possession. "Surely, many of these were sold?"

Delighted, he chuckled and clapped his hands, like a child with a treat. "I've been buying them back!"

I stared. "Do you mean, the purchasers are willing to part with them?"

"No, no. When a patron dies, the pictures often come back onto the market, and then I buy them myself. You see, I plan to leave them to the nation! All of them! Look here—"

He led me to a homely scene titled *A Country Blacksmith Disputing upon the Price of Iron.* "I did this many years ago, in the Dutch style. Wanted to show 'em I could do anything anyone else could do. I bought it back later on. And here—"

We stood before a view of ships in a harbor, titled *The Sun Rising Through Vapour,* a marvelous example of his fascination for depicting light as it appears through mist or cloud. In a quiet voice, he said, "This, and another, I have designated to hang, after my death, in the National Gallery between two Claudes."

There was immense pride in this statement, Mary, but not a shred of vanity. In the same vein, I have heard that the poet John Keats, dying of consumption before his twenty-sixth birthday, wrote to a friend, "I think I shall be among the English poets after my death." Great artists know their worth, and it is the only thing in the end for which they care.

During my circuit of the gallery, Mr. Turner now and then looked into my face and must have seen what pleased him, for at last he said, "This is all very well, but here is what I've brought you to London to see."

He opened a door to a large studio, wonderfully sky-lighted, which was clearly a workroom. I saw, on the walls and standing about haphazardly, a large number of oil paintings, some of subjects familiar to his *oeuvre*, others in which the subjects were not discernible. They appeared to be studies in pure color, the paint thick and sometimes applied with a palette knife as well as a brush. Although immensely more skillful than my own poor efforts, I saw at once the similarity in our quest for expressing something beyond the ordinary.

When I had studied these at some length, I turned and saw him smiling gleefully. "So, Miss Prudence, we have something in common, do we not?"

I scarcely noticed his use of my first name, so natural did it seem. I nodded silently, and he went on. "You needn't be surprised your oils don't sell. These don't either! The farther I move away from the recognizable, the more the public rejects my work. Look here."

He pointed to a striking painting, titled *The Opening of the Valhalla, 1842: Honor to the King of Bavaria*, where the suggestion of a palace appeared to float among clouds and mountains. "As I returned from Venice, I came through Bavaria and sketched this building, which King Ludwig was erecting as a shrine for the arts. When the painting was finished, I sent it to an exhibition in Munich, where no one took the least notice of it. It came back to me damaged, and with a bill for seven pounds for the shipping!"

I smiled, for I saw that his indignation was more feigned than real.

"And look here," he went on, leading me to a picture with one of his notoriously lengthy titles: *Snowstorm—Steamboat off a Harbor's Mouth Making Signals in Shallow Water, and Going by the Lead.*

He looked at me challengingly. "Do you understand it?"

I saw the outlines of a ship nearly inundated by swirls of sea and sky, the light coming fitfully through shafts of cloud, painted with an artistry that was deeply moving.

"Understand it?" I said quietly. "That is not the question, I believe. I *feel* it."

Mr. Turner looked at me thoughtfully. "Yes, that is what I wish. You see, I was on that boat as it left Harwich, and when the violence of the storm was at its height, I got the sailors to lash me to the mast. For four hours, I observed, not expecting to escape. One critic called it "soapsuds and whitewash," but that didn't offend me in the least, as I didn't paint it to be *liked*, but only to record the experience as it was."

Presently, Mr. Turner announced that I was to stay for the afternoon. Almost as an afterthought, he remembered to ask if I was free for the day, and when I assured him I was, he said, unflatteringly, that he didn't suppose I had other engagements.

"Hannah will give us something here for luncheon. Don't expect much."

I was led by the sour-faced Hannah to a cloakroom to prepare myself for the meal, which was served in a small breakfast room. I could see that no polish had touched the fine wood of the tables and chairs for many a year, but Mr. Turner took no notice of his surroundings. Over our plates of meat and cheese, with biscuits and a bottle of wine, he talked of the climate in which artists grow.

"It's the very devil for women, Miss Prudence. Take you, for example. You have a promising talent that's never been developed. If you'd been a man, you could have studied seriously and worked in a world of other painters. The very gentility of your background is a bar to such opportunities. You may never have been first-rate, but you'd have had the chance to find out. My father was a hairdresser, here in London, neither rich nor poor, but he gave me support for what I wanted to do. If I'd had a sister, would he have done the same for her? Probably not, marvelous man though he was. One day the world may be different, Miss Prudence, but not soon, I'm afraid."

He told me of his pleasure at being elected to the Royal Academy in his youth, and spoke of some of his great patrons, especially of Lord Egremont, who had invited him to his grand house at Petworth many times before the Earl's death in 1837. I knew that some of his finest paintings were hung there and expressed my regret that they were not available for public view.

At that, he summoned Hannah, asked for writing materials, and scribbled a message.

"Here. Take this. The servants will let you in whenever you like."

I hazarded a mild thank you but made no fuss, as I knew he would not like it.

And then, Mary, after our luncheon, he led me back to the studio and directed me to a chair. "Sit there, Miss Prudence. I like your face. You don't simper and smirk. I feel inclined to paint you. Never went in much for portraits, and I don't paint much these days, but I do as I like."

And with that he worked for perhaps two hours, then dismissed me without ceremony, but with a warmth more true for its lack of outward expression.

Two weeks later, the finished portrait arrived. It hangs in my bedroom, as it is too precious to me to share with others in the parlor or the dining room, and there it has been for nearly fifteen years.

Claire transcribed the rest of Prudence's letter, which closed with the usual salutations to Mary and her family, and sat back to think about this startling news.

Where was the painting now? Certainly Mrs. Vickers didn't have it, nor did she seem to know about it. Even at the time of Prudence's mysterious death in 1863, a Turner would have been worth a lot of money.

Today it would bring a fortune. It must have been sold, perhaps changing hands many times, and it could be anywhere in the world, in a gallery or in a private collection. She would certainly like to track it down, if only to see what Prudence looked like. Besides, a copy would make a great addition to the illustrations in her book.

Chapter

13

THE FOLLOWING FRIDAY EVENING was the date the Nolans had scheduled for the faculty group party. Sally and Adrian had gone out for the evening with Brenda and Garth, a natural foursome having developed, what with Adrian's faithful attendance at the cottage during the week since Cheryl Bailey's death. Claire had noticed that Sally, who had dated various young men since the term began but had formed no new alliance, now seemed to regard Adrian as a pleasant fixture and had even gone so far as to admit that she liked having him around better than the one who had been last year's favorite.

In the course of the week, things had gradually settled back to near normal among the Third Year Abroad students on campus, with that natural resurgence of life after the intrusion of tragedy. The faculty members were presumably less affected, as only George Foley—so far as was known—had had any personal acquaintance with the girl.

Barry and Frieda had made up their guest list as a

return favor to those who had invited them to parties during the first two months of their stay, and added some others Barry had come to know. With spouses and friends, it came to a group of some twenty-five people.

"They won't all come, of course," Frieda had said cheerfully over the phone when inviting Claire. "And those who do will be packed like sardines, but I think that makes a good party. No chance of sitting around in a circle making polite conversation."

Claire, getting dressed for the evening, looked glumly into the mirror. Neil had flatly refused to come, and though she had to admit he was right to decline, it didn't improve her mood.

When she had tried to urge him to come along, he had adopted that tone of quiet authority that no doubt had furthered his career but didn't do much for her. Learning that George and Caroline Foley were on the guest list, he had said, "My dear Claire, I'm not suggesting that Foley killed the girl, but he is certainly on our active list. There may be other faculty as well who will come to our attention. I simply can't turn up and engage in small talk under the circumstances."

She had known there were disadvantages to a relationship with a policeman, but more than that, she was dismayed by her disappointment. Once the pain of the divorce had attenuated, she had had no problem going to parties alone. Now, with Neil in her life, she wanted to walk in with him, feel the pleasure of being with him among all those couples. Damn! What had happened to her independence, to that comfortable state of not needing emotional support from anyone? Oh, well, life was full of trade-offs. Nobody said you could have it both ways.

It was an after-eight drinks party, and she had promised Frieda to come early. Deciding 8:15 was early enough to fulfill her obligation, she was surprised to find half a dozen people there and others coming in behind her. The Nolans were good hosts, friendly but casual, and Claire noticed they had already adopted the English practice of making only vague introductions and leaving people to mingle at will.

The drink of choice was gin and tonic, but Claire, who hated tonic, fell back on her standby, whiskey and soda. An hour into the party, she had chatted with an elderly professor of history, two wives whose affiliation she never learned, and a young man whose field was classics. Meanwhile she sampled Frieda's creative dips and nibbles, including a heavenly hot cheese affair in a chafing dish she remembered from parties in California.

During the years of her marriage to Miles, Claire had spent enough summers, holidays, and leaves in England to encounter divergent attitudes toward Americans. Most of their friends had been people Miles had known in the Home Office or other branches of government, who had treated her cordially in her role as someone's wife, but she had also had occasion to meet people in academic circles, where she found they were divided, like all Gaul, into three parts. There were those who genuinely liked Americans, those who scarcely noticed her nationality, and a third group who, for one reason or another, regarded themselves as inherently superior to those trans-Atlantic upstarts.

The Nolans' faculty group was no exception. Everyone so far in the evening had belonged to Types One or Two, and she had high hopes of escaping Type Three altogether, when she noticed Frieda talking with a tall man whose bony face seemed to be fixed in a permanent sniff. She also noticed that he couldn't take his eyes off Frieda, who was looking extremely sexy in a black skirt and sweater that on anyone else would have been nothing much. Far from flirting with her, the man looked more like the victim of a snake charmer, as she chattered, her dark eyes flashing up at him and away again. Just once, she looked steadily into his eyes for a moment, and Claire saw the man put his hands behind his back, as if afraid that he might reach out and touch her if he didn't exert restraint.

Across the room stood a tall woman, engaged in conversation, whose eyes nevertheless took in the colloquy between Frieda and the man before she turned away. Obviously, the wife, Claire thought.

Moments later, Frieda brought the man to her.

"Claire, darling, this is Dr. George Foley, Dr. Camden. His field is nineteenth century. I've told him about your work on Mary Louise Talbot." And Frieda melted away.

Testing the waters, Claire asked, "Are you interested in Talbot, then, Dr. Foley?"

"Not especially. Rather a popular writer, was she not?"

"Yes, quite."

"I see. It's a biography you're doing, is it?"

"Yes."

"I expect you'll have all sorts of footnotes and that kind of thing?"

"It will be annotated, yes."

"I believe you people are good at that sort of thing."

Claire took a deep breath. This was what minorities encountered all the time. "You people," indeed.

Giving George Foley an angelic smile, she said, "Yes, we do grub about mindlessly. It fills the time."

And she walked slowly away, seething as she refilled her glass at the drinks trolley.

A woman with straight dark hair and a sharply intelligent face approached. "Hello. I'm Muriel Roberts.

Barry tells me you're a colleague of his from California."

"Yes, Claire Camden."

"Do you mind sitting for a moment? My feet are agony."

"Love to."

They took two empty seats on a small sofa, and Muriel Roberts said, "I was about to rescue you from the beastly Foley when you walked away. Was he ghastly?"

Claire grinned. "He was, but how did you know?"

"I know George. We're not in the same department, thank God—I'm in art history—but we're on committees together from time to time. This is only his third year here at the university, but it was clear from the beginning that he hates academic women."

"He doesn't think much of Americans, either."

"The twit."

"But does he dislike women in general?"

Muriel laughed. "Not at all. The word is out that he has a roving eye, but whether it goes beyond chit-chat, I've no idea. Caroline keeps a sharp eye on him."

Claire had heard from Neil that Foley obviously knew Cheryl Bailey better than he had at first admitted, but it appeared that this rumor had not made the rounds of the faculty.

Putting George Foley out of her mind, Claire decided to seize the chance to ask about Prudence Halley's painting, without disclosing the source. No use giving away a chance for a small scoop if she was the first to learn the circumstances surrounding the painting.

"Since art is your field, I have a question for you, if you don't mind. I've run across a reference to a portrait by Turner."

Muriel said, "Do you mean J.M.W.?"

"Yes."

"Wonderful old boy, isn't he? But a portrait? He didn't do many, so far as I know."

"That was my impression, too."

"There's one in the Tate, and perhaps one at Petworth or somewhere. Actually, he's not my field—I'm Renaissance—but of course, we all study him early on, as he's one of our greats. Who was the subject of the portrait?"

"Not a well-known person, I believe. Still, I'd like to track it down. Where would I start?"

To Claire's relief, Muriel seemed only mildly interested. "The Courtauld in London has fairly complete records of provenance. That's probably your best source."

Claire thanked her, and they went on to talk about their respective research projects, comparing notes on the pros and cons of academic life. Both recognized that spark of mutual liking that can lead to friendship. Presently, Muriel looked at her watch and announced she must be going. "Let's meet again, shall we?"

"Love to."

Others besides Muriel were beginning to leave, while a few seemed to be happily entrenched. Claire watched as the tall woman appeared, dressed for the out of doors, and handed George Foley his coat.

"Shall we?"

It was not a question, and Foley nodded. "Of course, my dear."

Stiffly, they made their farewells to the Nolans and swept out the door.

It was after eleven when the last of the guests took their leave. Claire, on Frieda's instructions, had stayed to the end.

Stretched out on the sofa, she smiled. "A great party, you two."

"It was, wasn't it?" Frieda sprawled at the other

end of the sofa, while Barry poured two stiff g-and-t's, handing one to his wife. "Claire?"

"Thanks, no. I've had plenty."

Claire noticed they had both wisely held down their drinking during the party and were now ready to booze it up in compensation.

Barry bent over Frieda. "You were super, sweetie." They went in for a long kiss before Barry dropped into a chair and launched into the ritual talking over of the guests. Claire said nothing about George Foley's rudeness, not wanting to cast gloom on the proceedings, but she did mention her pleasure in meeting Muriel Roberts.

Frieda said, "The woman in the Art History Department?"

"Right."

Barry nodded agreeably. "Nice woman."

Claire hoped Frieda wouldn't go into her suspicious mode, and she didn't. Evidently Muriel Roberts didn't constitute a threat.

When the phone rang, she heard Barry say, "Hi, Neil. Yes, she's here."

Neil's voice was warm. "Is the party over?"

"Yes."

"Shall I come and see you home? I'm free till morning."

Claire laughed. "That's the best offer I've had tonight."

Chapter

14

OVER BREAKFAST THE NEXT MORNING, Neil bemoaned the lack of progress on the Cheryl Bailey case. "We're checking leads from all over the country. These chaps more often tend to stay roughly in the same area, but not always."

"You are thinking of a repeat killer, then?"

"Oh, yes, I'm afraid so. The total lack of motive is the compelling factor. Cheryl hadn't been here long enough to make enemies, even if she had been the type to do so. No family members present, no long-term associations with anyone in the British Isles."

"We haven't talked much about the racial factor, Neil. Could it be someone who hates black people?"

"We must take that into account, of course, but in this case it seems unlikely. In London or other large cities, there are racial tensions that we don't see much here in Devon."

Claire knew that the extensive door-to-door questioning over the pertinent area had yielded nothing. Except for one or two neighbors on Newton Lane who had occasionally noticed one of the young ladies walking along (including the "dark one"), no one appeared to have seen anything at all. Not too surprising, since the cottages were set back from the road and half hidden by trees.

Neil said gently, "I spoke with Mrs. Bailey again yesterday. A very courageous lady. She asked if it would help for her to come to Devon, and I had to say there is little she can do. We cannot release the body until the case is closed, and she's decided it's best to remain at home with her other children. I wish I had some sort of progress to report to her."

"I wonder if it really matters. If it were Sally"— Claire swallowed—"would I want revenge? Would I even care? The loss itself would be so devastating—"

Neil stood up and came around the table behind her, hands on her shoulders, bending to kiss the top of her head. Then he walked to the window and stared out at the rain streaking the glass. "We'll get the bastard, wherever he is."

At half-past six that evening, Neil came for Claire, then picked up Barry and Frieda, driving on through a sloshing rain toward the village of Bickford.

Earlier that day, when Neil had gone and Claire was back at work on Mary Louise Talbot, Sally had phoned to say that their foursome was going on to a party in Exeter that evening but Adrian wanted Claire and Neil to join them for drinks at the Priory first.

"Oh, darling, I don't know. We promised the Nolans to do Tandoori with them this evening, since Neil didn't go to the party last night."

"Well, why not bring them along?"

"Hadn't you better ask Adrian first?"

"Sure. He's here. Hang on."

In a moment Adrian took the phone. "Mrs. Camden? I'd be delighted to have Dr. and Mrs. Nolan as well. Seven o'clock, then?"

As they drove, Frieda, bundled in wool pants and sweater, cap and gloves, still shivered. "It's freezing. Is it going to snow?"

Neil laughed. "Not cold enough for that."

"Oh, lord. I hope Adrian's house is warm. It was such a gorgeous day when we were there for tea."

Neil turned into Newton Lane, following the curve of the road through the darkness, the trees obscuring the sparse dwellings on either side.

Frieda said what they were all thinking. "This is where Cheryl must have walked the day she was abducted. I guess no one saw her, Neil?"

"Not that we've learned."

Turning in at the cottage, Neil took the twisting graveled drive up toward the house and stopped at an area cleared for cars. From there, they followed a path through the garden.

Sally, Brenda, and Garth were already there, clustered around a roaring fire. Frieda went straight for the hearth, where Claire noted with amusement that she soon turned back and then front, learning that one side can be toasted while the other is still refrigerated.

The children, as Claire secretly called them in her mind, were drinking wine, which Claire and Neil accepted, while the Nolans took Adrian up on his offer of "something stronger."

Diffidently, he held up a bottle of Glenfiddich. "I found some whiskey in Mummy's cabinet. Will this do?"

"Absolutely!"

Adrian gestured toward the glasses. "Do you mind?"

"Of course." And Barry poured two generous glasses.

They chatted amiably about this and that, at first avoiding like the plague any mention of the murder.

When the others got into a discussion of current British politics, Claire, who had had enough of that in her years with Miles and his Home Office cronies, let her gaze wander around the room, studying the paintings visible from where she sat. Some contemporary streaks and blobs of not very high quality, in her inexpert opinion; a pleasant scene of French countryside, reminiscent of Daubigny; an attractive watercolor of a garden; two bewigged gentlemen on horseback; and above the fireplace, a portrait of a striking young woman in an evening gown, her dark hair caught up with a set of sparkling combs.

Turning to Adrian, beside her on the sofa, Claire said, "I'm admiring your pictures. Sally tells me your parents were interested in art."

"Yes, very much so. The one above the mantel is Mummy soon after she married my father. He commissioned it from a chap who came down from London."

"She's lovely."

Adrian glowed. "Yes, she was, even to the end."

"I'm so sorry, Adrian."

"Thank you. Sally and I agree that we're fortunate to have mothers we could be genuinely fond of. Not everyone does, you know."

"That may go both ways, I think. You and Sally are rather nice young people."

They exchanged a smile. Then Claire said, "I believe your—that is, Mr. Martinelli is a painter?"

"Jasper? Yes. Not bad, really. He did that one of the garden, and the two modern-looking ones over there. Don't know why he does those when he actually can draw, but Mummy liked all of them. She had them hung here, and I've left them where she wanted them."

"You have other pictures, I expect?"

"Oh, yes, though nothing frightfully interesting. I'd

show you, but most of the house is closed. We keep only a few rooms open, especially in the winter."

"Have you by chance anything by Turner?"

"Do you mean old J.M.W.? *The* Turner?"

"Yes."

"Oh, lord no, he'd be quite out of our range."

"I thought perhaps there might have been one from a former generation?"

Adrian smiled. "There are a number of family portraits scattered about, dating from the 1780s when the house was built, but the earlier Abbotts were philistines of the first order, I'm afraid. The interest in painting began only with my father."

"I see." Silly of me, Claire thought, to imagine my missing Turner could be here at the Priory, but it's probably in a private collection somewhere, one that isn't catalogued. No harm in asking.

When Adrian got up to refill wine glasses, and Barry seized the chance to give himself and Frieda another round, Claire noticed a movement in the darkness at the far side of the room. Someone was standing there, silently observing the company. Medium height, bearded. Of course, it was Jasper, materializing in his usual ghostly fashion.

Brenda's friend Garth broke the silence, addressing Neil. "Excuse me, sir, I know you cannot tell us anything confidential about—that is, about what happened to Cheryl Bailey. From what we've read in the news, it seems that no one has come forward who saw her walking along to the bus stop that morning. We've wondered if the man might have been driving along the lane just as she left the cottage and abducted her there."

Sally nodded. "In that case, he might even have been driving in the other direction, not toward the bus stop at all."

Brenda added, "Or he might have turned about and gone back toward the village."

Sally's gray eyes flared, and she ran a hand through her long blond hair. "It's just so hard to believe she would get into the car with a stranger."

The young people knew nothing of Professor Foley's admission that he had on one occasion driven along Newton Lane and picked up Cheryl at the bus stop, taking her on to the campus.

Claire said, "He might have pretended to need her help. I remember that in the Ted Bundy case in the States, several times he put his arm in a sling and lured his victims by asking them to help him carry something to his car—a briefcase, a carton, even a small boat. Then he easily overpowered them. Many of his victims were young college women who would be susceptible to helping a man with what looked like a broken arm."

Sally said, "Yes, Cheryl would do that, and probably we would too, wouldn't we, Brenda?"

"Yes, assuming the man was presentable-looking. One would never expect to be attacked by a man with a disabled arm."

Claire shivered. "Exactly."

At that moment, Jasper drifted into view.

Adrian said, "Ah, there you are. Wine?"

"Yes, please," and Jasper took the glass from Adrian, who said, "I believe you know everyone, except perhaps—?"

He looked questioningly at Neil, who held out his hand. "I'm Detective Superintendent Padgett. Mr. Martinelli?"

Jasper nodded, as the others exchanged murmurs of greeting, then stood leaning against the mantel, gazing absently into the fire as the conversation moved on to other topics. When someone asked Claire about her progress on the Talbot biography, she gave a brief description of the letters from Prudence Halley, saying nothing about the mystery of the missing Turner but mentioning that Prudence had met the painter on several occasions.

A voice seemed to float out of the flaming logs. "Genius."

Startled glances at Jasper, who looked at Claire. "Brilliant."

"Turner? Yes."

Jasper nodded. "Talbot describes a painter in one of her books. Obviously based on him."

Claire, who was setting down her wine glass, nearly sloshed it on the table. "Yes, *Eleanor*, 1865. You've *read* Talbot, Jasper?"

"Oh, yes. Several books. Jolly good plots."

Sally and Brenda, obviously convulsed with giggles, looked at Garth and Adrian, who were having their own control problems.

Barry, noticing nothing, announced that he could never make it through those three-volume monstrosities, while Frieda countered that he just didn't realize how fascinating those Victorians could be.

Apparently Jasper had reached the limit of his capacity for conversation, for he stroked his beard, made a vague gesture of farewell something like the Queen's royal wave, and murmuring, "I'll be off, then," oozed back toward the door through which he had entered.

Garth said, "Is he always like that?"

Adrian smiled tolerantly. "Yes. Mummy said he was a restful companion."

Some time later, when her group began to take their leave, Claire noted with pleasure that as they expressed their thanks to Adrian, Sally stood beside him, smiling. An attractive couple. Not that Claire was thinking of marriage at this point. Sally was only twenty. Plenty of time for that. What she hoped for was a happy relationship, one without turmoil, and this one looked promising.

Chapter

15

In a modest bungalow on a street not far from the town center of Kings Abbey, Hubert Hart sat at the dinner table with his mother, pushing the boiled potatoes around his plate with a fork.

At the double ring of the phone, the woman picked up the receiver. "Cora Hart, here." A pause. "He's here. Hold on a moment, please. Hubert, Reverend is asking if you'll take Sabbath school tomorrow?"

Hubert groaned and pursed his lips in distaste.

"Yes, Reverend, he'll be happy to. Thank you." She hung up the phone, eyeing her son severely. "Hubert, this simply won't do. I've said you'll do it, and do it you must."

"All right, then."

They ate in silence for a time. Then Hubert put down his fork. "Look here, Mother, I've done as you asked and not seen Nora McBain for many weeks, and it's no good. I love her and I want her if she'll have me."

Cora Hart's lips formed the tight grimace of disapproval Hubert had hated all his life.

He looked away, only to hear the harsh, cold voice. "Hubert, look at me."

Reluctantly, he looked. With not a trace of color on her doughlike face, her hair drawn severely back and twisted into a graceless knob, his mother was like a caricature of a woman, he thought. A vision of Nora floated past, her warm softness making a hollow ache in his chest.

"That young woman is no better than she should be. You've been brought up to better, you know you have. What would your father have said?"

He wanted to shout, "My father would have envied me, stuck with you as he was," but he said nothing. It was always better to let the litany run its course. Any response from him only prolonged the torture.

"You told me yourself when you first walked out with her that she'd lived a life of sin. You thought you could save her and make a decent woman of her. But let me tell you, Hubert, that kind never changes. She'd use you till she grew tired of you, and then it's off with the butcher or the baker, you'll see."

He had heard all this so often he could have repeated the phrases with her, like the responses on Sundays. Next he would hear about the young women at chapel.

"You're a fine-looking young man, Hubert, I'll say that if I am your mother. There's many a young woman at chapel who'd jump at the chance if you'd look about you. How would it be if you have children and your wife isn't a believer? With someone from chapel, you'd know you share the same views on the things that count in life, to say nothing of the afterlife."

Hubert's hands curled into fists, and he felt the anger pressing till he thought he would burst. Hold on, he told himself. She'll stop if I just hold on.

Like a singer pausing before the big aria, his mother

took a deep breath and plunged on. "You're a clever boy and you have good prospects. A clerkship for a solicitor is a cut above anything your poor father ever had. Don't you go throwing away your chances by making a bad marriage. A man with a common, vulgar wife is lumbered all his life."

Now Hubert shot to his feet, banging his fist on the table. "Nora is not common and vulgar! She's a woman anyone might be proud of. I won't hear you say another word against her."

And he snatched up his coat from the hook by the door and walked out, pulling the door shut with a bang.

At the Crown, Nora McBain wiped the bar counter and pulled two pints for a customer, who took them away to a table. Saturday night was always busy and this one was no exception. At least, the time went faster this way.

Ten o'clock. One more hour till closing.

Bert Crofts was coming along to see her home. Nice to be escorted by a policeman, even though he was off duty and not wearing his uniform. She'd been out with Bert a few times over the past few weeks. He was a good-looking lad, no doubt about it, but when he'd tried to maneuver her onto the bed, she'd headed him off.

Until two nights ago, that is. That night, when he walked her home, her mood was mellow, and she had made love with him. He'd stayed for a couple of hours afterward, talking till she fell asleep, and he'd slipped away, waking her only to lock the door after him.

Now, one of the regulars was chatting her up when her boss told her she was wanted on the phone.

Surprised, Nora went around the end of the bar to the wall phone and picked up the receiver. "Nora McBain here."

"Nora? Is that you?"

A man's voice, slightly hoarse. Something familiar about it.

"Yes. Who's speaking?"

"It's me, Mick."

"*Mick?* How did you find me here?"

"I rang up your mum and she told me."

"So, what do you want?"

"Just rang to ask how you are and all."

"After going on five years, you just rang up to say how am I?"

"All right. Don't get shirty. I know I hadn't ought to have waited so long. Things have been rough, see?"

"Oh, rough, have they? While I've been attending balls at Buckingham Palace."

"Yeah, I read you. So, how's the kid?"

"He's fine, no thanks to you. So what do you want, Mick?"

"I want to talk to you."

"Where are you?"

"Never you mind where I am."

Nora heard the proprietor call her name.

"Look, I can't talk now."

"All right. I'll come round to your place tomorrow morning."

Before she could answer, the line disconnected.

Back behind the bar, Nora was waiting on the next customer with shaking hands when the pub owner asked if she was all right.

"I'm fine," she said automatically.

"You don't look fine, Nora."

"Sorry about the phone call."

"Not to worry. You've never been one to hang on the phone. Anything I can do?"

"No, but thanks."

Thoroughly shaken, she went on with her work, smiling at the customers but without her usual glow.

At half-past ten, P.C. Bert Crofts turned up and ordered a pint, his eyes moving up and down Nora's body as she handed him his glass.

It was after eleven before the last customers departed and Nora finished cleaning up. Putting on her coat, she looked out of the window.

"Is it raining?"

Bert said, "No, but it's cold. Here, let me do that."

He wrapped her wool scarf around her neck, kissing her casually on the lips with the air of a man who knew more and better things were in store.

As they walked along the high street and turned into the neighborhood where Nora lived, Bert held her tight against him, keeping their steps in unison. Twice he looked back over his shoulder, hearing footsteps behind them. A man was walking slowly along, going in the same direction. No harm in that.

Not accustomed to noticing the moods of others, Bert was wrapped in his own anticipation of delights to come, so it was only as they went through the gate and up to her door that he remarked, "You're quiet tonight, luv."

He followed her inside the little caravan, where Nora turned up the heater. Kicking the door closed behind them, Bert put his arms around her, pulling off her cap and running a hand through her hair. As he bent to kiss her, he saw the tears moving slowly down her cheeks as she stood passively silent.

Astonished, he said, "What's up?"

"You'd best go, Bert. Thanks for seeing me home."

"So what did I do wrong?"

"No, it's not you. It's my husband. He rang me up at the pub tonight."

"Your husband? I figured as you was divorced—or free, anyhow."

"I would be if I could. I've never heard a word from Mick for five years until now."

"Then he isn't coming round?"

"No."

"Well, we needn't worry about him tonight, eh?"

Bert tossed his coat on a chair and slipped Nora's coat off her shoulders, running his hands down her back and pulling her against him. "I'll help you forget him, luv. Just give me the chance."

Nora pulled away. "No, Bert, not tonight."

Bert stared. "Come on, Nora, don't be daft. We had a good time the other night, didn't we?"

Nora nodded, reaching for a tissue to blow her nose.

"Do you still love this bugger, is that it?"

"No. It's just—I don't know. I have to think. I'll say goodnight, then."

Bert's eyes hardened. "If that's the way you want it."

Picking up his coat, he wheeled and went out the door, slamming it behind him.

Nora stood looking after him, then turned the lock on the door, took off her clothes, and slipped into her nightdress and a jersey.

Wearily, she sat on the chair by the table, running her finger around the coffee stains on its vinyl top.

Why had she cried over Mick? Did she still love him, still want him back? No, not on your life. It all seemed so long ago. They were only kids—she was fifteen when she got pregnant, and Mick only a year older. His mum tried to prevent them from getting married. Said Nora had trapped him, and how did she know the brat was his?

That was stupid. Mick knew, all right. He was the only one she'd been with, and he told his mum so. That was the only decent thing he ever did. She was five months along before they went to the registry office. Then some relation of his dad's got him a job in London—porter at a hospital. The wage was low but at least they could barely make it. The National

Health took care of her when the baby was born, and she would have gone to work soon after, but before she was able to find work, it was all over. Mick couldn't face having a kid. He was always at the pub with the lads, and soon it wasn't the lads. He took up with a girlfriend and sometimes didn't come home at night.

When Nora complained, he roughed her up. By this time, she thoroughly despised him. Any affection she had once felt for him was utterly gone, and when he finally took off, she was glad to see the back of him.

So why the tears tonight? She wasn't in the habit of analyzing her own feelings. She had simply taken what life dealt out and coped with it as it came. She didn't expect anyone to help her or even to care much what happened to her. Her mum was taken up with her own life and couldn't be bothered. Other than being fond of little Willie, her mum had never shown much affection to anyone. Of the men who had come and gone in Nora's life, some might have wanted to marry her but nobody wanted to take on a child as well.

That is, nobody but Hubert Hart.

Now her tears started again, pouring down her face and dripping off her chin. Hubert had been so good with Willie. Seemed genuinely fond of the child, unlike some of the blokes who had petted him just to please her. Too bad he was so taken up with his chapel and those ideas about making love being immoral and that.

She wiped off the tears, blew her nose again, and was crawling into bed when she heard a knock at the door of the caravan.

Bert Crofts had been gone only five minutes or so. Must have decided to come back and pester her again.

"Who is it?" she called.

"Nora? It's me."

Peering through the glass on the door, she saw a muffled figure she didn't recognize until a faint light fell on his face.

"Hubert?"

"Yes. Are you all right?"

"Yes."

"It's cold out here. May I come in?"

"Half a mo."

Nora slipped into her dressing gown and opened the door.

"It's late, Hubert. I was just going to bed."

His face white and pinched with cold, Hubert Hart stood just inside the door, looking at Nora.

"I had to see you. I followed you home from the pub, and I thought your boyfriend would stay, but I was glad to see he didn't."

Nora sighed. "He's not really my boyfriend, Hubert. He's a policeman. He walked me home so I wouldn't be alone. There's a killer on the loose, you know."

Hubert shuddered. "I know. How's Willie?"

"He's well. Turned five last week."

"I remember. I wanted to bring him something, but I was afraid you'd rather I didn't."

"Honestly, Hubert, I don't know what to say."

Her voice thickened, and Hubert put out a hand toward her, then drew it back. "Is something troubling you, Nora?"

"It's Mick. He rang me up at the pub this evening."

"Mick? Your husband?"

"Yes."

"What did he want?"

"That's it. I don't know. He said he'd come round to see me tomorrow."

Now Hubert put his hand on her arm. "I can see it distressed you to hear from him. I hope he won't make trouble for you."

Nora gave him a grateful look. "I hope not."

"I'd best be going. Take care, my dear." He bent and kissed her forehead, then turned and went out the door.

Nora fastened the lock, then stood silently thinking for a few moments before going back to bed.

Chapter

16

WHEN NEIL HAD ANNOUNCED he was free on Sunday, Claire looked skeptical. "Really free? Not hovering-by-the-telephone free?"

He grinned. "Truly. Until tomorrow, actually, barring a major crisis."

After their breakfast, Claire said, "It's time for Prudence. I've brought you up to date so far. Now you'll have time to read these. I've marked the parts of interest."

The next letter of any significance after Prudence's description of her dramatic visit to Turner when he painted her portrait recorded her visit to Petworth, the country home in Sussex of Turner's late patron, the Earl of Egremont. She exclaimed over the delight of seeing the great house, with what she called "its lines of simple elegance," and of strolling in the vast park. Most of all, she was overwhelmed by the privilege of viewing the magnificent paintings dating from the sixteenth century and culminating in the Earl's collection of Turners. Since there had been no train service there, she had taken a series of coaches and had stopped overnight at an inn, but she declared that the arduous journey "passed like a dream for such a purpose."

In the following letter, Prudence announced the arrival of her nephew, Eustace Halley, who had come to stay with her.

"My elder brother," Prudence wrote early in 1862, "has sent his son to spend some months with me. It came as a great surprise, as my brothers seldom take notice of my existence except with the greatest reluctance. It appears that the boy was sent down from Eton over some difficulty, in which he assures me he was not at fault. I don't know the circumstances, but he tells me that he was in honor bound to take the blame, although innocent of wrongdoing, for which I admire him. As he has shown some aptitude for drawing, my brother has asked that I find an instructor for him and that he work under my supervision for a time. I am sure he does not wish Eustace to pursue a career in the arts. I believe his desire is to keep the boy occupied until he decides upon a future course for him."

In another letter, Prudence mentioned that the nineteen-year-old Eustace treated her with affection, teasing her when she urged him to greater industry in his studies. "I'll never be half the artist you are, Aunt Prudence," he would say. "It's no good your trying."

In due course, Eustace formed a friendship with a young man whom Prudence referred to only as Spicer. Reading the passages marked by Claire, Neil looked up with a wry smile. "I note she doesn't mention Spicer's given name, nor does she call him *Mr.* Spicer. I deduce that, in the parlance of the day, he was 'not a gentleman.'"

"Exactly. I doubt if Prudence, with her unconventional attitudes, would have objected to him on that ground alone, but, as you'll see, she had serious doubts about his character."

"Yes. Here she says, 'Eustace spends much of his time now with young Spicer. I find him a cheeky fellow, and I fear he is leading Eustace into habits of drinking at taverns until late hours and neglecting his studies.'"

Now Claire handed him the final pages. "Here's the big one. This is the last letter she wrote before she was killed."

> The Laurels
> Sudbury, Devonshire
> 4 May 1862

My dear Mary,

I regret to impose upon your kindness, but I should like to ask for your advice. You are a mother, and although your children are still small, I believe your knowledge of the world is greater than mine, and I shall be most grateful to have your opinion on what course I should take.

My problem concerns Eustace. I am most distressed about him. He has twice asked me for loans of small sums, which he promises to repay when his monthly stipend from his father arrives. In the first instance, he did repay me, but subsequently he has asked me to wait. Then, three weeks ago, he asked me for a larger sum, stating that it was an emergency and that he would repay everything he owed to me when his money arrived.

When I saw the envelope from my brother in the post some days ago, I expected each day to receive the money, which I sorely need. It is true my brother has provided me with a small allowance for Eustace's board, but it is not sufficient, as the boy requires rather good wines with his dinner, which he expects me to supply. I was forced at last to ask him to repay the loan, and Mary, I am dismayed to report that he replied rather flippantly that he could not do so as he had lost money at the tables.

He has solemnly promised not to engage in gambling in future, as the sum sent by his father is barely sufficient for his personal needs, but I fear that the man Spicer, whom Eustace regards as a "jolly good fellow," may influence him adversely.

Another matter has caused me further disturbance. You may recall that I keep the portrait of myself done by Mr. Turner in my bedroom, as I feel it to be something too personal, too sacred, to be viewed by persons who would not share my reverence for his work. It hangs on an inner wall and is not visible from the doorway, and I keep the door locked at all times, so that my lodgers have no knowledge of the picture's existence. Only the woman who comes mornings has seen it, and she has been with me for many years and is, I am certain, quite unaware of the possible value of the painting.

When Eustace first came to me, I showed it to him with great pride, and he was duly astonished that such a thing existed, unknown to the world of art collectors. He remarked that it would surely fetch a good deal of money, but he saw that I had no desire to part with it at any price. I told him that I intend to leave it to the National Gallery in London, to be added to the collection Mr. Turner had bequeathed, and expressed the pride I feel in being able to present a hitherto unknown work by the great artist.

Recently, Eustace asked me to let his friend Spicer have a look at the painting, and I refused, telling him frankly that I do not like the man and would prefer that he break off his relation with him. Since that time, Spicer has rarely come to the house, but I fear Eustace still meets with him elsewhere.

Then a disturbing incident took place only last week. I had been out and returned earlier than I had anticipated. As I ascended the stairs, I heard sounds of scratching, as of metal upon metal. Puzzled, I stepped softly up to the top of the stairs and peered round in time to see the man Spicer at my bedroom door, attempting to insert a key into the lock.

I strode forward and confronted him angrily, asking him what was the meaning of this. His face turned red but he said airily, "Eustace asked me to bring something to him. This is his room, is it not?"

Knowing he had visited Eustace in his room in the past, I said, "You know quite well it is not. I shall ask you to leave my house and not return."

When I reported the incident to Eustace, he made light of it, saying he had indeed given his friend his own key to retrieve something for him and that the man must have mistaken the room.

Now, Mary, I must face the truth that Eustace was lying to me to protect his friend. My great fear is that the man Spicer intends to steal my painting, which would indeed bring a high price, either from a museum or from a private collector. It is painful to believe that Eustace would be a party to such a plan, but such is the influence upon him of this man, that I fear he cannot be trusted.

It is clear to me that I must send Eustace back to his father. My dilemma is this: shall I tell my brother the full circumstances of his son's behavior, or shall I simply say that I cannot have him with me any longer? It will be simple enough to cite ill health as a reason, although my health is in fact splendid.

I know that you will wonder why I hesitate, Mary. You see, for all his faults, I've grown fond of Eustace, and I believe he is fond of me. My brother has always been severe in his treatment of the boy, and I do not wish to make things more painful for him than need be. I should like your opinion, as I know so little of what is best for young people. If I do not tell, will Eustace believe that he has escaped punishment and thereby continue in his petty misdeeds? On the other hand, if I tell all to my brother, he will without doubt take severe measures against his son. Is it likely that such treatment will make Eustace face up to his shortcomings, or will the result be to make him bitter and all the more inclined to continue in his current path?

I am sorry to trouble you, Mary, but I shall be most grateful for any suggestions you may have.

Affectionately,
Your loving cousin,
Prudence

Postscript: As I very much fear that the man Spicer may attempt to gain possession of my painting, I am taking immediate steps to ensure its safety for a period of time until Eustace is gone and his friend has learned that the painting is no longer here and will give up any hope of acquiring it.

Neil shook his head. "And two days later she was dead."

"Yes. Poor Prudence. All we know from Talbot's journal is that the brother must have returned Mary Louise's letters to her, writing a note to inform her that her cousin had been attacked by an intruder and died of her injuries."

"So, what on earth happened? Did Spicer and the beastly nephew make off with the painting before she could dispose of it? Or did she spirit it away to safety before they could get their hands on it?"

"And was it really an intruder, or did friend Spicer zap her over the head in order to get at the painting? By the way, you haven't seen the newspaper accounts yet. Here are the photocopies. See what you think."

"Right. Let's have a look."

On Friday, Claire had made a quick trip to Sudbury to return the originals of the letters to Mrs. Vickers and to check for any newspaper accounts of Prudence Halley's death.

Sudbury may not have been very large in the 1860s but it was the market town for the surrounding area and had boasted a weekly newspaper known as the *East Devon Herald*. The local librarian had seemed pleased at Claire's interest and, after some searching, came up with issues beginning in the month of May 1862, their pages yellowed with age.

The first item, dated 7 May 1862, evidently came in just as the paper was going to press, for it merely stated that the body of Miss Prudence Halley of Cudworth Way, Sudbury, had been found on the floor of her home by her nephew, Mr. Eustace Halley. Police reported that Miss Halley had died of wounds to the head, and that the case would be investigated as a homicide.

A week later, the story received full play. Under the headline, "Brutal Murder of Local Lady Artist," the article repeated the facts and proceeded to more detail.

> Police are baffled by the possible motive for the attack on Miss Halley on Tuesday last. According to the police surgeon, her death was caused by a single blow to the head, administered by a blunt instrument. No murder weapon has been found.
>
> Miss Halley's empty pocketbook was found beside the body, but it is unlikely it had contained more than a small sum of money. When questioned, two ladies who lodge at the house stated they knew of no objects of great value on the premises. This was confirmed by Mr. Eustace Halley, nephew of the victim, who was stopping with his aunt for a period of months. Grief-stricken, the gentleman sobbed when questioned by police, stating, "My aunt was not a lady of wealth, and her few pieces

of jewelry were not taken. I can think of no reason for the attack upon her."

Upon examination of the body, the police surgeon placed the time of death at approximately two o'clock in the afternoon, two hours before the time at which Mr. Halley found his aunt lying on the floor in the passage beside the open door of her bedroom. The police were summoned and arrived on the scene at a quarter past four o'clock.

Asked his whereabouts at the alleged time of death, Mr. Halley replied that he was in the company of a friend, Mr. William Spicer, who confirms that the two men were together during the course of the entire afternoon until four o'clock, at which time Mr. Halley returned to his aunt's home and made the shocking discovery.

The two lodgers were also not at home at the time, having gone together to spend the day with a mutual friend at Seacombe, as was their custom each week on the Tuesday.

The Coroner's hearing on Thursday last returned a verdict of "murder by person or persons unknown." Police believe the crime may have been perpetrated by a person of unsound mind, and residents are cautioned to bolt their doors and to report the appearance of any persons of suspicious character.

Miss Halley was known locally as an artist of talent, whose sketches and watercolors, portraying scenes of Sudbury, have been sold in local shops.

Neil laid the first photocopy on the table and turned to the remaining sheets.

Claire said, "I'm afraid there's nothing of substance after the first one," and, after looking them over, Neil agreed. For the following two weeks, the articles, of diminishing length, more or less rehashed the initial facts, and the last one merely stated that the police had no further evidence in the case.

"Nothing after these?"

Claire shook her head. "I checked the next couple of months and found no further mention. According to Talbot's journal, the case was never solved. As late as 1872 there's an entry in which she mentions with sorrow that ten years have passed since her cousin's death and the killer has never been found."

Neil pondered. "So, we have three possibilities for the murderer. First, it was actually a mad intruder. Second, it was Spicer and Eustace together. And third, one of them—probably Spicer—did the deed and Eustace covered for him."

Claire nodded. "I'd go for the third one. Eustace was pretty sleazy, but I don't see him actually bashing his aunt with a poker, or whatever it was. Yet, we know he lied immediately to the police when he said there was nothing of value in the house. He must have come back, found her by the bedroom door—*open,* please note—and either knew or guessed it was Spicer who'd done the deed."

"Notice, too, that the two lady lodgers were always away on Tuesdays, something our mad intruder wouldn't know."

"Yes, and the cleaning woman came only in the mornings. So our crime takes place on a Tuesday in the afternoon. Then, the question remains: what happened to the painting?"

Neil frowned. "If Prudence found Spicer making off with it, one can believe he might have killed her. But what if she had sent it off to a place of safety before he turned up? It's possible he tried to force her to tell him where it was, and when she refused, he struck her in a fit of fury."

"Yes. And here's another problem. If Eustace wasn't a party to Spicer's plan, and came home to find auntie dead and the painting missing, wouldn't he have told the police what he suspected?"

"I think that even if he had nothing to do with the murder, he probably did conspire with his chum to steal the painting, and he knew Spicer would implicate him if he told."

Claire sighed. "We may never know. But whoever disposed of the painting, I'd like to find it now. I've been thinking, Neil. Prudence visited Petworth House. Wouldn't that have been a logical place for her to send her picture for what she believed would be temporary safekeeping?"

Neil grinned. "We have the day free. Why don't we go and ask?"

Chapter

17

GETTING TO PETWORTH HOUSE in West Sussex required a journey of several hours. There was no motorway, except for a segment skirting Southampton, and Neil followed a succession of A-roads along the south coast that eventually brought them to the great country house that Prudence Halley had visited nearly a hundred and fifty years ago.

As they drove, Claire filled Neil in on her recent research on Turner at the university library at Exeter, where she had consulted a number of books on the life and works of the painter.

"One thing I've confirmed right away is that he really didn't go in much for portraits, of either men or women. His notebooks contain sketches and drawings of figures, and in his private notebooks there are some surprisingly sexy sketches of couples in bed. He never married, but for years he had a mistress named Sarah Danby, by whom he had two daughters. Sarah's niece was the sour-faced Hannah who looked after the Queen Anne Street gallery, the one who opened the door to Prudence on her London visit. In his later years, a Mrs. Booth evidently took the place of Sarah Danby and cared for him until his death in 1851."

"So, what portraits of women did you find?"

"Only two in oils: one at the Tate called *Lady in a Van Dyck Costume*, and the one at Petworth, titled *Jessica*, subtitled *The Merchant of Venice, Act V, Scene ii.* Both of these were done in 1830, some seventeen years before he met Prudence, and the photographs show ladies in fashionable dress."

"Certainly not our Prudence. I'm trying to recall Act Five of *The Merchant.* Is that the scene where Jessica and Lorenzo talk about the night?"

"That's the one."

"One of the most charming scenes in Shakespeare, to my mind. How does it go? 'On such a night as this,' then something about Troilus."

Claire laughed. "Yes. I knew you'd ask, so I snatched Bea's Shakespeare off the shelf as we were leaving. Here it is. The two lovers vie with each other in praise of the night. Lorenzo says:

> *"The moon shines bright!—In such a night as this,*
> *When the sweet wind did gently kiss the trees,*
> *And they did make no noise; in such a night,*
> *Troilus, methinks, mounted the Trojan walls,*
> *And sigh'd his soul toward the Grecian tents,*
> *Where Cressid lay that night.*

"Jessica counters with Thisbe running from the lion's shadow, and Lorenzo replies:

> *"In such a night*
> *Stood Dido with a willow in her hand*
> *Upon the wild sea-banks, and wav'd her love*
> *To come again to Carthage."*

Neil smiled. "And then they begin teasing each other, as I remember. Lorenzo says, 'In such a night did Jessica steal away from Venice,' and then, what does she say?

> *"In such a night*
> *Did young Lorenzo swear he lov'd her well—*
> *Stealing her soul with many vows of faith,*
> *And ne'er a true one.*

"And he counters:

> *"In such a night*
> *Did pretty Jessica, like a little shrew,*
> *Slander her love, and he forgave it her."*

"Right. And it ends when Jessica says she would 'out-night' him, but someone's coming. A wonderful scene. We'll see what Turner's Jessica looks like."

They talked Shakespeare for a while, then lapsed into companionable silence. Presently, Claire said, "We may not learn anything about Prudence's portrait today, you know. I don't expect it's actually hanging in the Petworth collection, or it would have been listed in the books I've already looked at. There's just a chance, though, that it might be lurking in storage somewhere. Most major galleries have pictures in storerooms that are sometimes rotated or only hung during special exhibits. These are listed in their catalogues, of course, and maybe there's something like that at Petworth."

"And if not, we're having a good day out."

The weather had behaved with remarkable decency on their drive. Some rain squalls had quickly dissipated, and as they came into the village of Petworth and followed the signposts to the car park, pale shafts of sunlight struggled through the patchy clouds overhead.

As they walked long the path toward the west front of the house, Claire said, "I see what Prudence meant by 'simple elegance.' No fussy turrets, wings, projections. Lovely, clean lines."

"And gorgeous grounds," Neil added. "We'll take a stroll later."

When they had their entrance tickets and Claire had bought the guidebook, they agreed to tour first and ask questions afterward. Going up the oak staircase, they dutifully looked into the family bedrooms that had been opened to public view, then descended to the series of rooms containing the great works of art. An impressive number of magnificent Van Dycks were the jewels of the early years, as the Turners were the stars of the "modern" collection. The Turner Room held a dozen of his finest paintings, while the last of the rooms, the large North Gallery, housed another half-dozen, along with many works by his contemporaries.

It was here they found the *Jessica,* portrayed leaning from a window, wearing an odd, halo-like hat and a rather bland expression.

Neil said, "The flesh tones are good, but I don't see the flashing wit of Shakespeare's Jessica."

"I'm afraid you're right. Maybe that's why he didn't go on with portraits. He was much happier with scenery than with people."

Back at the visitors' entrance, Claire asked whether there were other paintings not on exhibit and was told by the gentleman in charge that, so far as he knew, there were none. "You see, the collection is permanent, with no additions or changes, as may be the case in museums. However, since 1947 this has been a National Trust property. You may wish to make further inquiries at the London headquarters of the Trust."

Claire expressed her thanks, and Neil said, "Now for a stroll."

They walked around the north end of the building and through the iron gateway into the grounds and deer park, landscaped by the incomparable "Capability" Brown, with its rolling greens, artificial lakes, and artfully placed trees and shrubs, although many, according to the guide, had been damaged and destroyed by the storms. In half an hour, they had circled back toward the house, and Claire said, "There's a tea room. Shall we?"

"Absolutely."

In a separate building beyond the courtyard known as the Domestic Block, they found the restaurant and consumed a pot of tea and a plateful of fresh buns and scones. Claire said, "As I thought, we didn't find out anything, but it's been a great day."

Neil set down his cup and looked directly into her eyes. "It's a day I'll not forget."

Accustomed to his English reserve, she felt a warm rush of pleasure. Putting her hand gently on his cheek, she said quietly, "For me, too."

As they left the tea room, Claire mentioned the old church they had passed on coming in. "It should be just beyond here, according to the guide. Shall we take a look at it?"

Neil looked at his watch. "It's getting a bit late. Why don't you go on, while I go back for the car? I'll collect you at the church in twenty minutes."

"Fine."

She made a stop in the ladies' room, coming out and almost colliding with a plump young man who was hurrying toward the tea room. For a moment, she couldn't place him. Then she remembered. Rodney Simms, the neighbor who had prompted Mrs. Vickers to look for the Prudence Halley letters.

Giving him a friendly "hello," Claire saw Rodney's

start of surprise and a glance to either side, as if he wished he could dash off without a reply. Then, he quickly recovered and oozed cordiality. "Dr. Camden! How lovely to see you!"

"How is Mrs. Vickers?"

"She is very well."

"She was not at home when I returned the letters last week. I left them with Toby."

"Yes, so I understand. Did you find them helpful?"

"Yes, very much so, thank you."

"Good, I'm so glad."

"Is this your first visit to Petworth?"

"Yes, it's lovely, isn't it?"

"You've seen the Turners, of course?"

Again, Rodney's plump face puckered in discomfort. "Yes. Quite marvelous. I was just going in to tea. Will you join me?"

"Thanks, no. I've had mine, but do go ahead."

With a look of relief, Rodney nodded. "Yes, I shall. Very good to see you."

And he scuttled off into the tea room.

What on earth? Claire shrugged. She had said nothing about the missing Turner to Mrs. Vickers, who confessed she hadn't read all of Prudence's letters. Claire distinctly remembered that neighbor Rodney had said he hadn't read them all either.

Maybe he hadn't read them on the day she first went to Sudbury, but after she left them with Toby a few days ago, Rodney may have decided to check them out after all. If he had read that last letter, he would know about the portrait, he would know about Eustace and Spicer, and he would know that Prudence said she was taking steps to secure the safety of her painting.

Was Rodney on the same trail she was? And if he should find the picture, would he meekly turn it over to the National Gallery, as Prudence's letter states was her intention? If so, why was he looking so guilty? If his intentions were honorable, he would have talked to Claire about it, even suggested they work together to find it.

Or was she imagining the whole thing? With a shrug, she turned and went out the far side of the building and along the short walk to the church.

In the dark interior, she walked down the nave and back along the aisles, peering into small side chapels where a few paintings were scarcely visible in the dusky light. A crucifixion, a nativity, and a solemn gentleman in a ruff. If she had vaguely imagined Prudence's Turner arriving at Petworth and being handed over to the local church, she could forget it. Nothing like that here.

A leaflet on a table gave the history of the building. Like so many churches in the British Isles and on the Continent, the existing building had stood on a much earlier site, and this one was no exception. The church had been burnt in Cromwell's day and rebuilt after the Restoration of the monarchy in the 1660s. All that remained of the original Norman church was the crypt below.

Lured by her fascination with ancient buildings, Claire followed the steps that led down to the dimly lit crypt, walking slowly along the stone floor and under the rounded Norman arches, where bodies had been entombed in the days of William the Conqueror. Empty now except for a stone altar at the end that held a pair of candlesticks and a brass vase, there was little to see. It was the echoing of sheer age, the image of monks shuffling across these stones in their unadorned garments, that made Claire shiver a little as she went back up the steps and out into the cold sunshine, where, moments later, Neil came for her.

Chapter
18

WHILE CLAIRE AND NEIL were on their way to Petworth on the Sunday morning, Nora McBain was nervously tidying up the interior of her caravan. She washed up the sticky dishes, scrubbed the little sink, and emptied the closet, neatly rearranging its contents. When she had put Willie's toys away in the chest under the freshly made bed, she took a soapy sponge and wiped the linoleum floor, all the while muttering to herself, *Why am I doing this?*

When he rang her up at the pub the evening before, Mick had said he would come round in the morning, and here she was doing a turnout as if she expected a visit from Princess Di. She knew Mick would notice nothing, but some flicker of pride impelled her not to let him find her place looking like a pigsty.

What did Mick want, anyhow, after all this time? What if he wanted to take Willie away? Could he do that? She had seen frightening cases on the telly where the people from Social Services took children away from parents they said were unfit. Was she unfit? She loved him so, and she'd always tried to do her best for him, but she'd had a bit of fun on her own now and then. Before she came back here to her mum, she'd sometimes had a bloke to stay the night while Willie slept, but she'd never done like some and left him alone while she larked about.

Still, why would Mick want him, anyhow? That couldn't be the reason for his coming. If he wanted money, that would be a laugh. By the time she paid her mum for the caravan and for Willie's keep, she scarcely had a quid for herself.

Nothing to do now but wait till Mick arrived, that is, if he came at all. He'd obviously been drinking last night. He might change his mind and never turn up. It was already ten o'clock, though she hardly expected Mick to be up with the birds.

Willie's voice called, and she opened the door to see his rosy face shining with excitement. "Granny's going to see Aunt Dodie and she'll take me along to play with Danny!"

Nora bundled him into her arms and squeezed, kissing the round cheeks. "Off you go, then! Be a good boy!"

Her younger sister, who lived over at Kings Abbey, had a new baby and would be glad to have Willie to play with her small boy. Nora noticed her mum hadn't asked her to come along, but no matter. Mum had her moods, and it was best not to notice. At least Willie would be gone when Mick came—if he did.

Close on to eleven o'clock, a man's voice called "Nora!" It didn't sound like Mick, and she peered through the window to see Hubert Hart looking anxiously at the caravan.

Holding open the door but not stepping back, Nora said irritably. "Hubert! You again? Sorry, this isn't a good time."

His face pale, Hubert frowned. "Has he come?"

"Who?"

"Your husband. You told me last night he was coming round today."

"Oh, so I did. No, he hasn't come, and you'd best go along before he does."

"Look here, Nora, just come out for a moment, won't you please?"

Nora hesitated, then put on a warm jacket and stepped outside. She saw there was no rain, no wind, even a few fingers of sunshine lighting the leaves of the elm tree.

Leaving the door of the caravan ajar, she stood looking at Hubert. "Come to that, it's Sunday. Why aren't you at chapel?"

A nerve twitching in his cheek, Hubert said, "I've decided to give up going to chapel."

"I'll wager your mum won't like that."

"That's right enough. She's—well—"

"Pissed off?"

"Nora! I wish you didn't use that kind of language."

Nora turned back toward the caravan. "I didn't sign on for a lecture, thank you."

Hubert pulled at her sleeve. "Don't go, Nora. I'm sorry. It's just a habit, you see. I've grown up like that and it's hard to change."

"I didn't know you *wanted* to change."

"The truth is, I do. I love you, Nora, and I'll do anything to have you, even if it means giving up all the things I've always believed in."

"You make it sound like you have to turn into a sinner for me."

Hubert stared at her fixedly. "You're so beautiful, Nora. I've never known anyone so lovely. I think of you day and night. I even dream about you. You liked me too, at first, didn't you?"

Nora sighed. "I did, yes, till you started making me out a wicked person and that."

"I wanted to save you from eternal damnation."

"There, you see, I don't care for that kind of talk. I'll take my chances, thank you, Hubert. Now, you'd best be off."

"Just one kiss before I go."

He cupped her face in trembling hands and kissed her lips. "I want you, Nora. Someday we'll be together, you'll see."

Half an hour later, Nora heard a knock and opened the door to Mick McBain. They stared at each other in silence, Nora thinking, "Is this the boy from the comprehensive I thought was so good-looking when I was a kid of fifteen? He's not yet twenty-three, and he looks like a wornout layabout."

Mick took off his jacket and sat down. "You're looking good."

Ignoring this, Nora said, "Coffee?"

"Not if there's anything better. A brandy? Gin?"

"You're hooked, are you?"

"I didn't say that. Coffee's fine."

She looked at his puffy skin and the fine red lines already beginning to lace his nose. "Look, Mick, when you work in a pub, you soon know the ones as need it."

"Okay, okay. I've had problems, that's all. I can quit when I like."

Silently, Nora made the coffee and poured two mugs. "Milk?"

"Thanks, no."

Nora stirred the powdered milk into her coffee, thinking, "We can sit here all day before I say a word. Whatever he wants, let him say it."

At last, Mick looked around the caravan. "Cozy, this. I see you're back of your mum's place. Does the nipper sleep here with you?"

"No, at the house."

"This his picture?" Mick bent over and looked at a colored snapshot stuck to the door of the little fridge. "Looks a bit like me, eh?"

"Not much, I'm glad to say."

"All right. I know I ran out on you, Nora, but I was just too young to have a family."

"You were older than I was."

"Sure, but women, they're better with babies and all. You understand."

"I understand, all right. Are you still with that slut you went off with?"

Mick blinked. "Who? Oh, haven't thought of her for years."

"Been plenty since then, right?"

Mick looked smug. "A few. I don't suppose you've been living like Mother Teresa yourself?"

"None of your affair what I do."

Mick's tone became conciliatory. "You're so right. I'm sorry for what I did, see? I'd like to make it up to you, but I don't know how to do that."

Nora stared. "If you mean, get back together, you can forget it. Over my dead body, as the saying goes."

Mick looked relieved. "No, I know it's too late for that. But I've got a problem and I need help at the moment. When I get back on my feet, I'll send you some money, that's a promise."

"Good. Then I'll retire to the south of France."

"Come off it, Nora. All I want is a place to stay for a time. You see, I owe money to some chaps who'll cut up rough if I can't pay up. They don't know about you or that I'm from Devon. I've been stopping with a friend but he can't keep me any longer. I have a chance to get out of the country, but I need a place for a week or so till it happens. Once I get away, I'll earn good money and I'll pay you back."

Nora snorted. "Where am I supposed to put you?"

"Well, I thought, here in the caravan. If you don't

want me here with you, you could stop in your mum's house with the nipper till I'm gone."

Nora stood up and slammed the palm of her hand on the table. "The only thing I want from you, Mick McBain, is to get shut of you. It'll soon be five years and I can divorce you for desertion. I don't know what you're up to. For all I know, you may be in trouble with the police. Whatever it is, I'm not having it. Now, just get out."

Mick shot out of his chair, eyes bloodshot with fury, and raised his arm. "Bitch!"

He stepped toward her and Nora stared him down. "And don't touch me, you bloody bastard, or I'll have you up for assault."

With a snarl, Mick snatched up his jacket and bolted out the door.

Nora stood still, staring after him, heart pounding, body shaking, but her eyes were bone dry.

Chapter

19

ON THE FOLLOWING TUESDAY, Claire set off with Frieda for a day in London, hot on the trail of Prudence Halley's lost Turner. At least, she hoped there *was* a trail to be hot on. The visit to Petworth with Neil had been a marvelous excursion but hadn't helped much in locating the painting. Now she'd decided to follow the suggestion of Muriel Roberts, the art-history professor she'd met at the Nolans' party, and try the Courtauld Gallery in London. With an early start, they had arrived at Claire's flat in Bedford Square not long after ten o'clock.

"Easier to park here, with my permit. We'll take a taxi down to the Strand."

Formerly housed among the buildings of the University of London, the Courtauld had now taken up handsome quarters in the right wing of Somerset House, premises that had been occupied by the Royal Academy of Art through much of Turner's career. In the ensuing years, a series of government offices had occupied that part of the building until the Courtauld took over.

"You'll love the collection," Claire told Frieda. "I've been through several times. I'll come to you when I've finished."

"How will you find me?"

"Don't worry. It's a small gallery, compared to the National Gallery or the Tate. Actually only two floors of paintings. I'll find you."

Leaving Frieda in the gallery proper, to the right of the entry drive, Claire crossed over, as she was directed, to the Witt Library on the left, where records were stored of the works of artists of all periods and nationalities.

For each artist the records were arranged by subject such as landscape, still life, historical, and so on. Claire asked for Turner portraits, duly filling out the required form, giving her name and address and purpose of inquiry.

She was then directed to the location of the files by a young woman who looked at her curiously. "Someone was here only last week, asking for Turner portraits."

Claire said, "That's odd, as he did so few of them."

"Yes, that's why I noticed."

Remembering her suspicions of Rodney Simms, Claire said casually, "It may be a friend of mine. A rather plump young man in his twenties?"

The young woman frowned. "Actually, I don't recall. It may well have been."

Following the direction down some stairs and through a series of rooms lined with shelves containing large green boxes, Claire found the Turner files. Rows and rows of Landscape and other designations, and at last a single box labeled "Portraits."

Claire's hope was to find some mention of portraits other than those on the lists she had seen, especially something of doubtful attribution. After all, Turner was old and in ill health when he did the Prudence

Halley portrait. It might well be kicking around somewhere with a question mark on its provenance, spurned by the major galleries of the world.

Unhappily, the box, when she opened it, contained no surprises. There were photographs of each of the works in the category, including the two known ladies, along with a couple of self-portraits and a photo of a work titled *The Artist and His Muse*. This one, marked "J.M.W. Turner?," did have doubtful attribution, as the question mark indicated. The problem was that it showed a rather stout man, seated with pad and pencil, while a plump lady, all bosom and draperies, leaned on his shoulder, obviously inspiring him to whatever he was doing. The lady certainly wasn't Prudence Halley.

Returning the box to its shelf, she went back up the stairs and signed herself out of the library, finding Frieda in the gallery proper, absorbed in the Impressionists.

Frieda looked up. "Any luck?"

"No, I'm afraid not."

"Too bad."

Half an hour later, Claire said, "I hate to drag you away, but we should go on to the Tate."

Frieda sighed. "It's a wonderful collection. I'll come back."

They emerged into the Strand, where Claire was looking for a taxi when she saw a number 77A bus lumber to a stop a few yards to their right. "Come on, Frieda. This will take us to the door."

As the bus creaked its way along the Strand and down into Whitehall, Claire acted as tour guide, pointing out Number Ten Downing Street, then the Houses of Parliament on their left, with the east end of Westminster Abbey at their right, Frieda loving it all. "We were only in London for a few days when we first came over, and it wasn't enough. I can't wait for

Christmas." Claire had offered the Nolans her flat for the holidays, happy to stay in Morbridge with Sally and Neil.

Along the Millbank, they came presently to the stop opposite the Tate Gallery. Peering over the wall, they saw the gray waters of the Thames moving sullenly toward the sea between the muddy banks of low tide, while a halfhearted drizzle misted their wool caps and dusted their coats with moisture.

Turning away, Claire said, "Let's go straight into the Clore first." They waited at the traffic light where the city had at last prudently provided a safe crossing zone after years of art lovers dashing across the wide street, dodging the speeding cars.

Turner had told Prudence Halley he intended to leave his paintings "to the nation," and he did so in his will, as Claire had read. According to the Turner bequest, they were to be kept together, and the National Gallery in Trafalgar Square had at first housed many but not all of them. With the building of the Tate Gallery at the turn of the century, most of the paintings had been hung there in a series of "Turner rooms." Then, a bequest from the Clore Foundation for a separate Turner building had resulted in the opening in 1987 of the new wing of the Tate, the Clore Gallery, where Turner's last wish was magnificently fulfilled.

While the architects of the recent addition to the National Gallery in Trafalgar Square had preserved harmony with the original buildings, the designers of the Clore had made no attempt to blend with the columned grandeur of the Tate. A small garden and reflecting pool led to the new wing, which was gently contemporary, its clean, geometric lines touched with trim of bright greens, reds, and yellows. Yet, veiled by enormous trees, it managed to merge itself pleasantly with the old exterior, and inside, the rooms were beautifully lighted.

Upstairs in the gallery, Claire and Frieda wandered through the rooms, absorbing the dramatic range of Turner's work, from the rich darkness of the Claude Lorrain period, the grandeur of scenes from myth and antiquity, the contrast of dark and light influenced by Rembrandt, the scenes of daily life from the Dutch school, and the overwhelming illumination of his visits to Italy, culminating in the late works, where pure color dominated over subject. There were few portraits of any kind, and only the one woman, the elegantly dressed lady from 1830 in the Van Dyck costume.

Standing before her, Frieda said, "It's interesting, but not exciting. How does it compare with the one you and Neil saw at Petworth?"

"This lady has a sort of cold elegance, but neither of them has a strongly marked personality. I've read that Turner loved the challenge of trying out the styles of painters he admired to show he could do what they could do—not so much for the benefit of others, but for his own satisfaction. Looking at this picture, I'd say it's well done but it's no Van Dyck. Maybe that's why he didn't go on with portraits. He was his own best critic."

"Seems likely. When he did Prudence, it was the whim of an old man who could follow his own impulse if he felt like it."

"Exactly."

After their brief tour, they went back down the stairs to the young man at the information desk to ask about the possibility of other portraits not on exhibit, or ones that might be listed as studies of doubtful attribution, and were told, after some searching, that there seemed to be nothing of that kind in their records.

"Have you tried the Witt Library at the Courtauld?"

"Yes, I've just come from there, and I've seen the one at Petworth."

Claire looked at her watch. "Twelve-thirty, Frieda. Ready for lunch? Let's try for the Whistler Room. If we hurry, we might get a table."

Although the Clore was connected at the gallery level to the Tate proper, from where they stood it was quicker to go outdoors and up to the main entrance. When their handbags had been checked for security—the IRA was busy with bombs in London again—they turned left down the stairs and managed to get a table for two in the dining room, with its charming murals.

"My treat," Claire said, before Frieda could see the hefty prices on the menu.

Over a bottle of Verdicchio and the excellent food, they talked Turner for a while, then moved on to other topics. When coffee arrived, Claire noticed Frieda had become uncharacteristically silent.

"Anything wrong?"

"Yes. There's something I need to talk to you about, Claire."

"Sure, go ahead."

"Well, no use beating around the bush. The fact is, I'm pregnant."

One look at Frieda's face and Claire repressed any cries of joy. "I gather this isn't necessarily good news. Is Barry unhappy about it?"

"He doesn't know. And for God's sake, Claire, don't tell him—or anyone."

"Of course. Whatever you say. But why shouldn't Barry know?"

"Well, actually he doesn't want more children, but that's not really the problem. You see, it's not his."

"Can you be sure?"

"He had a vasectomy years ago."

"Oh. Then it's someone you've met since you came to Devon?"

Frieda couldn't resist an impish smile. "That's right. Well, after we'd been here awhile. And then, after our first meeting, it was a couple of weeks before we got together, if you know what I mean."

Claire knew what she meant. "Didn't you use precautions?"

"That was the problem. I haven't needed to be on the pill since I've been with Barry, and in other instances, the guys were—that is, the same as Barry. And the first time here, I didn't really know it was going to happen."

"Did you get the pills afterward?"

"Well, it took a while to do it. We're signed up with a local doctor on the National Health, but I didn't dare ask him for the pills, in case Barry found out. I went all the way down to Plymouth one day, told a doctor there I was a visitor from overseas and had forgotten my pills, and he gave me some. But by that time it must have been too late."

Claire said gently, "There are other methods, you know."

"Yes, but you see, I'd told him the first time I was okay and I didn't want to admit I wasn't. I was sure I'd be all right once I got the pills. We were only together a few times before that, and I just didn't think it would happen.

"But Frieda, are you sure?"

"I'm afraid so. After I missed my period, I waited awhile, thinking it might be nothing, but several days ago I went to the chemist and got the test. It was positive. I did it again yesterday, and now I'm sure."

"So, what do you think you'll do?"

"There's not much choice, is there? I'll have to terminate. The crazy thing is, Claire, I'd just been half wishing I could have a child. I even asked Barry if he would try reversing the surgery, but he said no way."

"Would you want to keep this child, then?"

"Not if it isn't Barry's. I really love the old guy, you know, and I don't want to hurt him. I need to find out something, and I want you to help me."

"All right, if I can."

"You see, I know abortion is legal here, but I don't know whether the husband has to be informed. Can you find out for me, Claire? And right away. I can't very well ask our doctor, as you can see. I thought maybe you could ask around while we're here in London."

They took a taxi back to the flat, where Claire had planned to pick up a few extra items of clothing and some books to bring down to Devon.

Seeing Frieda shiver, Claire put her on her bed under the duvet. "Here, sweetie, snuggle under that. No use turning on the heat. We won't be here that long."

On the phone, she tried her own London doctor, a Pakistani woman whom she liked and respected, and learned she was on hospital calls. Referred to an associate, she asked Frieda's question and was told that technically the husband's consent was not required, but if the doctor knew the couple, he or she would no doubt urge that the spouse be informed. The woman is also required to indicate that mental or physical harm would result if she does not terminate the pregnancy.

Gathering up her things, she bundled Frieda into her coat. "Okay, let's try to beat the traffic."

There was no way to get through to the motorway without a struggle, but once on the M4, they moved along well, as the worst of the outgoing traffic hadn't begun yet.

When Claire told Frieda what the doctor had said, she seemed to cheer up. "Good. So long as it isn't absolutely required, I think I can handle it. I'll go back to the doctor in Plymouth again and tell him I'm not married and would be traumatized by having a child out of wedlock."

An hour later, Frieda had fallen asleep, her head against the back of the seat, a look of contentment on her face.

Claire looked at her fondly. What would have been for herself an emotional crisis of some magnitude was obviously not that for the happy-go-lucky Frieda. She probably would have made a good mother—affectionate and fun-loving—but Claire agreed that a child, at this time, was not right for any of them.

And now Claire realized that, from beginning to end of Frieda's uninhibited disclosure, there was one item singularly missing.

She hadn't told the name of her lover.

Chapter
20

ON TUESDAY, WHEN FREIDA HAD LEFT early to go to London with Claire, Barry Nolan slept in, dawdling over breakfast and puttering aimlessly around the empty house. He had no obligations on campus on Tuesdays, although he usually spent some time in his office during the day to check things out. The TYAs had turned out to be a pretty decent bunch, and if they'd had any tendency toward wild behavior, it had been subdued for the time being by the tragedy of Cheryl Bailey's death.

Around noon, Barry bundled up and set off for a walk. Might as well get something to eat while he was out. He still thought of noon as lunchtime, though he was getting used to the one o'clock custom. Going down the high street, he leaned over the old stone bridge and studied the water, racing over the rocky stream bed as if it had to meet a time table. Farther downstream, it would slow down and appear to meander peaceably along with all the time in the world. Like life, he thought. Sometimes helter-skelter and other times with patches of calm.

When he turned off onto a lane of neat row houses, he really knew where he was going—he had taken the same walk before—but it was easier to pretend to himself that he was just out for a stroll.

He heard the child's voice before he came to the caravan. "Rrrmmm, rrrmmm."

Looking over the gate, he said, "Hi, Willie."

The dark head turned as Barry opened the gate and stepped inside. The patch of grass where Willie played was little more than brown stubble, deadened by the frost that visited nightly. Still no snow, but it wouldn't be long now.

Barry knelt beside the boy, saying nothing, studying the curve of the round cheek, the look of concentration as the child moved his toys.

Then Willie looked up, the dazzling blue of his mother's eyes making Barry's heart twinge.

"Hello, Dr. Nolan. See this firetruck? He runs into the lorry—bang, bang!"

"I see."

Remembering his own boys, now grown and out in the world on their own, he wondered if he had been too hasty with Frieda about whether to have a child of their own. Did she really want it, or was it a passing fancy? She hadn't brought it up again, he noticed.

He'd loved his kids, had truly enjoyed each stage of their growth from babyhood on, more than most men he knew. And children liked him, too. He never talked down to them or spoke in the false voice adults often used. Maybe he should talk to Frieda about it again. But hell, he'd be pushing seventy when the kid went to college. Could he handle that?

Barry looked up to see Nora smiling at him. "I'm glad you came. Willie's been asking after you."

"Tell you what." Barry's tone suggested a spur-of-the-moment idea. "Why don't Willie and I go and get some takeaway and bring it back for lunch?"

Willie dropped his toys and stood up, looking pleadingly at Nora, who said, "Why not?"

She straightened the child's jacket and gave him a kiss. "Go along, then."

Walking with Willie's hand in his, Barry felt the lure of having a child again. Still, if he'd just wait a bit, there should be grandchildren. One son was already married, and he and his wife hadn't said they wouldn't have children, which in today's world practically meant they would. The younger one was still playing the field, but he might settle down one of these days. A grandchild. That would be something.

Later, back at the caravan, Barry opened the beer he had bought for himself and Nora and gave the child a soft drink. When they had eaten the pizza that had been Willie's choice, the little boy went back to his toys in the garden, happily sucking a lollipop.

Now, Barry settled back in his chair and gave Nora his crinkled smile. "So what's new, sweetie?"

Established now as a fatherly confidant, Barry enjoyed these little chats, with their hints of unstated sexual attraction. Once, when Nora had said, "Sometimes I think I could fancy you if you were a bit younger," he knew exactly the boundaries she set and made no move.

In answer to his question, Nora told him about Mick's phone call and visit. "He wanted me to hide him till he could get out of the country. What does that tell you?"

Barry nodded. "Big trouble, I'd say."

"Right."

"Was it upsetting to see him again, Nora?"

"After he phoned, it was, but when I saw him next day, you can forget it. He's turned into a drunken sod. I was ashamed to think he was Willie's father."

"Was Willie here?"

"No, he'd gone off with my mum, and I'm glad. Mick didn't even *ask* to see him. Some father."

They talked for a while about the murder of Cheryl Bailey.

Nora said, "You're acquainted with that detective superintendent. Do you have any inside information about what's going on?"

"No, I'm afraid not. I know they're still working full speed ahead on the case, following up even the remotest leads, but I gather they're not having much luck."

"The police know a lot of things that don't get into the newspapers."

"Yes, I suppose they do, but I think if they had a break, they'd be only too happy to let the press know."

Nora sighed. "I'm still afraid at night."

"You don't walk home alone?"

"Lord, no, but it's still scary. The other night Bert Crofts saw me home—he's a police constable—and I saw someone walking behind us, only I don't think Bert noticed."

"Did you find out who it was?"

"Oh, it turned out to be Hubert Hart. He came to the door later and told me."

"Hubert? The clerk in the solicitor's office in Kings Abbey?"

"Right. He came round again the next day. Says he isn't going to chapel anymore, but he still talks like a preacher."

For another hour, they chatted on, Barry encouraging her confidences and entertaining her with anecdotes of academic life, until he left to pick up his car and make a late-afternoon appearance on the campus.

On Wednesday, the day after her trip to London with Frieda, Claire was working in her study when

Frieda phoned to say she had an appointment with the doctor in Plymouth on Friday. "It seems they don't perform the surgery on this visit. I have to go back, so I'll let you know when."

Claire had promised to go along when the day came, but today she put in a solid day's work and rewarded herself with a romantic dinner and evening with Neil.

It was seven o'clock the next morning when the phone on her nightstand burred a double ring, bringing her from deep sleep to confused awareness. At the second burr-burr, her hand groped for the phone. Any call at an unusual hour brought the automatic blip of fear. Something wrong with Sally?

"Hello."

"Claire, it's Barry. Is Frieda there?"

"No. Why?"

Now she heard the croak in his voice. "She's not here. I thought she might have gone to your place."

Claire sat up. At seven in the morning, Frieda would not be out for a stroll, or out anywhere in the cold, unless she had to be.

"What do you mean, not there?"

"Just what I said. She's gone. Oh, God, Claire, I don't know what to do. I guess I'd better tell you what happened."

Claire pulled the pillow up behind her and leaned back, ready to hear another Nolan crisis saga.

"Sure. Tell me."

"Well, last night we got into an argument, and I sort of lost my temper and swatted her one."

Not for the first time, Claire thought. "Okay. So, then what?"

"She grabbed up her coat and stuff and went out the door. Said she didn't want to stay in the same house with me."

"What time was this?"

"About one-thirty in the morning."

"Has she done this before?"

"Yeah, once in a while. But she always comes back. We'd had some drinks, and I figured she'd be back soon, so I stretched out on the sofa and dozed off. I just woke up a few minutes ago. I'm scared, Claire. You know that killer is loose. What if he sees this woman walking alone?"

"Did you call the police?"

"Not yet. I thought she might be at your place. Where else could she have gone on foot?"

"Maybe she went to a hotel. Why don't you check around, and if you don't find her, you'd better report it to the police."

"Right. I'll do that." Then Barry's voice broke, and sobs came from deep in his chest. "Oh, God, Claire, what'll I do without her?"

Claire went to the kitchen, made a pot of coffee, and phoned Neil to fill him in on what was happening.

"I know the Nolans have a terrible track record for domestic tiffs, but Barry's sure she would have let him know by now where she is."

Neil said, "I wonder if perhaps this time Frieda decided to give him a real scare, not realizing its implications. If she's not at a hotel, could she have gone to someone's house for the night?"

"I doubt it. I'm the only candidate for that, and she didn't come here. She and Barry are really careful about keeping up appearances with the English faculty. She'd never go to one of them."

"Might she have accepted an offer from a stranger?"

"Yes, it's remotely possible. Maybe she hitched a ride with someone. I know it's an idiotic thing to do, but remember, they were both sloshed, and Frieda is no shrinking violet."

In the end, they agreed there was nothing to do but

wait. The usual policy of taking no definite police action for twenty-four hours, which had been suspended in the case of Cheryl Bailey, was appropriate here, where the likelihood was that Frieda would turn up of her own volition.

What Claire couldn't say to Neil at this point was the thought that had crossed her mind almost from the beginning. Had Frieda gone to the nameless lover who was the father of her unborn child? If so, did he live in Morbridge, within walking distance? Or did she phone him to come and pick her up? But was he free? What if he were married? No sanctuary there.

Claire had just put down the phone when she heard the doorbell and found Barry standing there.

Distraught was a gross understatement for Barry's condition. She brought him to the kitchen, poured him coffee, and watched as he took it in hands that shook. His eyes, bloodshot and watery, gazed into hers with desperate pleading. "What'll I do, Claire? She was everything to me. You know that, don't you?"

"Sure, Barry, I know that. But look, she's probably trying to teach you a lesson. She'll be back."

His head dropped to the table, his forehead on his circled arms. "No, no, she's gone. I know it. I'll never see her again."

Claire, watching as sobs shook his body, began to feel wisps of fear tingle her spine. It really wasn't like Frieda to do this. Even if she wanted to frighten Barry, she would know that Claire would be worried and would probably have phoned her by now to say she was all right.

Barry stopped to take a long shuddering breath, the way children do when they cry, and Claire said quietly, "Barry, dear, did Frieda take her handbag or any money with her when she left?"

He gave her a dazed look and thought for a long

minute. "No, she just put on her coat and gloves and her wool cap, and shot out the door."

"Could she have had money in her coat pocket?"

"No, I don't think so. She never did, as far as I know."

Claire thought, no money, no credit card. It didn't sound good.

Seeing that empty reassurances were doing nothing for Barry, she made some slices of toast, spread them with blackberry preserve, ate some herself, and watched as he mechanically chewed. A little food would do him good, whether he knew what he was eating or not, and it did have the effect of calming him down.

Well and good, but when she suggested he should go home and see if Frieda had turned up, the calm vanished and hysteria took over. "No, no! Claire, let me stay here! I can't go back there and be alone—I can't do it!"

"But, Barry, if she comes back, she won't know where you are."

Voice still shaking, he choked, "Yes, she will. I left her a note saying I was coming here and to call you."

"Okay. What about campus? Do you have a lecture today?"

A blank look. "Today? What day is it?"

"It's Thursday."

"Oh, Thursday. Yesterday was Wednesday. I did my lecture yesterday. I only have office hours today."

"Shall I call and cancel them for you?"

"Oh, yes, please. I can't talk to anybody."

"And what if the police try to reach you?"

"The police?"

"You went to the station and reported Frieda missing, didn't you?"

Tears leaped out of his eyes, as if somebody had pressed a button.

"Yes, yes, I did. Oh, God, it's so awful."

Claire patted the heaving shoulders and went to her study, where she called both the TYA office on campus and the Morbridge police station, giving her number where Barry could be reached if he did not answer at home.

It was nearly ten o'clock that morning before Claire worked out what to do with Barry. She suggested he go for a walk, but he shuddered and said he couldn't bear to see people. She handed him the morning paper, but it fell from his hands, his unfocused eyes looking at her piteously.

She thought, *What does one do with a large, helpless child? Of course, television.*

Gently, she led him to Bea's cheerful little "morning room," put him in a deep chair with a footstool, and turned on the TV. Its effect was magical. He sank back into an instant stupor. The American craze for talk shows had made its way across the Atlantic, and Barry watched with glazed eyes as the host, a dandy with blow-dried hair, fielded questions from women whose husbands abused them both physically and emotionally. Two minutes of his glib implications that the husbands were the blameless victims of shrewish wives was enough for Claire.

For a moment, she wondered if Barry would be disturbed by stories of abusive husbands, but it was clear from Frieda's accounts of their battles that neither of them saw him in those terms. Besides, Claire knew that Barry wouldn't take in a word that was said but was merely soothed by the familiar sound of the tube.

Quietly, she slipped out of the room.

Chapter

21

BACK IN HER STUDY, Claire forced herself to concentrate. Surely, they would hear from Frieda soon and everything would be all right. She switched on her word processor and brought up the current file.

In her biography of Mary Louise Talbot, Claire had already passed the date 1865, when the novel *Eleanor* came out, but now, in light of the Prudence Halley letters, she had gone back to expand her discussion of the novel.

In the kind of biography Claire was writing, the emphasis was as much on the social and cultural background of the period as on the events of Talbot's life. Especially in the case of a minor writer like Talbot, what she ate for breakfast was less significant than how she dealt with prevailing customs and attitudes.

Eleanor was a gold mine of clues to Talbot's scorn for Victorian conventions. On the one hand, she acceded to the tastes of her reading public by making Eleanor an exceedingly pretty young woman and giving the painter the looks of a dashing buccaneer. On the other, she managed to take some adroit potshots at contemporary attitudes. While Eleanor's parents reacted in horror to their daughter's wish to marry a man who was socially unacceptable, Talbot countered by giving a sympathetic portrayal of the artist.

A passage early in the novel set the stage for the conflict that followed, as Eleanor Dexter and her mother sit at the breakfast table in their town house in London:

Mrs. Dexter put down her fork. "Eleanor, I should like for you to come with me this afternoon. We have several calls to make. I have ordered the carriage for three o'clock."

"I'm sorry, Mamma, I have an engagement."

"What sort of engagement, may I ask?"

"I am not a child. I shall soon have my twentieth birthday. Surely I need not consult with you about my movements?"

"In that you are quite mistaken, my dear. While you are in your father's house, you must conduct yourself with propriety."

Eleanor's black brows drew together. "Are you suggesting that I do not do so?"

"How can I judge when you decline to tell me what sort of engagement you have made?"

"I did not decline to tell you. I simply objected to being questioned. My engagement is to visit the gallery of Mr. Howard Grover to view his paintings."

"Mr. Grover? Surely you do not mean that extraordinary young person whom you met at the seaside and brought to the cottage when the servants were out?"

"Yes, and he is extraordinary, but not in the way you mean. He is an artist of great talent who is gaining recognition. He is already a full member of the Royal Academy and he is not yet twenty-seven."

Mrs. Dexter sighed. "Eleanor, you may recall that I

returned to the cottage at the seaside and met this Grover person as he was leaving the house. He is not a gentleman, my dear. His speech might have been that of a footman, and his manner was awkward, to say the least."

Her dark eyes flashing, Eleanor rose from the table. "You need not have him to tea, Mamma, if you object to his manner. I shall simply look at his work and hope that I may learn something of value for my own painting."

Unperturbed, Mrs. Dexter sighed again. "It is all very well for a young lady to be accomplished in drawing, as you are, my dear. It is quite another to regard it as a serious occupation. It is quite time for you to think of your future."

"You mean, to marry, of course."

"Certainly I do. I can't think why you refused the offer of your cousin, but naturally your father and I will not press you to marry a man whom you positively dislike."

"Thank you, Mamma, that is very kind indeed. I do not dislike my cousin. I simply do not wish to marry him. Now, if you will excuse me?"

"Yes. You may take Betty with you, if you wish to visit Mr. Grover's gallery."

At four o'clock that afternoon, Eleanor and her maid arrived at the number in Harley Street on the card given her by Howard Grover. The door was opened by a maidservant who left them standing in the dark vestibule while she went to announce Eleanor's arrival.

A moment later, a door burst open and Howard Grover strode forward, both hands extended. "Miss Dexter! Please come in."

Leaving Betty in the company of the servant, Eleanor followed her host to a sitting room, where she expected tea to be served. Instead, Grover led her to the fireplace, where a large painting was hung over the mantel. It was a landscape, dramatically portraying a lake surrounded by hills, with light coming through the foliage of towering trees.

"Do you see?" Grover tossed his head, the dark locks falling back over his forehead, his eyes moving eagerly from her face to the painting. "The great Claude Lorrain is the master of scenes like this. I haven't matched him yet, but I shall. Someday, I shall!"

Eleanor said nothing, but her heart lifted at the sight of his eager face.

"Come along, now."

She followed him up a flight of stairs to a large room, its walls covered with oil paintings. Slowly, they made a circuit of the room, where seascapes and scenes of the English countryside mingled with pictures inspired by the invigorating influence of his recent trip to France. Eleanor did not speak, but at the end of the tour, her glowing eyes spoke for her.

The artist studied the young woman who stood before him, noting her straight black brows, the dark hair piled high and drawn smoothly back from her face, the fine lines of nose and mouth, and most of all the dark eyes so eloquently expressive.

"Miss Dexter, you don't simper. I like that. Will you sit for me?"

Without hesitation, Eleanor said, "Yes, Mr. Grover. I shall."

Claire put down her copy of *Eleanor* with a smile, amused at Talbot's transformation of Prudence and Turner into a romantic couple.

After an hour or so of selecting passages for quotation and writing a draft of new material, Claire looked in to see how Barry was doing and was pleased to find him asleep, his head dropped awkwardly to one side, his breath coming in little snorts. Poor old Barry. Best thing for him was to get some rest.

Back in her study, she tried to get back to work.

No luck. She looked at Bea's clock on the mantel. After eleven o'clock. Surely Frieda would have called or come back by now, however furious she had been with Barry the night before. No use phoning Neil. He would be in touch if there was any news.

Trying not to give way to fear, she went to the kitchen, put the kettle on for a pot of tea, and checked the fridge for what to give Barry for lunch later on. An omelette and salad would do, if she could get him to eat.

The double ring of the phone on the kitchen extension made her jump. "Hello."

"Claire? Neil. Is Barry Nolan there?"

"Yes."

"Good. Will you put him on the phone, please?"

Claire heard Neil's solemn, official tone. "Look, Neil, if it's bad news, can you tell me first? Barry's in pretty bad shape."

A pause. "Yes. Perhaps that will be best. We have found the body of Frieda Nolan."

"Oh, God, how awful. Where?"

"Out here on the moor. Near Monk's Cross."

"You're there now?"

"Yes. I came out to confirm the identification."

"I see." ·

Then the official manner changed and his voice lowered. "I'm so sorry, darling. I know you were fond of her."

Claire swallowed. "Yes, I was. I'll get Barry now. Hold on."

When Claire switched off the television, Barry awoke, looking confused, then suddenly aware of where he was.

"Barry, dear, I want you to be ready for some very bad news."

His eyes searched hers but he said nothing.

"They've found her."

"She's dead?"

"Yes. I'm afraid so."

Barry's head dropped and a long, shuddering sigh racked his body.

"Neil needs to speak to you on the phone."

Slowly, like a very old man, he got to his feet, leaning on Claire's arm as they made their way to the kitchen.

Claire saw Barry listen like a docile child as Neil repeated the news. After a moment, he put the phone down and stood without moving.

Claire put her arms around him, stifling her own grief. "I'll do anything I can to help."

Barry nodded. "Yes. Come with me."

"Go with you where?"

"They're sending a car to take me to—to—"

"To where she is?"

"Yes."

"Of course I'll come if you want me to."

By the time the police car arrived, Claire had given them each a cup of tea and helped Barry into his outdoor gear before putting on her own. The day was clear but cold, Bea's outdoor thermometer hovering near freezing.

The driver, a young woman police constable, remained deferentially silent as they drove out of town, and Barry, quiescent now, sat with his head dropped forward on his chest.

At the outskirts of Morbridge, the driver took a road that climbed sharply, winding through a wooded area fringed with scattered houses and breaking suddenly into the undulating hills of the open moorland. Deadened by the cold, the gorse made patterns of dark brown patchworked with the mossy grays and greens where water formed pools and bogs or trickled in half-frozen streams over the rocky soil. Claire felt the compelling fascination of the bleak landscape, much of it unchanged for centuries, as they passed ridges topped with the granite outcroppings of the tors or swept past hillsides where sheep and moorland ponies nibbled the sparse vegetation.

The driver had turned onto a secondary road, and now Claire saw the familiar shape of Hound Tor on her right as they approached. Wasn't it near here that Cheryl Bailey's body had been found? Yes, there was the small stone circle, only the tips of the upright stones visible from the road. The kistvaen would be there, enclosed by the circle. She and the Nolans had driven out to see the spot soon after Cheryl's death.

Claire looked at Barry to see if he remembered. Not a chance. Staring down at his feet, Barry was in a world of his own. Not once had he even looked to see where they were going. Just as well, she thought, feeling his pain.

If it was Cheryl's killer, would he have used the same burial spot again? No. They drove on, passing the spectacular granite pile known as Bowerman's Nose for its resemblance to a man in profile, and going on another quarter of a mile.

Now Claire remembered. Monk's Cross was one of the ancient stone crosses that dotted the vast area of the moor. Many, she knew, were far from the roads, where only intrepid hikers could view them, but this one was easily accessible, standing only twenty yards or so from the road. Some of the old crosses were partially weathered away or had begun to lean like the Tower of Pisa, but Monk's Cross was perfectly formed and stood straight, its massive gray stone over seven feet high.

The cross itself came into view before they came closer and saw the police cars and the familiar tape enclosing the site. The officer parked the car and opened the door for Barry, who gave her a dazed look.

She said quietly, "Will you step this way, please, sir?"

Barry got out of the car and looked at the low wall of broken stone that stood between them and the stone cross. Several people could be seen bending over some object on the other side of the wall.

Barry shuddered. "Claire, come with me."

"All right."

The officer guided them around a pool of water and up the slight rise to an opening in the wall, where Neil came to meet them.

Claire said, "Barry wanted me to come," and Neil nodded. "Of course. Just here, Dr. Nolan, if you please."

As the others stepped back, they could see Frieda lying against the wall, her winter coat neatly buttoned, her gloved hands on her chest, dark curls framing her face under the wool cap that covered her ears, a muffler circling her throat. At a glance, Claire thought she looked as if she might be asleep, until she saw the gray-white face. Not a hint of life there.

Barry cried out, "Oh, doll—" and took a step toward the body but was stopped by Neil's arm.

"I'm so sorry, Dr. Nolan, but we must touch nothing at the moment. The doctor has confirmed your wife's death but made no further examination. I've asked you to come here to tell us first if this was the way your wife was dressed when you saw her last."

Barry stood still as a stone, gazing down at Frieda.

"Dr. Nolan?"

"What? Oh, yes. She looked just like that."

"Thank you. We shall need to take a statement from you, if you will please come into the station this afternoon."

Barry nodded. "Yes, all right."

Then he turned to Claire. "Take me away, Claire, take me away."

Chapter

22

THE EVENING, NEIL CAME TO CLAIRE'S PLACE around nine o'clock. "There's nothing more I can do till tomorrow, love, and I thought it might help if I came for an hour or so."

Claire felt a warm rush of affection for this man, so reserved, but sensitive in the ways that counted. The tears she had been pushing back all day broke through at last, and she clung to Neil, burying her face on his shoulder.

At last she fished a tissue out of her pocket and wiped her face. "Brandy?"

"Yes, good idea."

Sitting by the fire, leaning against Neil's comforting body, she asked, "What's happening with the investigation? Are there any leads at all?"

Neil looked solemn. "One thing seems clear. It's the same chap again. When they took the body to the morgue and removed the clothes, they found the same mark."

"The 'C'?"

"Yes. Carved between the breasts, as with Cheryl Bailey."

"And the cause of death?"

"The pathologist will do the PM in the morning and we'll know more then. I'll be there."

Claire murmured condolence, knowing that the requirement for the senior officer to attend the postmortem was a part of his duty Neil most disliked.

Now she said, "Poor Frieda. Her way of life wasn't mine, but she was such a dear."

"Do you want to talk about her?"

"Yes, darling, thanks. It would help."

Starting back over the years she had known Frieda, first as a graduate student in her seminar, then as Barry's wife for the last five years, Claire recounted incidents from their days in California, laughing over some of Frieda's antics, then recalling their recent day in London.

"There's something I think I should tell you, Neil. The postmortem is going to reveal that Frieda was pregnant. I doubt if it will have any connection with her death, but it will be pretty hard on Barry when he learns about it, as he had a vasectomy years ago. It might be better if you know about this now."

"It couldn't be his child then?"

"No. She told me she was having a relationship with someone here in Devon."

"Was she planning to keep the child?"

"No. In fact, she had an appointment on Friday in Plymouth to arrange to terminate the pregnancy. I had promised to go with her when the surgery was scheduled."

"Do you know who the father is?"

"She didn't tell me, and I honestly don't know. It could very likely be someone we've never met."

"Did the father know?"

"I'm sure she hadn't told him. She was concerned

about not letting Barry know, either, as you might guess."

Neil pondered. "I'm glad you told me this, darling. We'll try to break it to him gently, if it can be done."

Claire topped off their glasses from the decanter. "Poor Barry, he's absolutely shattered, even without this news. He's going to need a lot of propping up, I'm afraid. I gave him some lunch, and he chewed like a cow with a cud, having no idea what he was doing. I gather he got to the station all right?"

"Yes. I didn't do the interview myself, but my officer said he seemed stunned. He answered everything dutifully but as if from outer space."

Claire nodded. "I was sure he'd come back here afterward, but he phoned earlier this evening to say he would be okay and not to worry. I think he'd already had a few drinks and will have quite a few more, till he conks out."

Then, at last, Claire talked about the fear that had obsessed her since the moment she heard of Frieda's death. Everything had pointed to the same killer: the woman walking alone, the body buried—or at least deposited—in the same part of the moor. Now that the mark of the "C" confirmed the theory, her terror for Sally was intensified.

"I've seen Sally today," she told Neil. "She's pretty upset about Frieda. She was as fond of her as I was."

"Good job you put extra locks all round her cottage."

"Yes, and she and Brenda are making sure they are never alone, even for short periods. Before this, we could still have some hope that Cheryl's murder might be the only one, but now we know it isn't. And now it would seem the man must live somewhere in this area."

"I'm afraid so. One advantage is that it will make it somewhat easier for us to concentrate our investigation. We may have a better chance of nailing him before he can kill again."

They talked on until Neil reluctantly had to leave, saying an affectionate good-night and promising to try to get away the next evening, if only for a short time.

When he had gone, Claire sat staring into the dying fire and thought about Neil and their future. In another year, he would be free to marry. By that time, she would be back at her university in California. Forty-six years old. Much too young too retire. She liked her job, but more important, she liked her independence.

So, how did Neil fit into this picture? His livelihood was bound up entirely with the CID, where his rank was very high indeed. His son was at school in England. He couldn't turn up in California and announce he wanted to be a detective, and at forty-eight, he certainly wouldn't quit to raise begonias.

Claire would be happy to go on as they were, but would Neil be content with a long-distance relationship? For her husband Miles, superficial and charming, it had been perfectly satisfactory, but she wasn't sure it would suit Neil. They had avoided talking about it, as the question needn't be faced for some time to come. It was only on occasions like tonight—when she felt the urge, like Elizabeth Browning, to count the ways she loved him—that thoughts of the future took front stage. Leery of commitment after her divorce, she now felt she could trust Neil, and it was a good feeling.

When Claire awoke the next morning, it was to see through her window the first snowfall of the year. The flakes, teased by the wind as they fell, clung to trees and shrubs and already lay thinly over the grass of Bea's garden.

Still haunted by the vision of Frieda's body, the

dark curls framing that dead-white face, she thought, What if the snowfall had begun a day earlier? Would Frieda have rushed out of the house if it were snowing? Probably not. Nor would the killer have been as likely to roam the streets looking for a victim. And there might have been footprints in the snow where she was lying, instead of the hard soil of the moor.

Back in her study, after her breakfast, she expected to hear from Barry and was surprised when noon came and no word. Picking up the phone, she dialed his number and waited through half a dozen double rings before he answered.

"Hello." Barry's voice was thick with sleep.

"Barry, dear. It's Claire. Did I wake you? I'm sorry."

"No, it's all right, doll. I need to get up, I suppose."

"Are you all right?" Silly question, but what else does one say?

"Sure. I'm okay."

"Do you want to come over for lunch or dinner?"

Long pause. "Maybe dinner."

"Fine. Come about six o'clock. By the way, it's snowing, but it's light so far. Should be no problem driving."

"Snowing?" Now his voice broke. "Oh, God. She's missing it. She was so excited, waiting for the first snow."

Claire swallowed hard. "Look, dear, eat some breakfast, will you?"

"Okay."

"Promise?"

"Sure."

Claire checked her supplies and decided she'd better stock up at the local supermart in case the snow turned serious. It looked as if half the population of Morbridge had the same idea, she thought, as she waited in a long line with her loaded basket. Ahead of her in line, she saw the enchanting Nora McBain, from the Crown, holding the hand of a cherubic small boy and chatting with Jasper Martinelli, his dark straggling beard almost tangling with his shoulder-length black hair.

When they had passed the checkstand, she saw through the window that Jasper put Nora's bags into his car along with his own, as she and the child climbed into the front seat. Anything doing there, Claire wondered, or just a chance meeting? Jasper seemed too inept to organize a love affair, but after all, he had married Adrian's mother. Maybe she had made all the moves. Adrian had told Sally his mother was besotted with the man. No accounting for tastes, Claire thought with a shrug.

Later that afternoon, Sally called and announced she would come to spend the night with her mother, "if it's all right?"

"Of course it's all right, darling."

"Garth is planning to stay over with Brenda, and I thought they might like to be alone. Adrian's having dinner with a friend somewhere."

"Barry's coming for dinner. He'll be glad if you're here."

Wanting to add, "Drive carefully. Lock your car doors," Claire refrained, working hard at not being a hovering mother.

By five o'clock, when Sally arrived, the light snowfall had stopped and the wind had died, leaving a white, still world.

"It's so gorgeous! I love the snow!" Sally's face glowed, then her eyes turned solemn, as she threw her arms around her mother. "Frieda would have loved this, wouldn't she?"

They talked about Frieda, about Barry, about the whole tragedy of two deaths so close to themselves, and when Barry came, Sally hugged him while they both wept.

Through drinks and dinner, Barry seemed to derive comfort from talking about the Frieda of the past but found it too painful to speak about the circumstances of her death.

When he had gone, promising to take one of Frieda's sleeping pills if he couldn't sleep, Claire and Sally tidied the kitchen and went upstairs to change for the night. In gowns and robes, they curled up in Claire's room for the kind of chat they both loved, Sally giving the latest bulletins about her studies, her professors, and her friends, then asking her mother the standard question, "What's new with *la Talbot?*"

Claire was deep in a discussion of *Eleanor* when the doorbell rang. Almost ten o'clock. Maybe it was Barry again. Downstairs, Claire looked through the peephole and saw Neil.

"May I come in?"

"Of course, darling."

When she had gone through the ritual of the double locks and the chain, she took one look at Neil's face and asked, "Trouble?"

He nodded. "Are you alone?"

"No, Sally's upstairs. Here, let me take your things."

Neil stood still, his eyes searching her face. "No. I can't stay. I must ask you a question, Claire, and it's absolutely vital that you tell me the truth."

Puzzled, she said, "Naturally."

"It's this. Did you by chance mention to Barry or Frieda, or to anyone, what I told you about the mark on Cheryl Bailey's body?"

"Of course not!"

"Not to anyone at all? I would understand if perhaps you didn't fully realize the importance of the information."

"I certainly did realize its importance, and I certainly didn't mention it to anyone."

Neil frowned. "It was very foolish of me to tell you about it. This might cost me my career, you see."

Now Claire's anger flared. "You don't believe me? Why would I lie to you?"

"I understand it's difficult at times to admit that one has, no matter how innocently, betrayed a confidence."

"What you're saying is that Barry may have found out about the mark and you assume it must have come from me, is that it? Come on, Neil, there must have been dozens of people who knew about it. All your officers, for a start."

He shook his head. "No. Only myself and my senior officer knew. We saw at once how vital it was to keep it under wraps."

"Well, then, what about the pathologist who did the postmortem, and others on his staff?"

"Only three persons there knew of it, and they are all professionals with no connection to Barry Nolan."

"Okay. You told me you had the HOLMES computer system checking all over the country for similar marks. That must mean dozens of people knew."

"Yes, but you see, we didn't describe the mark we were seeking. We asked for records of *all* marks on homicide victims that had any sort of symbolic shape or design. We got a few crosses, a swastika, and so on, but nothing like this one."

"So it comes back to me, is that it?"

Sorrowfully, Neil said, "You were close to the Nolans, Claire."

Calm now, Claire said carefully, "What does this have to do with Barry, anyhow?"

"I'm not at liberty to say."

"Oh, I see, I'm not to be trusted. Oh, God, Neil,

this is crazy. Look, I didn't tell anyone *anything*. You'll simply have to take my word for it."

"Yes, all right. Thank you. I must be going now."

Stunned, Claire watched as he walked slowly to the door, turned the knob, and went out without looking back.

Chapter

23

THE NEXT DAY, Sally stayed on after breakfast, holed up in Bea's morning room with her books and notes, planning to finish her current essay and run it off on Claire's word processor before going back to the cottage. She was still there when the electrifying phone call came at noon.

"Claire? It's Barry."

"Are you all right?"

"No! I'm at the police station. *They've arrested me!*"

"*What?*"

"Well, not actually arrested, I guess. They call it 'helping with their inquiries,' but they're acting as if I killed Frieda, and they're asking me all sorts of questions about Cheryl Bailey. They're over at the house right now, making a search."

"They can't do that without a warrant, Barry."

"It's okay. I told 'em to go ahead. What could they find? Look, Claire, I called because I'm going to need a lawyer. Can you find someone for me?"

"Yes, I'll try."

"I need somebody who handles criminal cases. I understand most of them don't."

"You're at the Kings Abbey station?"

"Yes."

"All right. It's Saturday, but I'll do my best."

"Thanks, doll. I've gotta go now."

Sally, who had come out when she heard the phone ring, saw the shock on Claire's face. "What's happened, Mums?"

When Claire told her, Sally said, *"Barry?* Poor old Barry wouldn't kill anyone!"

"I wouldn't think so, either. The thing is, I must try to find a solicitor for him."

Sally shook her head. "Must be a big mistake."

Claire began by leafing through her mother-in-law's address book, then realized she was reluctant to involve Bea's friends in the problem. The office at the university would be closed on the weekend. Who else?

What about Muriel Roberts, the art-history professor she had met at the Nolans' party? Claire checked the phone book for Exeter and found the number. *Pray that she's home.*

"Muriel Roberts here."

"It's Claire Camden. We met at the Nolans two weeks ago."

"Yes, of course, Claire. Delighted to hear from you. I've been intending to ring you, but one gets inundated."

"Exactly. The same for me. I have a problem, and I wonder if you can help."

When Claire had filled her in, Muriel's common-sense response was consoling. "Can't see Barry Nolan in the role of murderer, but let's do what we can. I'll give you the home number of a solicitor friend in Exeter. She doesn't do criminal work herself but she's sure to know someone who does. Let me know if you find someone."

Two phone calls later, Claire was given the home telephone number of a solicitor in Exeter who, according to Muriel's friend, took criminal briefs.

A brisk voice answered. "Maurice Webb here."

Claire told him the circumstances and was pleased to hear his response. "Yes, yes. I'll pop over to the station and speak with Mr. Nolan. You are in Morbridge, Mrs. Camden?"

"Yes."

"I shall need to speak with you, if I may."

"Oh, yes, please. I'll be at home all day and evening."

"Very good. I shall give you a ring before I arrive."

Much relieved, Claire reported to Sally that she had found a lawyer for Barry, describing Maurice Webb's manner on the phone.

Sally said, "He sounds really peppy. I was afraid you might get one of those languid types with the old-school tie who act as if everything in the world is beneath them."

They talked for a while about why the police would suspect Barry, agreeing that Neil and his officers must have some sort of evidence to go this far in the questioning.

Sally said, "Of course, the husband or wife is always the first suspect in any homicide, but what can the evidence be?"

"Maybe Barry will know."

Later that afternoon, when Sally had gone back to the cottage, Claire thought long and hard about Neil's question to her the night before. It was disturbing enough that Neil didn't at once believe her that she told no one about the mark on Cheryl's body. Now, if Barry were a suspect, where did the "C" mark fit in?

If Barry didn't know about the mark, then, given

other evidence, he could be accused of killing both Frieda and Cheryl, on the assumption that only the killer would use that mark.

But if Barry *had* somehow learned about the mark, although certainly not from Claire, it could mean that he had used that knowledge in some way. The only scenario that seemed possible was that he *had* killed Frieda and had made the mark on her body to lead the police to believe it was the other killer.

This must be the dilemma that faced Neil. If Claire had admitted telling Barry about the mark, Neil would know which of the two possibilities to pursue.

She had been angry at Neil's manner the night before, but she was sure that, on reflection, he would know she was telling the truth. He would probably drop in again this evening, and they could work it out.

Meanwhile, it was after four o'clock before she heard from Barry.

"Claire, it's me." Barry may have been an English professor, but in conversation, he didn't bother with the finer points of grammar. "I'm home. Say, thanks for getting that fellow Webb. He's a go-getter, all right."

"Barry, have they told you what evidence they have that makes them think you're—that is, that you—"

"That I'm a murderer?" His voice went flat. "It's okay, Claire, you can say it. Yes, they told me some things but Webb told me not to talk about them, so I'm not."

"Can't you tell *me?*"

"No, he says not anybody. I better follow his orders."

"Yes, you're right. Mr. Webb's on his way over here. Anything I can do to help?"

"I'm okay for now, but he says if they arrest me, we'll need to have money for bail. We don't know how much yet."

"I haven't got much, Barry, but I might be able to help a little. Let's see what happens. Do you want to come over for a meal?"

"No, I'm fine." He didn't sound fine, but she heard a clink that sounded like a refill was going on.

Ten minutes later, Claire opened the door to a short, fiftyish man, his head bald in the center and fringed with a ring of salt-and-pepper hair.

"Mrs. Camden? Maurice Webb."

"Please come in."

Webb stamped snow off his boots and briskly hung his overcoat on a hook by the door, revealing a gray pinstriped suit and a bow tie.

Claire led the way toward the fire. "Please sit down. Will you have tea, or a sherry?"

"Sherry, if you please."

She handed him his glass and sat down with her own.

Webb's small, expressionless eyes studied her face. "Mr. Nolan tells me you are old friends, as well as both members of the faculty at the university in California. Is that correct?"

No chitchat about the weather. No bedside manner, or whatever you call it for a solicitor. Straight to business.

Claire was amused but pleased. "Yes, that's correct."

"I want you to tell me everything you can about Mr. Barry Nolan and his wife, anything at all. Only the truth can help us, Mrs. Camden."

"Yes, I see."

Without hesitation, Claire described the stormy ups and downs of the Nolan marriage, including occasional mild physical violence. More difficult was the task of telling him about Frieda's affair and pregnancy, but since Neil knew it all anyhow, it was no use concealing it from Barry's lawyer.

"You see, Mr. Webb, although outwardly it would

not seem so, the Nolans were extremely fond of each other."

"Yes, yes, I understand that. The reverse may also be true. I've seen marriages of the utmost propriety but without a shred of affection. Now, Mrs. Camden, if Mr. Nolan had learned of his wife's pregnancy, under the circumstances you describe, what do you believe would have been his response?"

"He'd have been furious, but I doubt if he did know, or I think he'd have told me. Has he told you what they were quarreling about that evening?"

"No, but if he had done so, it would be privileged information. I *can* say that he admitted to striking his wife, as he tells me he has already told you of that fact."

"Yes, he did. He also told me the police have searched his house."

"Yes. It is most unfortunate Mr. Nolan had given his permission before obtaining counsel. However, he seems confident there is nothing incriminating on the premises."

"He's probably right. You see, Mr. Webb, given everything, I simply cannot believe that Barry would kill Frieda. He adored her, and learning of her infidelity would not have been cause, in my opinion, for more than anger. I doubt if he's been entirely faithful himself."

"Exactly. I thank you for your frankness, Mrs. Camden. Friends of the accused often try to obfuscate matters they believe to be detrimental, causing in the end all sorts of difficulties."

"Mr. Webb, Barry tells me that if he is actually arrested, he will need money for bail. Have you any idea how much it might be?"

"Depends on the charge, and of course upon the magistrate. Some are more lenient than others. However, let us not borrow trouble. We shall cross that bridge if we come to it."

Webb put down his empty glass, gave a quick tug at his bow tie with both hands, and stood up. "Thank you, Mrs. Camden. I must be off."

When he had gone, Claire smiled to herself. Was Maurice Webb another Wemmick, the law clerk in *Great Expectations,* who appeared to the world as an automaton of business efficiency, without an ounce of sentiment? Did Mr. Webb, against all assumptions to the contrary, go home to a miniature castle, complete with a much-loved aging father, or perhaps to a warm and adoring family?

Claire warmed up some leftovers in the microwave, watched television for a while, then curled up on the sofa with a book, waiting for Neil to phone or to arrive at the door.

Nothing. By eleven o'clock, she gave up and went to bed.

Tomorrow was Sunday. Surely she'd see him then.

Chapter
24

On Sunday morning, Claire phoned Neil at his flat in Kings Abbey and found him at home. Deciding her best course was to behave as if there had been no misunderstanding, she said, "Hi, darling. Are you free today?"

"Well, technically so, but I plan to spend most of the day at the station."

"Oh, I see. Can you get away for a quick meal?"

A pause. "Yes, I expect so. What time?"

"Seven?"

"Yes, all right. Till seven."

The icicles still hung like stalactites in his voice. Oh, well, Claire figured they could talk it out when he came.

She decided she needed a day off from Mary Louise Talbot. Since it was already December, she wrote some Christmas cards to friends in California to get them off early, did some minimal housework, had her daily chat with Sally on the phone, and answered a recent letter from Bea in Istanbul. Bea had finally

177

heard the news about Cheryl Bailey from a friend in Morbridge. Nothing to do but assure her that Sally was being extremely cautious and urge her not to worry.

Needing some exercise, she walked into the village to post her letters, her footsteps echoing in the tranquil silence of the Sunday afternoon. The shops were closed, all the householders no doubt at home carving the weekly joint. There was one couple strolling among the trees on a path by the little river. As Claire crossed the bridge, she noticed a tall, thin man, thirtyish, and a young woman who gazed up at him when he spoke, as if his words issued from the oracle at Delphi. As the man's head turned, Claire recognized the bony, arrogant face of Professor George Foley. Another of his students, without doubt. In just such a way, Cheryl Bailey must have been mesmerized by Foley. He certainly didn't charm Claire, but she wasn't a twenty-year-old. With a shrug, she dropped her letters in the slot and turned back toward home.

Neil arrived soon after seven, receiving her conciliatory kiss but responding with little enthusiasm. Over drinks, she tried to talk about their problem, assuring him once again that she had told no one at all about the mark on Cheryl's body.

"You do believe me, don't you?"

Neil said, "Yes, of course I believe you," but his whole demeanor cried out, "I want to believe you, but I can't be sure."

Claire said, "I saw George Foley this afternoon, with what looked like another enamored student."

Neil murmured "Mmm" but asked no questions.

Claire tried again. "What on earth is going on with Barry Nolan? Do you honestly think poor old Barry killed Frieda? To say nothing of Cheryl Bailey?"

Stony silence.

"Look, Neil, this is ridiculous. If you don't want to

tell me what's happening, then let's forget it and talk about other things."

A great idea, but no good in practice. Neil asked about the Talbot project but only half listened to what she was saying. Claire switched to asking about his son, whose school holidays would be coming up soon. "Is he going to his mother?"

"Yes, he'll be with Janice and her parents until the New Year, then come back here to me until the term begins. And what are Sally's plans?"

"Her housemate Brenda is going to her home in Kent for the entire holiday. Sally's going to spend a few days there, then come back here with me until after Christmas. Then she's going to London with her father and his friend Pierre.

Silence.

Claire tried again. "So, you'll be free for Christmas. Will you spend it here with us?"

Neil's eyes avoided hers. "That's very kind of you. Yes, thank you."

It went on like that throughout their meal, both making painful efforts at inconsequential conversation.

Only when he was ready to leave, coated and gloved against the cold, did Neil break out of his shell. His dark eyes, filled with pain, looked into hers for the first time that evening. "I do love you, Claire. You know that."

When the door closed behind him, Claire fastened the locks and went back to the fire.

Only a few nights ago she had sat just here, wondering about their future—hers and Neil's—thinking with pleasure that she believed she could trust him utterly.

She never thought that *he* might not trust *her*.

But why? Nothing had happened that would make him doubt her, or so it seemed to her. Yet, how well did they really know each other? A few casual meetings over a year or two. Then, last spring, coming together with passion and seemingly with mutual respect. Seven months of times together when he could come to London or she to Devon.

Would it be different if their circumstances had allowed them to live together? The daily contact of living in the same household reveals plenty of things about people, usually unexpected ones, both good and bad. If he had lived with her for all that time, wouldn't he know by now that it was simply not in her nature to lie to him, especially about something as vital as the "C" mark?

It was obvious that Neil wanted to believe her but equally obvious that he couldn't be sure and was tormented by his uncertainty. His parting protestation that he loved her carried the uncomfortable suggestion that he forgave her for lying and loved her in spite of it. Not a reassuring prospect for the future.

It was frustrating not to be able somehow to prove she was telling the truth. Maybe circumstances would eventually do that for her. But was that really the point? The fact remained that he didn't trust her now.

She remembered the theory in psychology that people accuse others of their own shortcomings. Did Neil sometimes tell lies himself and therefore suspect others of doing the same? She hadn't had the least hint of that in his nature, but nothing had come up to test that theory until now. Nevertheless, she knew that, had the circumstances been reversed, she would have accepted *his* word without question.

In the days that followed, neither of them wanted a repeat of that miserable Sunday evening, each assuring the other on the phone that they were simply too busy to meet. Perhaps on the weekend?

Claire was surprised to hear little from Barry, who had gone back to his campus duties and seemed to be spending the evenings at home alone with his liquid consolation. On Tuesday evening, Muriel Roberts asked her for drinks and they went on to dinner at a local bistro, talking over what little was known about the Nolan case and generally sharing the beginnings of a comfortable friendship.

Working on the biography was a welcome refuge from thoughts of Neil. One point Claire wanted to make in her discussion of the novel *Eleanor* was that the development of the love affair between Eleanor and the artist, Howard Grover, presented some interesting problems for Talbot as author. In giving a sympathetic portrayal of their attachment, the Victorian author had to tread carefully. Her publishers depended heavily on profits from the powerful lending libraries like Mudie's for their survival, and editors knew that Victorian matrons kept a sharp eye on what their daughters read. Anything that openly encouraged young ladies to thoughts of revolt would be penciled out before it ever got into print, and Mary Louise Talbot needed the money to support her growing family. No way would she go back to genteel poverty. At the same time, her own impatience with Victorian prudery made its way through her work whenever she could safely get by with it.

In the novel, when Eleanor announced that the artist wished to paint her portrait, her mother gave her consent, so long as the maid Betty was to be present in the studio. Talbot traces the growing attraction between the lovers as they converse during the sittings. Howard Grover speaks freely about growing up as the son of a shopkeeper and tells Eleanor anecdotes of his life in the streets of London and about his early experiences in becoming a painter. The maid Betty sees nothing to fear. Her mistress could never take up with the artist, she reports to her fellow servants, as "he's no gentleman, for all his high-flown talk about art and such."

They first declare their mutual affection after half a

dozen sittings. On this occasion, when the tea was brought in, Betty was excused, as was the custom, to go to the servants' hall.

Grover frowned at his canvas. "Please take your tea, Miss Dexter. I want to try to get this right before the light goes."

Quietly, Eleanor poured a cup and walked across to where he stood at the easel, setting the cup on a table at his elbow. "You must have this, Mr. Grover. It will do you good."

She studied the picture. "It's impossible to see one's self, is it not? I can see the resemblance, of course, but do I truly look so aloof?"

He looked at her in surprise. "Aloof? Not at all."

"Perhaps sad, then."

Now his eyes held hers. "Are you sad, Miss Dexter?"

"Sometimes."

His heart beating, he looked into her eyes. "I am extremely sorry to hear it."

In a whisper, Eleanor said, "I am happy when I am here with you. My life is otherwise empty, a pointless round of social obligations."

"These do not give you pleasure, Miss Dexter?"

"Very little."

Eleanor returned to her chair and Grover worked on in silence. At last, he put down his brush and walked to the window. With his back to Eleanor, he said, "I have thought a great deal of what you have just told me, that you are happy when you are here with me."

Now he turned to face her. "I believe you know what I should like to say to you, Miss Dexter, but our circumstances make it impossible for me to speak."

Eleanor rose and looked directly into his eyes. "I know what others might say, Mr. Grover, but for myself, I am aware of no circumstances that should keep us from saying whatever we wish."

For a moment, he stood transfixed. Then with a cry of joy, he sprang forward and took her in his arms. "Miss Dexter! *Eleanor!* You know that I love you!"

He bent toward her and she lifted her face to receive his kiss.

"My love, my darling, will you be my wife?"

Eleanor looked into the face of the man she had come to care for so deeply. Her voice trembling, she said, "Yes, I shall be proud to be your wife!"

Needless to say, both Eleanor and Grover knew the course of true love was destined to run into major roadblocks and agreed to move slowly to prepare Eleanor's family for the news. In the following week, when she came for her sitting, they continued their plans.

When Eleanor came into the studio, she sent Betty to fetch a shawl from the cloakroom for her, stepping quickly into the arms of her lover.

As they parted, she said, "You are to come to a reception on Thursday week. I shall introduce you to my father, and then perhaps you can invite him to come here to see my portrait."

Grover kissed her once more, then laughed and pointed to the easel. "There it is, my dear."

Eleanor stared. Her portrait was gone. Only a solid white ground greeted her astonished gaze. "What happened?"

"The more I looked at it, the less I liked it. It simply did not catch you as I see you, my darling, especially now, when you glow with a radiance I want to try to reproduce. I shall start again, and this time it will be worthy of you."

When Betty returned, she found them both laughing, and heard her mistress say, "Will there be something to show in two weeks' time?"

"Oh, yes, I can work rapidly when I must. These past weeks I've had no incentive for speed."

This remark sent them off into gales of laughter again, to Betty's mystification. Her mistress had indeed been in gay spirits of late, but the vagaries of mood among the gentry had always puzzled Betty, who thought that if she herself had no work to do, lovely clothes to wear, and endless parties to attend, she would be happy always.

True to his word, Grover had a nearly finished portrait to show to Eleanor's father when he came to the studio, but the visit scarcely produced the result they had hoped for. Mr. Dexter merely nodded, pronounced the portrait "very fine, very fine indeed," and walked out, instructing the artist to send him the bill when it was finished. Eleanor then invited Grover to take tea with the family, where her mother treated him with stiff courtesy and her father ignored him altogether.

In despair, Eleanor finally announced that she and the artist wished to be married and that Grover intended to call upon Mr. Dexter to ask for her hand. The result was predictable. The man was "unsuitable," and "there is no more to be said."

Putting down her notes, Claire stood and stretched. It was Thursday afternoon, and she was ready for a break. Depressed by the rift with Neil and uneasy about Barry Nolan, she was assailed by a restless desire to get out of Morbridge. More than a week ago, she had sent a note to Mrs. Vickers in Sudbury, asking for information about other descendants of the Halley family, and had had no reply. Knowing the lady worked in a shop all day and had son Toby to cope with, she decided to spare her the necessity of writing or phoning. Why not just drop in about five-thirty, as Mrs. Vickers arrived home from work?

That morning, a steady downpour had melted the snow, and by late afternoon a nasty wind was whipping the rain into shapeless whorls. In a mood to welcome a battle with the elements, Claire set off, stopping at the edge of town for petrol. Self-service had arrived, even in places like Morbridge, and the station roof only partly protected her from lashes of icy water as she filled the tank and dashed inside to pay the bill.

It was already dark by the time she reached the A-38, and soon after she turned off to Sudbury, the rush-hour traffic going into the town began building up. No problem. She wasn't expected, anyhow. It felt good just to be out. If Mary Vickers wasn't at home, she'd go back into Sudbury for a meal and try the house again. Anything not to be at Bea's place, wondering if the phone would ring, if Neil would be calling to make everything all right again between them.

Painful recollections of Frieda, so lively that day they had come to Sudbury together, stirred in her mind along with puzzlement about Barry. What if he had found out Frieda was pregnant? What if she had flaunted her lover to him? Claire had assured the solicitor, Maurice Webb, that Barry wouldn't have been enraged enough to kill. But could she be wrong? Barry seemed to be truly shattered by Frieda's death, but wouldn't that be true even if he *had* killed her?

Forcing her mind back to the street signs of Sudbury, she worked her way through the town and, in spite of the dark, found Cudworth Way with no problem. It was quarter till six when she stopped in front of The Laurels. The wind had worked itself into a minor frenzy as she stepped out of the car and ran, head bent, for the door. Mopping rain off her face, she rang the bell. No answer. At least, she supposed the bell had rung. Impossible to hear anything with the racket the wind was making.

She tried again. Still no answer, but lights shone from the windows on the ground floor and from the floor above.

Surely the thrifty Mary Vickers wouldn't go out and leave the house with all those lights blazing? Claire knocked with her gloved hand but could hardly hear the sound herself. She banged harder, and saw the door move slightly. Turning the knob, she found the door unlocked, and a mighty gust of wind blew it nearly out of her hand as it swung inward to the hall.

Stepping inside, she pushed hard against the wind and managed to close the door behind her. She was surprised to see that the doors on either side of the hall were open and the rooms lighted, as the custom in most English households in the winter was to heat only the rooms being used by the family. The parlor, where she and Frieda had sat having tea with Mary Vickers and Toby and their neighbor Rodney Simms, was surely not in daily use, and when she walked into the empty room, it was icy cold.

Crossing the hall, she peered into a room where a television and two easy chairs confirmed that this was the family sitting room, now empty.

Claire called out, "Mrs. Vickers?"

No answer, and no one in the adjoining kitchen.

Back in the hall, Claire was about to leave when she heard a muffled sound from somewhere above. Now she noticed, beyond the small Turkish carpet in the entry, a trail of very wet footprints leading toward the stairs. Walking tentatively to the foot of the stairs, she heard sharp sounds of banging, as if furniture was being moved about or something thrown to the floor.

She called again, this time raising her voice to a shout. "Mrs. Vickers?"

The noise abruptly stopped.

She must be there. Claire hesitated only for a moment. Ordinarily, she would have retreated rather than face someone who would have every right to demand what she was doing wandering around the house uninvited, but she was sure that sweet, timid Mary Vickers was the type who would apologize for not having heard the bell.

At the top of the first flight, she called out again, getting no reply, but she saw that the wet prints went on up the stairs. The lady must be in the attic, then.

Not wanting to startle her, Claire clumped loudly up the uncarpeted stairs. Now she saw why there was no answer to her call.

Mary Vickers lay motionless on the floor at the entrance to the attic.

Chapter
25

CLAIRE KNELT BESIDE MARY VICKERS, speaking her name but getting no response. She picked up her hand and pressed the fingers, hoping to get a return of pressure. Nothing.

Was she alive? Claire looked at the white face, remembering Frieda lying on the ground near Monk's Cross. No, this was different. Bending over, she put her ear to Mary's chest. Surely there was a faint heartbeat? She must get to the telephone.

As she stood up, her back to the attic doorway, she heard a sound behind her and felt a sharp blow on the back of her head. Her knees buckled, and she could hear herself moan with pain as a pair of arms pulled her backward and flung her to the floor of the attic. The full weight of a body pressed on top of her, pinning her down.

Then hands lifted her head to pull her wool muffler up and unwind it from around her neck. Terrified, she tried to think of basic rules of self-defense. A knee to the groin first. But when she tried to make her legs function, she could only struggle helplessly against the weight of the attacker.

Now she felt hands around her throat, cutting off her breath. Groggy from the blow to her head, she remembered something about pulling the small fingers of an attacker's hands, not the thumbs. Forcing her numb brain to guide her, she felt along the hand to the last finger, at the back of her neck, lower than the others. Yes, there it was. She pulled hard and felt the finger lift, but not enough to free the hand from her throat.

Desperately fighting for breath, she felt her eyes begin to close as consciousness ebbed away, when suddenly the hands released their hold. Dimly, she heard a scuffle, a thud, and a voice shouting, "Hoy, wait up there!"

Footsteps thundered down the stairs, and after a pause, someone climbed over her, muttering "Sorry!" Then she heard the loud clumping of other feet on the stairs, in hot pursuit.

Each breath she took was like a gift from the gods. Forget the pain in her throat. She rolled to one side and saw the still inert body of Mary Vickers. Too weak to sit up, she lay quietly, hammers banging away in her head.

The silence was broken by the sound of thudding feet coming up the stairs. Was the attacker coming back? He'd been chased away by someone, hadn't he? But what if he had overcome the other person and was coming back to finish the job?

Then she heard a hearty voice shouting, "It's me, Mum!" and saw Toby Vickers bending over his mother, holding her hand and kissing it. "I rang up 999. They're coming with the ambulance."

She watched as Toby tore off his jacket and laid it over his mother, crooning, "You'll be fine, Mum. They'll be here soon."

Then Toby lifted his head and saw Claire, who had inched her way out of the dark attic. "Dr. Camden? Din't know it was you! What was the bastard after, anyhow?"

Trying her voice for the first time, Claire found she had only a hoarse whisper. "I don't know, Toby, but thank you for what you did."

Before the ambulance arrived, Mary began to regain consciousness, moaning softly but unable to speak, and soon afterward, the crew came and took both women to the hospital.

The report on Mary Vickers was that she had suffered a skull fracture that was not life-threatening but that would keep her in the hospital for a few days.

When the doctor then examined Claire, he announced firmly, over her protests, that she was to remain overnight for observation. Resigned, she phoned Sally to say she had met with a minor accident but there was no cause for alarm. It was the end of term and Sally was due to leave the next day for her visit to Brenda. When Sally insisted on coming to the hospital, Claire said she must not go out in the storm and put the doctor on the phone to assure Sally there was no need to come.

"You go along with Brenda, darling, and have a lovely time. I'll call you there when I get home tomorrow."

Lying in the hospital bed, Claire had to admit she was glad to be there, and glad of the medication that eased the pain in her throat and head.

A police officer came to ask her if she could identify the intruder, and hearing her hoarsely whispered "no," he said, "We won't trouble you further tonight, Mrs. Camden. Someone will speak with you in the morning."

A few minutes later, Toby came in, and Claire

smiled at him in thanks, whispering, "How's your mother, Toby?"

He brushed a hand across his face, where tears had left smudges of brown. "Doctor says she'll be all right. I know you mustn't talk, Dr. Camden, but I want to know. Did you see the bloody bloke's face?"

"No, I didn't. It was dark in the attic. Did you?"

"No. I chased after him but he got the jump on me, see? When I pulled him off of you, he knocked me down and dashed off down the stairs, and all I could see was his back. By the time I went out the front door, I heard a car start up and roar away down the road."

A nurse glided in and looked sternly at Toby. "You must go, sir."

"All right, Sister. Sorry."

By morning, Claire's voice was still hoarse but definitely better, helped by the analgesic spray she could apply herself.

Presently, a fatherly-looking police officer arrived from the Sudbury force to take her statement.

She described arriving at the Vickers house, seeing the lights burning, and finding the door unlocked.

"There was no one on the ground floor," she went on, "but I saw wet footsteps on the stairs."

"Can you describe these, Mrs. Camden?"

"Not really. They seemed to be rather jumbled up."

"The first two sets of stairs have a carpet strip, do they not? The marks were visible on the carpet?"

"Yes. At least, it was obviously wet. I could see the drops of water and what looked like marks made by shoes or boots."

"Did they appear to be made by more than one person?"

"Yes, I believe so."

Now she described hearing noises from above and climbing the stairs to find Mary Vickers lying on the floor near the open door to the attic. "Then something struck the back of my head and I was pulled inside."

The officer's eyes looked at her with compassion and he shook his head. "I don't know what we're coming to with all this violence, that I don't. Now, can you tell me if there was light in the attic at that time?"

"No, it was dark."

"You could not see the face of your attacker?"

"No. He must have dragged me several feet inside the door, as I could see a faint light from the landing but nothing inside the attic."

"Have you any impression of the size of the attacker?"

"It's so difficult to say. He used his body to pin me to the floor. His weight was certainly oppressive, but I would guess him to be of average build, not excessively heavy."

"Did he speak at all?"

"No, but he sort of grunted and breathed heavily as he"—Claire shuddered—"as he choked me. And I'm afraid that's all I know."

The officer sighed and stood up. "Thank you for your help, Mrs. Camden. You've been most courageous. I hope you have a speedy recovery from your injuries." And with his head moving from side to side as he contemplated the ills of the world, he took his leave.

By midmorning, when the doctor had examined her and announced that she was free to leave, she dressed and was about to ask the nurse to call for a taxi when Toby turned up.

"Morning, Dr. Camden. Your car's at our place, in' it? Want a lift?"

"Yes, thank you, Toby."

She walked out with him to the lobby, wondering if he meant to put her pillion on his motorbike, when she saw the round face of Rodney Simms, who said, "My car's here. Shall we?"

The wind and rain of the night before had subsided, and the air was still, under a sullen sky. As they drove through the town, Claire saw broken branches of trees lying like twisted sticks where the storm had flung them down, and, as they passed along the esplanade, the rocky shore was littered with debris, exposed by the retreating sea at low tide.

Back at The Laurels, Toby insisted they both come in for a coffee before Claire set off for Morbridge. She watched in amusement as Toby placed her solicitously in the parlor, where two space heaters glowed at full force.

"The coffee's ready. If you'll excuse me, I won't be a moment," he said, sounding for all the world like his mother. "Give me a hand, Rodney?"

Five minutes later, Toby walked in, carefully bearing a silver tray, laid with cups, saucers, milk, and sugar, while Rodney followed with a plate of toasted scones.

Toby handed them their cups and passed the scones, then took his seat, sipping his coffee. If he had begun to remark on the weather, Claire was sure she wouldn't have been able to keep her composure, but he lapsed into a more familiar persona.

"If I ever lay my hands on that bloody bastard, he'll know a thing or two."

Claire said, "I'm glad you arrived when you did, Toby."

"Right. I'm only sorry Mum didn't stay for the film."

"Film?"

"See, we was all booked to go to the cinema with Rodney and a friend of his, to see some film about art."

Rodney interposed. "The life of Gauguin."

"Right. So Rodney and I are waiting there at the cinema when Mum comes along from work and says she's changed her mind and is going home to do some things for Christmas. So Rodney and I go along inside. His friend hasn't come but Rodney says he'll find us. The film starts and I watch for about ten minutes, and it's dead boring, so I take off for home on my motorbike, despite the rotten weather."

Rodney rolled his eyes upward at Claire, conveying the futility of trying to inculcate Toby with culture.

"So, I park my bike in the shed and lock it up for the night. I see all the lights burning and I wonder what Mum's up to, and when I don't find her, I go on up to the attic, and there she is, lying on the floor. Then I hear sort of grunting noises, and it looks like somebody's being attacked, so I hop in and pull the attacker's arms back. He must've been that surprised, but he leaped up and drove his fist into my middle. I doubled up and fell, and I couldn't breathe for a bit. Then I climbed over this person—'course I didn't know it was you, Dr. Camden—and chased the bugger down the stairs, but he got away."

Claire said, "I think you were very courageous, Toby."

The boy looked genuinely surprised. "Anybody would have done the same."

When Rodney added his opinion that Toby had been a hero, the boy turned slightly pink. "Leave off, Rodney. What I'd like to know is, what was he looking for in the attic? The place was a shambles. Everything tossed about, and Mum had just tidied it up not long ago. Why didn't he take the silver?"

Toby held up one of his mother's silver teaspoons.

Claire saw Rodney turn his head and gaze blandly out of the window. Now she was sure Rodney knew about the missing Turner. No exclamations of wonder about what might be in the attic. But Rodney certainly could not have been responsible for what happened the evening before. Unless? What about the friend who didn't turn up at the cinema? Could he have come to make a search, assuming no one would be at home? If so, it must not have been in collusion with Rodney, who had probably already made his own search long since, or Claire was much mistaken.

An hour later, back in Morbridge, Claire found the message light blinking on the telephone. Call Barry. Call Maurice Webb, the solicitor. Nothing from Neil.

First, she looked up Brenda Gilbert's number at her home in Kent and chatted with Sally, assuring her she was fine.

Next, Barry. But there was no answer at Barry's place.

Now for Mr. Webb.

"Mrs. Camden, thank you for ringing."

"Has something happened? I've tried reaching Mr. Nolan and he is not at home."

"Yes. Mr. Nolan was charged today in the death of his wife."

"Oh, dear. Is there anything I can do?"

"At the moment, he is in temporary custody. As the charge is manslaughter, not murder, I was able to secure a reasonable sum for bail. Mr. Nolan believes he can meet the requirement, but if he falls short, he may wish to ask you for assistance."

"I see. I could probably manage a few hundred pounds, no more."

"Thank you. I shall inform you if your help is needed. I have asked for a preliminary hearing, of the type known as 'old style,' in which the Crown presents its case and the defense may question its witnesses but does not present its own case. Our hope is that the magistrate will dismiss the charge on the ground of insufficient evidence."

Ever the automaton of efficiency, Maurice Webb rang off, and Claire knew it was useless to ask him what evidence the prosecution might have.

Neil certainly wasn't telling her anything.

She would have to wait for the hearing to find out what was going on.

Chapter

26

By late that afternoon, Barry Nolan was able to scrounge together enough money for his bail. Since it was still morning in California, his bank was open, and the total sum of his and Frieda's savings was wired to his bank in Devon.

Claire invited him for Chinese takeaway and found him more animated than he had been since Frieda's death. Bringing his own supply of gin and tonic, he made up a pitcher and poured himself a whopper.

"I'm glad I was able to make the bail without asking for your help, Claire, but thanks for your offer."

"Mr. Webb told me he got a reasonable bail for you."

"It seemed like a lot to me—over fifteen thousand dollars—but he says it's very good. You see, a big factor is that the police have my passport, so they feel pretty confident I can't leave the country. I get all the money back if the charges are dropped or if it comes to trial and I haven't run off."

"Do you have to put up the whole amount?"

"Yes. They don't have bail bondsmen over here. At home, we would only need ten percent of the amount, but Webb tells me the amounts are usually set higher over there, so it sort of evens out."

Mildly surprised that the carefree Nolans had managed to save that much on a professor's salary, Claire said, "I'm glad you had enough, Barry."

He gave her a sheepish look. "The truth is, a lot of it was Frieda's from her divorce, but we'd put it in a joint account when we were married."

His face crumpled and tears spurted from his eyes. "Oh, God, Claire, I loved that gal."

Claire patted and murmured, and when his weeping had subsided, she said, "Barry, do they really have any evidence against you?"

He reached for the pitcher. "Hasn't Neil told you?"

"No. Actually, I haven't seen him this week. He's been tied up with all this."

At that, Barry gave her a surprisingly sharp look. "Trouble in River City?"

Claire nodded. Leave it to Barry to notice anything to do with personal relationships.

"Nothing serious, I hope."

"No, I'm sure it will work itself out."

Claire had to clamp her teeth to keep from telling Barry what her problem was with Neil, but she had known from the beginning that it was out of the question to do so. Now that Barry had been charged in Frieda's death, the "C" mark must figure in some way in the police theory of the case. If she spoke a word to him about the mark, it would constitute the very betrayal of confidence Neil suspected her of.

After their meal, Barry switched to brandy, gradually sliding back into the somnambulistic state he had been in for the past week. As he was leaving, he gave her a hug. "You've been great, Claire. Hope things work out with Neil. That guy doesn't know how lucky he is."

On Sunday, Neil came again to spend the evening, obviously trying to behave normally but saying nothing about the issue between them. Although Barry's hearing had been set for the following Thursday, Claire said nothing about the case.

When Neil asked if he might stay for the night, Claire hesitated, and he said quickly, "Perhaps another time."

Each day, Claire phoned to inquire about Mary Vickers, learning from Toby that she was recovering more rapidly than expected. On Monday, the phone was answered by the lady herself.

"How kind of you to ring, Dr. Camden. I feel quite myself again, thank you, barring a bit of a headache. I'm so sorry I have not replied to your inquiry about the Halley relations. Were you coming to ask me about it?"

"Yes, but it's not at all urgent, Mrs. Vickers. Whenever it's convenient."

"I shall write soon to a cousin who may have some knowledge of present descendants. Meanwhile, we are baffled by the incident of Thursday evening. Whatever could the intruder have been looking for in the attic?"

Claire had decided it would be foolish to worry Mary Vickers with the theory about the Turner painting. Obviously, if Rodney Simms knew about it, he had not told Mary. Claire wanted a little more time to find it, if she could. If not, then she would tell her the whole story.

Instead, she said, "I suppose some people store valuables in their attics."

"Yes, the police said as much. Thank you for ringing, Dr. Camden."

With Sally gone, Claire spent the days before Thursday buried in work. She had read through a stack of contemporary writings about the painter Turner and found that many of these, while acknowledging his genius as an artist, treated him with ill-disguised contempt for his lowly origins as the son of a London barber and for his lack of the polished manners required by society.

These unkind opinions culminated in the year 1862 with the publication of *The Life of J.M.W. Turner,* the first full-length biography of the artist, written eleven years after his death. The author followed the Victorian party line by launching an attack on the character of the artist, and there could be little doubt that this spurred Mary Louise Talbot to write what constituted an impassioned defense of Turner in her novel *Eleanor.*

In words that must have made Talbot seethe, the biographer wrote: "Whatever his genius, the artist cannot be admired unless he is a true gentleman in mind and heart." Turner, with his "uncultivated intellect" and "underbred manner," was simply outside the pale. When he was known to have made a good deal of money from his work, this was portrayed as showing "the mean, grasping spirit of a petty tradesman." Even when the author gave examples of Turner's friendship with families of "high moral character," these were turned against him with disparaging complaints that he failed to benefit from such fine company to "improve his own demeanor, which was sadly lacking in the finer sensibilities."

True enough, when the biography appeared, it was attacked by certain perceptive critics as everything from "unreliable" to "scurrilous," but the general public read it with approval.

Prudence Halley's letters would certainly have enhanced Talbot's interest in Turner and his work. Now it was clear that the death of her cousin, only a few months before the publication of the deplorable "life," precipitated Talbot's defense.

Many passages in the novel demonstrated Claire's thesis that Talbot defended Turner through the vehicle of *Eleanor*. At first, the Dexters simply refuse to take Eleanor seriously when she declares her desire to marry Howard Grover. Her mother says it is "quite out of the question," and when Grover comes to call upon Mr. Dexter to ask for Eleanor's hand in marriage, her father displays no anger, only a haughty disdain at the absurdity of the question, adding that if such a marriage should take place, Eleanor would receive no money of any kind from her family.

In a charming scene, Grover takes Eleanor to meet his father, who still lives above his shop in the neighborhood of St. Paul's Cathedral. Eleanor is moved by the artist's devotion to his aging parent and by the old man's intense pride in his son's achievement. Telling her mother of this visit, Eleanor gets a typical response.

"My dear Eleanor, I am certain that persons in that walk of life are quite capable of feelings of affection. That is not a recommendation to bring such a person into our own family circle. Surely you understand that you would be cut off from ordinary social intercourse if you should be foolish enough to marry such a person."

"But that would not be a great loss to me, Mamma."

"Then think of your sister. She has just come out this year, and an unsuitable marriage on your part would have a most unsalutary effect upon her prospects."

Eleanor sighed. "If you would but make an effort to know Howard—Mr. Grover—Mamma, you would come to understand the nobleness of his character."

"I have now met Mr. Grover on several occasions, Eleanor, at your insistence, and I see nothing in him. He talks very well about his art, but an obsession with a single subject is scarcely a recommendation for his presence at the dinner table. Your father has been very lenient with you, in my view, in permitting you to meet with Mr. Grover from time to time."

Eleanor smiled bitterly. "Yes, I am sure I should be most grateful, with Betty or the footman dogging our every footstep as we walk in the park or visit museums. I understand only too well that Papa believes I will grow tired of my 'fancy,' as he calls it, if I am not absolutely forbidden to see my friend."

"And why not? It seems to me that if the man truly cared for you, he would not ask you to make the sacrifice of your fortune and your connections to take such a step."

"He has said that to me from the beginning, Mamma, and now he believes that he should go away, to give me time to be certain of my own mind. You will be happy to know that in a week, Mr. Grover leaves for Italy, where he will remain for several months, studying the great artists of the past and working diligently at his painting."

Mrs. Dexter's face was alight. "Your father will be immensely pleased with this news, Eleanor. I shall suggest that you be permitted to exchange one letter each fortnight. Will that be agreeable to you, my dear?"

If readers of *Eleanor* had only wondered up to this point if J.M.W. Turner was the prototype for Howard Grover, they would soon be in no doubt, for the letters written during Howard's sojourn in Italy were unmistakably based upon the artist Turner's experiences there. Talbot took many liberties with dates—for example, the real Turner did not visit Italy until the age of forty-four—but Howard's exuberant descriptions of the paintings he did in Rome and especially of those in his beloved Venice made the identification clear.

In her sympathetic portrait of the artist, Talbot went as far as she dared in taking potshots at the Mrs.

Grundys of the day. What Talbot could not do in her story—and this must have been a source of exasperation to her—was to allow the "unsuitable" marriage to take place.

Had she been willing to forgo the profits from the lending libraries, she might have got by with it, but her attitude throughout her career was a practical one. Push as far as you can, but play the game in the end. She never thought of herself as a writer of great literature, preferring her comfortable role as a purveyor of popular fiction, but fiction well written and laced with doses of social criticism.

In *Eleanor,* the painter returns from Italy, the lovers are unswerving in their devotion, and when Eleanor cannot secure her parents' consent, they plan to elope. At this auspicious moment, the artist falls ill from a fever he contracted in Italy, and after a series of touching scenes, he dies in Eleanor's arms.

Now Talbot faced her final problem. Just as a young woman could not make an "unsuitable" marriage and be portrayed as living happily ever after, it was equally impossible for the novel to have a tragic ending. Two years pass, during which Eleanor mourns her lover and is consoled, at a respectful distance, by the cousin whose proposal she had earlier rejected. At last, she comes to admire him for his steadfast devotion, and in the closing chapter, she realizes that she has come to love him, and the requisite happy ending is achieved. As a final gesture, Eleanor gives Grover's portrait of her to the National Gallery, as a tribute to his memory.

By Wednesday evening, Claire had done the final revisions on her discussion of *Eleanor* and was tidying up her study when Sally arrived with Adrian in tow. Sally had traveled to Kent with Brenda and Garth, and the arrangement had been that Adrian would come for her on the last day of the visit and bring her back to Morbridge.

Now, Sally reported on the pleasures of the visit, then asked what was happening with Barry Nolan. "You said on the phone that his preliminary hearing is tomorrow, Mums? Is it all right if we go?"

"I don't see why not. There is a public gallery."

"Good. Do you want to come along, Adrian?"

"Yes, all right, if you like."

Sally said, "Mums, what does Neil say about all this?"

Claire smiled. "He can't very well discuss it with anyone, can he, dear? We'll find out tomorrow."

"Okay. Adrian, shall we bring in the tree now? We found a little beauty in the woods near Brenda's place."

Adrian added, "It just fit into the boot. I'll fetch it."

Claire brought out the boxes of trimmings Bea had stored in a cupboard, and for hours, Sally and Adrian strung berries and hung the ornaments Sally remembered from childhood Christmases here in Bea's house. Claire, assailed with painful memories, felt again that Neil's presence in her life had made it all easier to bear, but forget the self-pity. She had survived before Neil came along, and she would do it again.

Chapter
27

THE PRELIMINARY HEARING for Barry Nolan began the next morning in the Magistrate's Court in Kings Abbey. In a building dating back to George IV, the courtroom was dark-paneled, and the visitors' gallery was a true gallery, raised above the well of the court itself. Several rows of seats on risers, behind a railing, gave spectators a view of the proceedings below, unlike newer buildings, in which the visitors' area was often on floor level.

Claire had arrived early, climbing the narrow stairs and getting a seat in the front row. *Like going to the theater,* she thought irreverently.

The court was already buzzing with activity. Solicitors and clerks, their hands full of documents, came and went, consulting, chatting, occasionally exchanging a laugh. Then a door at the back opened, talk was quenched, and everyone arose. To the time-honored sound of "Oyez, Oyez," the magistrate swept in, his black robes flying behind him, and the court was called into session.

Visitors began to fill the seats in the gallery, Claire holding two places for Sally and Adrian, who arrived as the first case was called. Glancing over her shoulder, Claire was surprised to see Jasper Martinelli among the spectators, and a few places beyond him sat a tall woman who looked vaguely familiar. Of course, Caroline Foley, wife of the professor. For all her airs, Claire thought, she's not above vulgar curiosity.

For more than an hour, the magistrate heard pleas in several cases that proved to be routine, if not for the accused, at least for the functioning of the court. In two cases, bail was set, and in the third, the man was remanded to custody.

It was eleven o'clock when the case of Barry Nolan was finally called, giving rise to a stir of interest. Murder, or manslaughter under mysterious circumstances, was not an everyday affair, and an old-style hearing on such a charge was rare enough to draw what Claire saw were obviously members of the press in a section to the side of the courtroom.

When Barry was brought in, he was placed on a low dais behind a railing, with his back to the gallery above, and facing the magistrate, who sat on a higher dais, across the well of the court. Facing the magistrate were the adjoining tables for the defense and for the Crown prosecution, and behind them, the tables for their respective clerks.

Maurice Webb sat at the defense table, looking over a sheaf of notes. "As a solicitor," he had told Claire earlier, "I am empowered to appear myself at the magistrate's hearing. In the event Mr. Nolan is bound over for trial at the Assize Court, I shall of course brief a barrister to conduct his defense at that time."

Claire caught a glimpse of Neil Padgett and was sure he glanced upward and saw her, but neither of them made a sign of recognition.

The magistrate began the proceedings by looking toward the Crown prosecutor. "Mr. Keating?"

A fair, pink-cheeked young man in his twenties rose to his feet. Must have been admitted to practice the day before yesterday, Claire thought.

The plea of "not guilty" was duly entered, and young Keating called his first witness, who was sworn in and took his place in the box.

Identifying himself as a farmer who lived a mile or so from Monk's Cross, the man described driving along the road at about half-past ten o'clock on the morning of Thursday, the thirtieth of November, and seeing a dark shape on the ground not far from the cross.

"There's a bit of low stone wall there, and I thought from a distance it might be one of my sheep, but then I stopped my car and walked over, and when I came close, I saw it was the body of a woman lying against the wall."

"Was the body on the side of the wall visible from the road?"

"No, 'twas on the other side."

"Then how is it you were able to see it as you drove?"

Patiently, the man explained. "The road curves right round as I come from my place toward the cross. There's but a dozen yards or so of the wall and then it peters out. Coming round the curve, you can see inside that bit of wall plain as day."

"Thank you. What did you do next, sir?"

"I bent over and touched the lady, and I could see she was dead, no doubt about it. I went back to my car and drove into Morbridge, as that's the nearest police station, and told them what I found."

"Thank you, sir." Young Mr. Keating turned to Maurice Webb, who waved away any wish to question the witness.

The farmer stepped down and the policeman who had been on duty was called. He described following the farmer to the scene and reporting by car radio to police headquarters in Kings Abbey.

The next witness was the doctor who had performed the postmortem examination of Frieda's body. A distinguished physician who served as the Home Office forensic pathologist for a broad area of the west country, he was duly sworn and took his place in the witness box.

Keating began, "Can you tell us, please, what was the apparent cause of death?"

The doctor took a notebook from his pocket but did not open it. "The case was an unusual one. There were pressure marks visible round the neck, but upon examination, no evidence of internal damage nor signs of strangulation were present."

The doctor now opened his notebook and glanced at it. "There was a wound to the back of the head, but this too was not of sufficient severity to cause death."

"Can you describe the nature of the wound, please?"

"Certainly. It was not inflicted by a sharply pointed instrument, such as a knife, nor was there evidence of a weapon of concentrated striking zone, such as a hammer. It could have resulted from a blow from a rounded object, or more likely from a fall, as its position on the back of the head is consistent with a person falling backward, the head striking the floor."

"Thank you."

"Further examination produced no indication of other wounds to the body, nor of poison or other foreign substances in the intestines. There was, however, clear indication of myocardial infarction. In simple terms, the deceased died of a heart attack."

"Was there evidence of heart disease in the body, sir?"

"No. One would expect to find such evidence, although in some cases, fatal seizures of the heart may occur without prior heart damage."

"In your opinion, Doctor, what could be the cause of such a sudden attack?"

"Extreme stress, fear, shock—any of these may, in rare cases, precipitate such a result."

"Thank you. Are there further findings of significance?"

"Examination revealed that the deceased was pregnant, the fetus having reached a development of approximately nine weeks."

"From the postmortem examination, sir, is it now possible to estimate the approximate time of death?"

"Not positively. Examination indicated that the last meal was consumed some six to seven hours before death occurred. Evidence of the time the meal was consumed would be suggestive of the time of death."

"Thank you, Doctor. That will be all."

Again, Keating turned to Maurice Webb, who murmured, "No questions," and the doctor stepped down.

As the next witness was being sworn, Sally whispered to Claire. "Now we know why the charge is 'manslaughter,' not 'murder.' I never believed Barry would intentionally kill anyone, least of all Frieda." And Claire nodded agreement, thinking that if she hadn't been cut off from Neil, she would have known this all along.

"Your name, please?"

A young man with black hair and dark, liquid eyes answered. "Sunil Mukherjee."

He gave his address, which Claire recognized as the street where the Nolans lived.

"Your occupation, sir?"

"I am a medical doctor. My practice is in Morbridge."

"Now, Dr. Mukherjee, will you please describe the

position of your residence in relation to that of the accused, Mr. Barry Nolan?"

"Yes, sir. We live directly across the road."

"Thank you. On the night of the twenty-ninth of November past, or in the early hours of the following morning, were you at home?"

"Yes, I was."

"Will you describe what you saw on that occasion?"

"Yes. At about half-past one in the morning, I saw Mr. Nolan come out of his front door, carrying someone in his arms. He unlocked the door of his car, which was standing in front of his house, and placed the person on the rear seat of the car."

"Was the person in a sitting position at that time?"

"No, sir. The person must have been lying down, as I could not see her."

"You say 'her,' Dr. Mukherjee. Was the person in question a woman?"

"I cannot say positively that it was a woman, but I could see a wool cap on the person's head which resembled one often worn by Mrs. Nolan. As only two persons occupy the house, I assumed it was she."

"What did you do then?"

"I thought the lady might be ill, and I considered stepping out and crossing the road to offer my assistance, as I am a physician. However, the night was extremely cold, and I was wearing my pajamas and a dressing gown. Before I could put on my coat, I saw Mr. Nolan enter the car and drive off."

"Now, Dr. Mukherjee, will you tell us how you happened to be at your window at that hour of the night?"

The young doctor smiled. "Yes. I was walking the baby. Our son is one month old, and he suffers from the colic. My wife and I often take it in turns to walk with him when he wakes in the night and is unable to sleep. As I walked back and forth, I looked out the front window of my house."

"Were you personally acquainted with the Nolans?"

Again, a smile. "Yes. They were most friendly to my wife and myself. Mrs. Nolan admired our little son and said on one occasion that she regretted having no children of her own."

"Thank you, sir." Keating turned to Maurice Webb, who now rose for the first time.

In his quiet, matter-of-fact voice, he began. "Dr. Mukherjee, looking to the night in question, or rather the early hours of the morning of the thirtieth of November, do you recall whether or not your infant awoke on the preceding night at a similar hour?"

"Yes, I believe so."

"And what about the following night?"

"Yes, very likely."

"Is it fair to say that the child, at this stage, awakens each night, often in the early hours of the morning, and that you or your wife are likely to be walking with him at various times during the night?"

"Yes."

"Sometimes more than once in a given night?"

The doctor smiled ruefully. "Yes, sometimes that is so."

"From my own experience, I recall that on such occasions, one is awakened from a sound sleep and is often groggy and not particularly alert, is that not so?"

Mukherjee said evenly, "If you are suggesting that I was not aware of the time nor of what I saw, you are much mistaken."

Unperturbed, Webb nodded. "On what date did you first convey this information to the police?"

The doctor paused. "Let me see. I believe it was on the Saturday."

"That would be on the second day after the occasion in question?"

"Yes."

"Can you explain why you did not come forward earlier?"

"Certainly. The police questioned everyone in the neighborhood on the Friday. I was not at home, and I had not mentioned to my wife what I had seen the night before. She naturally told the officer she had seen nothing. That evening, she told me about the inquiries into the causes of Mrs. Nolan's death, and that was when I remembered. I rang the police on Saturday and reported what I had seen."

"Thank you, sir. No further questions."

After some discussion with counsel for either side, and some shuffling about in the courtroom among the clerks, the magistrate declared a recess until two o'clock and retreated to his inner sanctum.

Chapter
28

STUNNED BY THE EVIDENCE of Barry's neighbor, Claire followed Sally and Adrian down the stairs, no one speaking until they had found a table at a small Italian restaurant on the next street.

Then Sally exploded. "What on earth was Barry doing, carrying Frieda out to his car in the middle of the night? It looks as if we were all wrong and he really did kill her!"

Claire frowned. "I suppose we'll have to hear his side of the story, but I must say he certainly kept *me* in the dark. There I was, oozing sympathy and coddling him, while he pretended not to know where she was or what had happened to her."

Adrian said, "Sally was most distressed when Mr. Nolan was accused of the crime."

Sally's indignation seethed. "Yes, I was. I hugged him and told him how sorry I was. And all the time he must have known she was dead! We should have known Neil wouldn't have had him charged unless they had some real evidence. Didn't he tell you about it, Mums?"

"No, it wouldn't be proper for him to do that, would it, dear?"

Sally gave her mother a shrewd glance but said no more.

By the time they got back to the courtroom, other visitors had taken their front-row seats, and they found themselves in the fourth and last row of the gallery. In front of Claire and to her right sat Jasper Martinelli, talking with a plump young man who proved to be none other than Rodney Simms. Exchanging greetings, Claire introduced Sally and Adrian to Rodney, who said to Adrian, "I believe we've met?" and Adrian politely replied, "Yes, I expect so."

So Jasper and Rodney were acquainted. The first time she met Rodney, the day she and Frieda went to Sudbury, Rodney had mentioned having read Mary Louise Talbot's novels on the recommendation of a friend. Jasper had certainly read Talbot, as she had learned the night they had drinks at Adrian's place. Odd that Rodney had never spoken of the connection. He must have known, through Jasper, that Claire's daughter lived at the cottage below the Priory. Or would he? Jasper was so uncommunicative about anything that didn't interest him, that he might have known the Queen and never mentioned it to a soul.

Just as the magistrate entered and took his place, an attractive, dark-haired man in his thirties burst into the visitors' gallery and squeezed into a place along the last row at Claire's left. She heard him ask, "Is this the Nolan case?" He looked somehow familiar, yet she was sure she had never seen him before.

Turning her attention back to the court, she saw that the next witness for the Crown identified himself as the detective sergeant who, along with a police constable, had searched Barry Nolan's house on the day he had first been taken in for questioning.

Keating asked, "Will you tell us please what items

214

you found that may have pertinence to the charge against the prisoner?"

"Yes, sir. We took a pair of walking boots. Just there." He pointed to a bag on the prosecution table.

Keating handed the bag to the sergeant, who opened it and produced a pair of stout leather boots. "We noted that the soles were encrusted with moss and other material that looked like the wearer had been walking on the moor. As they were still damp, it seemed as if it had been recent. Since the body was found on the moor, we took the boots along for examination."

The boots were duly entered into evidence.

"Please continue, Sergeant."

The sergeant indicated another bag on the table. "If I may, please?"

Keating handed him the bag, and the sergeant extracted a small carton, a bottle, a small plastic wand that looked something like a thermometer, and a printed sheet. "This is known as a pregnancy test, sir. These are the printed instructions."

"And where was this material found?"

"In the trash basket in the bathroom, sir."

"Thank you, Sergeant. Questions, Mr. Webb?"

Webb carelessly waved a hand, and the sergeant stepped down.

Now a gray-haired man was sworn and entered the box, identifying himself as a member of the Home Office Forensic Science Service. Asked first about the material found on the boots, he replied that the shale, limestone, feldspar, and mica, along with moss and grasses, formed a combination similar to that of samples taken from the location where the body had been found. All of these, it seems, may be found in various parts of the moor, but the particular juxtaposition of these strongly mirrored those of the area in question.

Mr. Webb rose and spoke mildly. "As your work is confined to the laboratory, sir, you may not be aware that Mr. Nolan was taken by the police to the scene where the body of his wife was found. It is therefore not surprising that the materials on his boots match those at the scene."

With a glance at the magistrate, he sat down with an air of having disposed of a troublesome detail.

Next, a pharmacist was called, who examined the pregnancy test material, as shown to him by the police. "The red mark in the small window just here indicates a positive reading."

"How accurate are tests such as this one, sir?"

"Approximately 98 percent."

"Then, the assumption is that the person who used this test was more than likely to be pregnant?"

"Yes."

Again, Maurice Webb waved him away.

As the witnesses came and went, Claire, looking over the shoulder of Jasper Martinelli, saw that he held a sketch pad and drew clever likenesses of each one, amusing himself, between sketches, by doodling in spirals or odd-shaped figures.

Now, she heard Keating say, "The Crown calls Detective Superintendent Neil Padgett," and there was Neil in the witness box, looking so beautifully solid and trustworthy that Claire caught her breath. "I love that man," she said to herself. "How could this be happening to us?"

It soon became clear that it was Neil's job to pull together the bits and pieces of evidence and present the case for the prosecution in an orderly fashion.

Keating began, "If you please, sir, will you tell the court the steps leading to the recommendation to the Crown prosecution that a charge of manslaughter be brought against the prisoner?"

"Yes. On the morning of Thursday, the thirtieth

day of November, Mr. Nolan reported to his local police station in Morbridge that his wife had disappeared. His statement at that time was that she had gone for a walk at approximately half-past one o'clock in the morning and had not returned to their house.

"At ten minutes before eleven that same morning, the Morbridge police were informed that the body of a woman was found on the moor near Monk's Cross. The officer on duty drove to the location and confirmed the finding, as you have heard. At ten minutes past eleven o'clock, his call was received at police headquarters in Kings Abbey. I myself accompanied the officers to the scene, arriving at approximately twelve o'clock. I was then able to make the first identification of the body."

"You were personally acquainted with the deceased?"

"I had met Mr. and Mrs. Nolan socially on a few occasions, but there was no close acquaintanceship."

"Thank you. Please go on."

"I then sent for Mr. Nolan to confirm the identification, which he did at approximately one o'clock. I requested that he come into the station later that afternoon to make a statement, as is customary in all unexplained deaths."

"What took place at that interview, sir?"

"I did not conduct the interview myself, but my officers reported that Mr. Nolan repeated his statement given that morning. When asked why his wife had elected to go out at such an unusual hour, he stated that they had had an argument, that she had left the house in a fit of pique, and that he had subsequently fallen asleep and was unaware that she had not returned until the morning.

"On the following day, Saturday, two matters of significance occurred. First, at the postmortem on the body of Mrs. Nolan, it became clear that, although there was some slight bruising around the throat, the cause of death was heart failure, not strangulation.

shall return to that point in a moment. Second, we received the statement of Dr. Mukherjee, as he has given it in evidence at this hearing. If indeed Mr Nolan had carried his wife to his automobile at half past one in the morning of thirtieth November, then his previous statement must be regarded as false. Whether Mrs. Nolan was still alive or was already dead at that hour is not known, although the presumption would be the latter."

Claire wondered why Mr. Webb didn't object to Neil's conjecturing at this point but decided Webb must know what he was doing. Probably biding his time, she thought.

Neil went on. "I interviewed Mr. Nolan again that afternoon, first giving him the official caution that his words would be taken in evidence. When confronted with the statement of Dr. Mukherjee, Mr. Nolan denied he had taken his wife anywhere and stated that the doctor must be mistaken. When asked what was the nature of the quarrel with his wife, he declined to specify its nature but insisted that the matter was a trivial one.

"I then asked him if he would give his permission for the police to search his house, and he said certainly, there was nothing anyone could find, and he handed me his ring of keys. I then sent two officers to his home.

"We took a recess to await the result of the search. It was after receiving the information concerning the pregnancy test that I asked Mr. Nolan if he had had the surgery known as a vasectomy, making it impossible for him to produce children."

Now Claire seethed. Neil knew about that because she had told him about it. So, he was not above using his personal knowledge to bolster his case. Not exactly Mr. Halo, for all his looking so incorruptible.

"And what was his reply, sir?"

"He acknowledged that he had had such an operation some years ago. I then asked him if he was aware that his wife was pregnant, and at that point, he stated that he would answer no further questions and wished to secure a lawyer."

Young Keating, glancing at Maurice Webb, said smoothly, "Mr. Nolan was of course within his rights to make such a request, and no imputation of guilt or innocence would ensue from his declining to answer further questions?"

In noblest tones, Neil said, "Absolutely none. I at once ceased all further questioning."

"Thank you, Mr. Padgett. Now if you will, please explain to the court the theory that led to the present charge?"

"Yes. As we have seen, there was clear evidence in the Nolan house that Mrs. Nolan had taken a pregnancy test. If her husband found this evidence and read the instructions, he would learn of his wife's pregnancy. However, the mere fact of her taking such a test, even if the result were negative, would in itself provoke suspicion in the case of his being unable to procreate. The assumption is that any man in such circumstances would be more than usually incensed, and that the quarrel that took place would be more than a trivial one.

"If the husband, in the course of such an altercation, placed his hands round the neck of the wife and pressed sufficiently to cause her to believe her life was in danger, it is probable that her fear would be intense, in fact, that it could be severe enough to cause the failure of the heart which the pathologist tells us was the actual cause of death. A commonplace argument would be unlikely to produce such genuine fear.

"Pursuing the theory, the victim falls to the floor, striking her head sharply. Within minutes, the husband realizes she is dead, but he is not certain whether the cause was strangulation or the blow to her head as she fell. He only knows that he has killed her. In panic, he remembers the recent finding of the body of the young American student on the moor. If he takes his wife's body out onto the moor and leaves it there, surely the police will assume she was the victim of the other killer."

Claire noticed there was no mention of the "C" mark. That was still under wraps.

Neil went on. "He remembers the location of the kistvaen below Hound Tor where the young victim had been buried, but when he drives along the road, he is unable to find the place in the dark. Now he recalls Monk's Cross, with the fragment of stone wall, not far from the road. There is no question of digging a grave in the rocky soil. He simply places the body on the far side of the wall and returns to his home, hoping he has not been seen.

"Now we come to the mossy material found on the boots of the accused. His counsel has suggested that these found their way there when Mr. Nolan was called to identify the body. However, I was present myself on that occasion, and it is my recollection, and that of my fellow officers, that the boots worn by the accused at that time were not the same as those presented in evidence here today."

Now, Keating turned to the defense table. "Mr. Webb?"

To Claire's surprise, Maurice Webb waved his hand. "No questions." And Neil stepped down from the witness box.

Wondering what sort of sketch Jasper had done

of Neil, Claire leaned forward and stretched to her right to peer over his shoulder, but all she saw was Jasper flipping over to the next page of his sketch book.

Oh, well, no problem. She wasn't sure she wanted to see a portrait of Neil right now, anyhow.

Chapter

29

AFTER NEIL'S TESTIMONY, a uniformed officer was sworn and entered the box.

"Your name, please?"

"Police Constable Bert Crofts, sir."

Claire and Sally exchanged glances, and Sally whispered, "The little creep with the bedroom eyes."

Keating glanced down at a page of notes in his hand. "Now, Constable Crofts, I understand you have evidence which may suggest a motive for the accused to dispose of his wife."

Crofts' eyes swiveled up toward Keating and back to the floor, his body twisting awkwardly. No sign of the sexy swagger today.

"Well, sir, it may be nothing at all."

Keating read from the paper in his hand. "I believe you were heard by a fellow officer to state that you 'knew the reason he did it,' and that you were referring to a reason for Mr. Nolan to kill his wife. Will you please repeat what you said on that occasion?"

Crofts looked like a weasel in a trap. "All I meant

was, sir, as Mr. Nolan spent a good deal of time with a certain young lady and seemed to be that fond of her."

"Have you reason to believe this—er—fondness was reciprocated?"

"Yes, sir. The young lady said to me on one occasion as she wished she could be married to someone like Mr. Nolan."

"You are personally acquainted with the young lady in question?"

"Yes, sir."

"Will you please describe the nature of your acquaintance with her?"

"We've been out here and there half a dozen times or so."

"I take this to mean you had what might be called a romantic association with the lady?"

Now Bert Crofts couldn't repress the smirk of the satisfied male. "You might say that, sir."

"Did you perhaps have some inclination toward marriage with the young lady yourself?"

"What, me? No, sir." Crofts must have sensed this was ungallant, as he added piously, "I can't afford to think of marriage at this time, sir."

"To your knowledge, Constable, were there frequent meetings between the young lady in question and the accused?"

"Yes, sir."

"You saw them together?"

"Several times at the Crown, yes. Other times, she told me she had seen him."

"I believe that will be all, Constable. Mr. Webb?"

The defense counsel gave Bert Crofts a contemptuous glance. "No questions."

As Claire expected, the next witness was Nora McBain. There wasn't exactly a gasp in the courtroom, but there was a perceptible stir as Nora's fresh beauty shone out in the drab surroundings. When she had taken her place in the box, she looked directly across the room at Barry Nolan with a look of melting pity, then turned her eyes back toward Keating, who asked her to state her name, address, and occupation.

Keating drew from her the fact that she was separated from her husband and intended to seek a divorce in the near future on grounds of desertion.

"Thank you. Now, Mrs. McBain, will you please describe to us the nature and extent of your acquaintance with Mr. Nolan, the accused?"

Softly, Nora said, "He's been very kind to me. He's often come into the Crown, sometimes with his wife, poor lady. Twice he walked me home after closing, and several times he's come to visit with me and my little boy during the day."

"Do you believe that Mrs. Nolan was aware of the occasions when you met with the accused outside of the premises of the Crown?"

Nora hesitated. "I'm sure I don't know, sir."

"Please remember that you are under oath. Did Mr. Nolan suggest that these meetings not be mentioned to his wife?"

"He did say as she was a bit jealous, sir. But she had no reason to be, I assure you."

"We have testimony that you made the statement that you wished you could be married to someone like Mr. Nolan. Is that correct?"

Nora looked up in surprise. "I may have done. He is a very kind man."

"Did you ever say something of that kind to Mr. Nolan himself?"

Nora looked over at Barry, clearly wondering whether or not this information had come from him. Seeming to get no help from that quarter, she sighed. "I did tell him as I wished I'd met someone like him before I married the one I did."

"Is it possible Mr. Nolan might have interpreted this to mean that you would be willing to marry him now?"

"But that's daft. He's already married."

Silence hung in the air as the full implication of this made its way into Nora's head.

Keating waited a full beat before turning to Maurice Webb.

Instead of his usual brisk hop, Webb took his time getting to his feet.

"Just one question, Mrs. McBain. Now that Mr. Nolan is free, would you wish to be married to him?"

Nora's eyes were pure sapphire. "I'm very fond of Mr. Nolan, but I think of him more as a friend or a father, not as a lover. And I'll tell you this, I'll never believe Mr. Nolan killed his wife!"

"Thank you."

Claire was surprised that Neil and the prosecution had even considered calling Nora McBain. She knew they were obliged to present at this hearing their full case for the benefit of the defense, but surely they had talked with Nora and knew what her testimony would be. Still, just because she, Claire, believed Nora, it didn't mean that a potential jury would do so. One look at Nora might be enough to convince them that a man Barry's age would be tempted to go pretty far for such a prize. The question, no doubt, was not what Nora believed but what Barry believed.

Now there was some stirring about in the courtroom, the prosecutor conferring with Neil Padgett, and the clerks shuffling papers. Sally, looking at her watch, said to Claire, "Adrian thinks we should be going, Mums. I'll call you tonight to find out what's happened with Barry."

Knowing they had a date to meet friends for dinner and a film, Claire smiled good-bye, just as Maurice Webb stood up to make a formal statement of "no case to answer." Young Keating then made a brief summary statement for the Crown, essentially reviewing the testimony that had been given and emphasizing the reliability of the police evidence.

During a pause that followed, in which the magistrate scribbled some notes and consulted with his clerk, Claire saw Jasper Martinelli leave the gallery, while Rodney Simms remained in his seat.

Claire wondered if the magistrate would dismiss the charges against Barry, but it didn't seem likely, and, indeed, after some time, the magistrate announced that the accused would be bound over for trial at the Assize Court on a date three months hence.

Now the matter of bail arose. As Maurice Webb argued to keep the bail at the figure already set, the visitors in the gallery began to file out, and Claire was about to follow when she noticed some folded sheets of paper under the bench where Jasper Martinelli had sat. Curious to see his sketch of Neil, she bent down and picked up the sheets, folding them over again and stuffing them into her handbag.

Downstairs in the waiting room, she heard the dark-haired stranger asking to go into the courtroom.

"I've got to talk to the guy who's on trial!" American. No mistaking that accent.

The bailiff at the door stood firm. "Sorry, sir, you must wait until the court is no longer in session."

As the man turned away, Claire asked if she could help. "I'm a friend of Mr. Nolan from the States."

The man gave her a look like Stanley meeting Livingstone. "Are you Claire Camden?"

"Yes."

"I've heard a lot about you. I'm Sam Crane, Frieda's brother!"

It was after five o'clock and fully dark when Sally and Adrian arrived at her cottage. Following their usual routine, Adrian came in with her, checked over the house to be sure there were no intruders, and announced he would run up to the Priory to change and be back in half an hour.

Sally bolted the door after him and went up to take a quick bath. With Brenda gone for the holidays, she was still nervous at being alone in the cottage, and as she waited for the hot water to make its way through the pipes, she imagined that their creaking noises were footsteps.

Telling herself not to be so silly, she laid out wool pants and a sweater, and the handsome leather boots that were an early Christmas gift from her mother, who had said she might as well start wearing them now in the cold weather.

Lying in the hot bath, she wondered about Barry Nolan. She hadn't seen much of life in a courtroom, but common sense told her that the magistrate would see enough evidence against Barry to send him to a trial. The testimony of the neighbor doctor walking his baby sounded pretty convincing to Sally.

When she had toweled off and put on her robe, she was startled to hear the sound of the doorbell. Adrian already?

Stepping into her bedroom slippers, she ran down the stairs and peered through the small window in the front door. Someone was there but it was too dark to see.

She switched on the dim light over the door and saw the figure of a woman, half turned away. She wore a tasseled cap over her head and ears. Her long dark skirt fell to her ankles, a shawl covered her shoulders, and in her arms she cradled an infant wrapped in a blanket.

Sally called through the door, "What is it?"

At that, the woman turned and gave one glance at the window in the door. Now Sally saw that her face was covered with a scarf, so that only her eyes were visible. With a quick motion, the woman turned her back to Sally, bent over, laid her bundle on the floor of the porch, and darted rapidly around the corner of the house.

Without a second thought, Sally unbolted the door and stepped out. As she bent down to pick up the infant, she heard a step behind her and felt strong arms pull her backward. Something was pressed against her mouth and nose, and the sickening smell of ether engulfed her.

Chapter

30

THE MOMENT THE DARK-HAIRED MAN identified himself to Claire as Frieda's brother, she could see the resemblance that had teased her mind when he first walked into the visitors' gallery of the courtroom. His smile had all of Frieda's charm, as he told her he had heard about her from his sister.

"I've heard about you, too, Sam. You're the big brother from New York City, aren't you? Frieda was very fond of you."

"That's right. Living on opposite coasts, we haven't seen much of each other in recent years, but I loved my little sis."

"I loved her too, Sam."

"This has been a real shock, Claire. Barry called me two weeks ago and said it looked like she'd been killed by some guy on the loose. I offered to come over right away but he said there was nothing I could do, so I said I'd come later. We'd talked about sending the body back home for burial."

"You've met Barry, then?"

"Yes, a couple of times. Seemed like a nice guy but I figured him as a wimp. Wouldn't have seen him as a murderer, but I guess you never know. I talked to him yesterday on the phone and he told me he'd been accused but he swore it was all a mistake. I thought I'd come over and see what was going on. I got a flight out of Kennedy and came in this morning. Just got here in time for the afternoon session."

"Yes, I saw you come into the gallery."

"Right. I asked the fellow next to me what had happened in the morning, and he told me about the autopsy and how Frieda had actually died of a heart attack. They figured it was brought on by fright when she thought her husband was trying to kill her, but I've got some news that may be important. I'd better talk to his lawyer."

The door from the courtroom opened, and Barry came straight toward them.

"Sam!" Quick tears formed in his eyes. "It isn't what you think, Sam. I thought the world of her, honestly."

Claire turned to Maurice Webb, who stood to one side. "What happened with the bail, Mr. Webb?"

"We managed to extend it till time of trial."

Introductions were made and Sam said, "Look, I don't know what really happened, Barry, but there's something I found out lately Mr. Webb here ought to know about."

Maurice Webb gestured them to a quiet corner of the room and asked Sam to go on.

"Okay. Last week, I went in for one of those routine physicals and the doc was taking what they call my history. When he heard that both my dad and my older brother died in their thirties of a heart attack, with no warning of heart trouble, he ran some tests, and the next day he told me I was very lucky, as my tests showed I was okay. He was sure, though, there was something hereditary in my family that caused the deaths, only some of us got it and others didn't."

Maurice Webb said, "Was it congenital hyper-cholesterol?"

Sam nodded. "That sounds like it, all right. It seems that in people who have this condition, the body forms huge amounts of cholesterol, and suddenly, bingo, you're gone. No warning. The doc asked me if I had other siblings, and I told him my sister had just died in England, only I thought she'd been murdered. When I heard today that she actually died of a heart attack, I figured this might be what happened to her."

Barry stared, his body shaking like a tree in the wind. "Oh, Sam, maybe that's it. Maybe it really wasn't my fault! I can't believe it!"

Maurice Webb's small eyes studied Barry without expression. "Mr. Nolan, I must warn you that you must not say anything before witnesses that may in-criminate you."

Barry said, "I don't give a damn about incrimina-tion. All I care about is that maybe I didn't really cause her to die. Oh, God, I loved her so much! Look, I'll tell you what really happened."

Webb tried again to protest but saw it was useless.

His voice thick, Barry went on. "That story about how she went out for a walk at one-thirty in the morn-ing was all hogwash. Sorry, Mr. Webb, but I had to say something, didn't I? When the police first ques-tioned me, I told them to go ahead and search my house. I never thought about the pregnancy test, but if I had, I wouldn't have worried. I didn't think it would have any meaning for them anyway. As for the stuff on my boots, I never gave it a second thought. Everything out there on the moor looks the same to me.

"Anyhow, here's what really happened. I did find the pregnancy test, just the way the police said. I dropped a full aspirin bottle into the wastebasket, and while I was digging around trying to get the aspirin back, I found the box and the test stick. When I saw what it meant, I really blew my stack, and Frieda didn't argue or fight back at all, the way she usually would. She just said she was really sorry, and the guy didn't mean anything to her, but I put my hands around her throat and said I'd like to strangle her, only I wasn't serious and she knew I wasn't.

"Then I pulled my hands away and she stood there looking at me with this strange expression on her face, almost like she was listening or something. I was yelling at her and she didn't answer, and I was furious and I said, 'Why don't you say something?' And then I gave her a shove and she fell straight back like one of those dummies kids play with. She didn't put out an arm to break her fall, she just went right over and I could hear the crack as her head hit the floor.

"She lay perfectly still, and I thought for a minute she was faking. Then I heard this sort of whistling breath, and I got down beside her and I could tell about a minute later she was dead. It was horrible. I did some ambulance service when I was a student, and it doesn't take long to know when somebody's really gone. I started to the phone to call 999, and then I remembered something I had heard."

Barry turned to his brother-in-law. "You see, Sam, one of my TYA students was murdered about a month ago, and they hadn't found the killer yet. Somebody told me about a little mark he had made on the girl's body, and that only the police knew about it and it was very important not to tell anyone."

Claire's head shot up. "Barry, *who told you?*"

Startled, Barry said, "I promised not to tell."

"Forget that. I *must* know. *Tell* me!"

"Okay. It was Nora."

"*Nora?* How did she find out?"

"I don't know. She said somebody told her."

Claire subsided. "All right, thanks. Go on with your story."

"Well, I figured if I made the same mark on Frieda, and took her out on the moor, where Cheryl Bailey had been found, of course the police would think it was the same killer. And I suppose at first they did. If that guy across the street hadn't seen me taking her out to the car, it would have worked."

Sam erupted. "Say, Barry, that was a pretty rotten thing to do to my sister's body."

"I know. I'm really sorry, Sam. It wasn't as if I had *meant* to kill her, you know. I just thought nobody would believe me and I was scared to death."

Claire said, "Look, Barry, why didn't you just tell the truth from the beginning? Say it was an accident?"

"But I wasn't sure it *was* an accident. Until Sam told me today about this heart attack business, I thought maybe I *had* caused her death, even if I didn't intend to. That's what manslaughter means, isn't it, Mr. Webb?"

"That's a reasonably good definition, yes."

"And you go to prison for that."

"Usually that is so."

"Okay, when the police accused me of manslaughter, I figured once I'd told them a lie, I'd better just stick with it and maybe they couldn't prove anything. Now, it's all changed."

Claire expected some vigorous protest from Maurice Webb at Barry's flagrant admission, but none came. The solicitor's face remained impassive, and his voice was uninflected. "Perhaps, Mr. Nolan, we should ascertain whether or not your wife in fact had the cholesterol condition before we leap to conclusions."

Barry's euphoria dropped a few levels. "I suppose you're right. But if she did, what happens now?"

"That I cannot say. We shall take it all in good

time." And Webb shook hands with Sam and made courteous exit.

Barry said, "Sam, come on over and I'll put you up at my place."

For answer, Sam gave him a cold stare. "No, thanks, I'll find a hotel."

Turning his back, he took Claire's arm and moved away. "Can I call you tomorrow, Claire? I'll stick around till we find out what to do about the body."

"Sure." She gave him her card. "Call me any time."

It was after six o'clock when she got back to Bea's house in Morbridge. Hanging up her outer wraps, she turned up the thermostat for the central heating and wandered out to the kitchen. Not really hungry after the lunch at the Italian place, she poured herself a glass of wine and sat down in her favorite chair, too tired to light the fire. No hurry about checking for phone messages. Sally was out with Adrian, and she'd given up expecting Neil to call.

Now she thought back to the things that had puzzled her about Barry's reactions from the time of Frieda's death. For all his sorrow and anguish, he had never expressed anger at the hypothetical killer. It was all, "I loved her," but not, "Let me get my hands on the guy who did this." Then there was his refusal to talk to Claire about it. She had been surprised at his meek acquiescence when Mr. Webb told him not to discuss the matter. Restraint wasn't in Barry's character. Most significant was the absence of protest against the accusation. Looking back, she realized there were no cries of "I'm innocent!" when he was charged, only a kind of hangdog resignation.

But why not, as Sam had asked, tell the truth in the first place? Whatever he believed he had done, why not face up to it?

She knew the answer to that one. Barry was weak. It was weak people who lied, hiding in the proverbial sand in the hope that trouble would somehow go away.

Neil believed she had lied to him. Now she knew the truth about Barry and the C mark, but that didn't alter the fact that Neil hadn't believed he could trust her. Did he see her as a weak person?

Wearily, she got up and walked slowly into her study. May as well check the phone. Yes, the light was blinking.

Adrian's voice. "Mrs. Camden? Have you seen Sally? I can't find her!"

Sally? What did he mean? She was with him. They were going to meet friends for dinner and a film.

Was this an old message?

Hands shaking, she pressed the rewind button. No, all the old messages had been erased. There it was again. "Have you seen Sally? I can't find her!"

Another light was blinking.

Neil. "Claire, please ring me at Sally's cottage the moment you come in."

Pressing the buttons for the familiar number, Claire heard the double ring. "Detective Superintendent Padgett here."

"Neil? What's happened?"

"Have you heard from Sally?"

"No. I thought she was with Adrian."

Neil's voice wavered. "I'm afraid it may be very bad news, darling. We believe she has disappeared."

Chapter

31

SALLY CAMDEN LAY QUITE STILL. At first, even with her eyes open, it was too dark to see, except for a faint glow of light far away.

Then, as her eyes adjusted to the dark, she saw that the light came from a tiny lantern hanging along a wall somewhere beyond where she lay. Where the wall was touched by the light, it appeared to be of stone, and when she felt around her, she knew she was lying on a mattress and the floor beyond it had the rough, cold texture of stone.

Where was she? In some kind of cellar?

Her mind drifted away and she closed her eyes again.

Images floated. She was being carried. Then she was lying down, and hands were moving gently over her bare body, down her arms, then over her breasts and abdomen, down her legs and feet. Then a mouth had touched her lips lightly, and a voice had whispered, "Cynthia! Cynthia!"

Someone thought her name was Cynthia. Odd. If

only she could wake up, perhaps she could remember, but a drowsy numbness engulfed her.

And why was her body naked?

She was wrapped in something soft and warm. She ran her fingers over the fabric. A quilted comforter.

Why was she so thirsty? She remembered her head being lifted and being given something sweet to drink from a glass. Now, through the darkness, she saw a wink of light at her left, a foot or so away.

Turning on her side, she reached slowly with her right hand and touched a round object. With some effort, she managed to raise herself onto her left elbow and bring the object toward her.

A glass. Putting it to her lips, she recognized the same sweetish liquid she had been given before. She didn't like the taste, but she took several swallows. Anything to quench her thirst.

Lying back again, she sighed and pulled the quilt around her. As her eyes closed, she remembered again the whispering voice.

"No time now, my dearest. Later. Later."

Claire drove out of Morbridge and onto Newton Lane toward Sally's cottage, her heart like a stone. No rational thoughts formed in her brain. Only the drumbeats of denial throbbed through her body.

Not Sally. Not Sally. Not Sally.

At the cottage, she pulled her car onto the grass to avoid the two police cars standing in the drive.

Neil came to meet her on the walk to the front door. "Claire, darling." His arms surrounded her and pulled her close. "I'm so sorry. We'll do everything we can to find her."

Stiffly, she stepped back and stared at Neil. "What happened?"

"Adrian will tell you."

Claire walked swiftly into the cottage, where Adrian

gave her a hollow-eyed look. "Mrs. Camden! I'm so sorry. I shouldn't have left her, but we arranged matters as we always did."

"Never mind, Adrian. Just tell me what happened."

"We came back from the hearing at a quarter past five. I went in with Sally and checked out the house. We agreed to change and that I would come for her in half an hour. I heard her bolting the door as I left."

"Yes. What then?"

"At a quarter till six, I drove down and stopped my car in the drive, expecting to see her at the window, as was our custom. When I didn't see her there, I thought perhaps she wasn't quite ready, so I went up the walk.

"As I came near, I saw that the door was open and I was truly alarmed. I called out, 'Sally, I'm here.' There was no answer. I searched the cottage, and she was simply gone."

"She must have opened the door. It had to be someone she knew."

"Yes, I agree. That's when I rang you up, Mrs. Camden. Sally's car was still here. The only thing I could imagine was that perhaps there had been an emergency and you had come for her."

Claire looked at her watch. Quarter till seven. An hour ago.

Neil said gently, "Claire, I'd like you to look over Sally's room to see if you can tell what clothes she might be wearing."

Mechanically, Claire moved toward the stairs, Neil behind her.

On Sally's bed lay the clothes she had laid out, and on the floor the boots Claire had given her. She stooped and lifted one of the boots, running her finger over the soft black leather. Holding it against her chest, she walked to the closet and carefully moved each hanger. Summer clothes had been pushed to the far side, and among the winter things, Claire couldn't recall any dress or blouse that wasn't there. Jeans and wool pants were another matter, and turning to the chest of drawers, she saw that the stacks of sweaters included ones dating back to Sally's high school days. No possibility of knowing what might be missing.

Still clutching the leather boot, she moved to the bathroom.

Neil said softly, "She had evidently had a bath."

"Yes, I see."

Claire went back to the bedroom and walked again to the closet.

"Are you looking for her dressing gown?"

"Yes. Only her summer robe is here. I don't see the winter one she's been wearing. Her grandmother is giving her a new one for Christmas."

"What does it look like?"

"Blue wool with satin piping. Rather worn."

A brief search revealed no sign of the robe.

"Might she have left it at the dry cleaner?"

Claire shook her head. "I took it with my cleaning last week and returned it to her the next day."

Neil said, "Shall we look at her coats?" and Claire, setting down Sally's boot, followed him down the stairs.

Standing before the row of hooks by the entry, Claire stared at the two jackets and the heavy wool coat. Woodenly, she said, "They are all here."

Officers with torches were conducting a search of the area around the cottage, and a constable had arrived carrying several small objects in plastic bags.

"We can't see well in the dark, sir, but here are some bits as might be helpful."

Claire and Adrian looked at the collection—a glove, a lipstick, an empty billfold, a cigarette lighter, a notepad—and shook their heads. Nothing belonging to Sally.

Another officer spoke to Neil, who in turn asked Claire if she had a recent photo of Sally to be photocopied and released to the press.

She sat at the little table in the corner and opened her handbag, taking out extraneous objects and piling them on the table until she found her billfold. Silently, she handed Neil a wallet-size picture.

As she slowly began to put the items back into her bag, some sheets of paper fell onto the floor, and a young police officer quickly retrieved them, laying them on the table for her. She thanked him without bothering to look at them, and sat for a time staring at the wall beside her, as if its flowered pattern held some intricate clue to the ills of the universe.

At last, her eyes turned back toward the table and wandered to the top sheet where it lay, half unfolded. A series of doodles: a row of circles, another of flower petals, and across the bottom of the sheet, some elaborate drawings surrounding a crescent, looking something like the initial letters in a medieval manuscript. Now Claire saw that the letter in all of the drawings was a "C."

Her numbed brain flickered, but it was some moments before the signals connected. These were Jasper Martinelli's drawings, made at the hearing today. Quickly, she turned the pages, with their sketches of the witnesses, and on two other pages, she found variations on the same letter, some shaded in, some with floral elaboration.

"Adrian, I have a question."

"Of course, Mrs. Camden."

"Wasn't your mother's name Cynthia?"

"Mummy's? Yes, it was."

Matters moved swiftly when Claire showed Neil what she had found.

He turned at once to Adrian. "Where's Jasper Martinelli?"

"I don't actually know where he is, sir. He said yesterday that after the hearing today, he would be away for a few days. We don't live in each other's pockets, but normally we inform the other if we're to be away."

"Did he take his car, do you know?"

"Oh, yes. At least it's not in its usual place up at the house."

"When did you see him last?"

Adrian paused. "It would be at the hearing this afternoon. As Sally and I were leaving, I believe he was still there."

Claire confirmed this. "Yes. I saw him leave a few minutes later."

"You did not see him subsequently, Adrian?"

"Not to speak to. I did hear him come in, while I was in the bath. As I was dressing, I heard his car go down the hill."

"What sort of car does Jasper drive?"

"It's a dark blue Vauxhall sedan, about eight years old. It was Mummy's car, you see."

"Do you know the number plate?"

Adrian looked blank. "I'm afraid not."

"Never mind. We can trace it."

Neil scribbled a note and handed it to a constable, who immediately went to the telephone.

"Now, Adrian, may we have your permission to search your house and grounds?"

"Yes, of course. Do you think Jasper—that is—?"

"We know nothing at the moment. Now, is there another way to reach the Priory without going up the drive that comes here by the cottage?"

"Yes. If you go along Newton Lane for a quarter of a mile, you'll see a sharp turn back to your right.

It's an old service road and a bit rough, but it will bring you along the ridge as far as the ruins."

"Good. As I understand it, Mr. Martinelli came down this drive at what must have been about half-past five o'clock today. You then drove your car down about fifteen minutes later. Is that correct?"

"Yes, sir."

"And so far as you know, no other car has traveled the drive since that time?"

"That is correct."

"Then, as soon as I have completed a phone call, I should like for you to take your car on to the alternate route you described and lead the way. My officer will follow, as I suspect it's difficult to find in the dark."

"It is, yes."

Briskly, Neil went to the phone and gave orders for police in a wide area to detain a man of Jasper's description, driving the Vauxhall with the number obtained by the constable.

Instructing one officer to report to him at the Priory if the ground searchers came up with anything significant, Neil waited until the others had gone. Then he turned to Claire and took her hands in his. "Will you leave your car and come with me?"

"Yes."

In the back of the police car, the driver screened off from them, Neil said, "We'll find him, Claire."

"What good will that do?"

"He may have taken her with him."

Claire's voice was bitter. "In her bathrobe?"

"We don't know that. You said she might be wearing jeans and a sweater."

"And no coat."

"He may have a coat for her."

"Cheryl Bailey was nude when you found her."

"But she was wearing clothes when she left the house. Her clothes are still missing, remember."

"He's probably killed her already."

"Remember that Cheryl had been given barbiturates. That means she must have been kept alive for some time. Certainly he couldn't have taken her out to the moor in the daylight."

"But it's dark now. He needn't wait."

Following Adrian, the police car bounced wildly over what was little better than a rutted path, and at last came to a stop. In the clear, cold air, the fragments of the ruined abbey stood in grim silence, evoking the ghosts of monks who had once walked peacefully in their precincts.

Neil pressed her hand, then sprang quickly from the car as the driver opened the door for Claire.

Following Adrian, who lighted their path with his torch, they reached the Priory, where two of the searchers had arrived.

"Our orders were not to go inside, sir. Is that correct?"

"Yes, but we shall do so now."

Consulting with Adrian about the arrangement of the house, Neil gave orders for the search, directing Adrian to give his officers access to the closed-off portions of the house and reserving Jasper's quarters for Claire and himself, accompanied by a constable.

Claire understood that the others would be searching for Sally, while Neil would be looking for evidence against Jasper. Going up the grand staircase, they came to the floor above the drawing room, where they found the living quarters of the two young men. Neil opened the door to Adrian's rooms and they saw a pleasant sitting room and an adjacent bedroom, both elegantly furnished and tidy. A large bath and W.C. lay between those and Jasper's quarters. Here the furniture was equally fine in the bedroom, where clothes and books were tossed carelessly about. His second room was his studio, presenting a scene of organized chaos.

While Neil and the officer began in the studio, Claire wandered back to Jasper's bedroom. On the bedside table was a framed photograph of Jasper and a woman who could only be Adrian's mother. Although the woman was still beautiful in her fifties, a stranger would suppose the photo to be that of mother and son, not man and wife, especially since Jasper looked even younger with his beard neatly trimmed.

A jumble of items covered the top of the chest, and Claire was about to turn away when she saw a bright gleam under the edge of a small sketch pad and pulled out a piece of jewelry, a charming little diamond brooch in the shape of a C.

When he saw it, Neil grunted, "The bastard's obsessed."

Half an hour later, with an officer stationed by the telephone, they were drinking the coffee Adrian had brought to the drawing room when a constable came in carrying a large plastic bag.

"We found these buried down in the straw stack, sir."

Carefully, he lifted out a black jacket, a striped sweater, and a pair of jeans, all matted with grass and twigs.

Everyone in the room looked at Claire in agonizing silence.

Hammers in her chest, she took a deep breath and walked over to look closely at the clothing.

"No, they are not Sally's. But there's something—I don't know—"

Neil stepped over and turned up the label of the jacket. "The Broadway. Does that mean anything to you, Claire?"

"But that's a department store in California!"

Her eyes met Neil's. "Of course. Cheryl Bailey.

Jeans and her black windbreaker. The girls didn't know which of her sweaters she wore, since they didn't see her that day, but they were sure of the other things."

Neil took Claire's arm. "Let's step out here." And he led the way to the hall. "We were just saying that Cheryl may have been alive for some hours. It's possible he may have kept her somewhere in this house. I'm going to call for more lads and check every inch of the place again."

Claire stood still. Two images came together in her mind. The ruins of the old abbey they had just passed, and the day they went to Petworth and she visited the old church.

"Wait, Neil. Let me ask Adrian a question."

Neil beckoned and the young man appeared.

"Adrian, is there a crypt under the old abbey?"

Startled, he stared at her, and repeated "A crypt?"

They waited, watching as Adrian's face lost its puzzled expression. "Yes, Mrs. Camden, there is a crypt, but nobody's been there for years."

"Where is the entrance to it?"

"Let me think. You go down past the old wine cellar—"

Neil stopped him. "Do many people in the community know about the crypt?"

"No, not at all."

"Does Jasper know?"

"Jasper? Yes, of course. Mummy and I showed it to him ourselves."

Neil seized his arm. "Let's go!"

Chapter

32

WITH ADRIAN LEADING THE WAY, they went down a staircase to the rooms below, where the original kitchens and pantries of the house dated from two centuries earlier. Down a stone passage, they passed the open door to the wine cellar and came to a heavy oak door, iron-banded, that creaked when Adrian lifted the bar and pushed it open.

Adrian flashed his torch, revealing a narrow stone passageway, the ceiling so low that both he and Neil bent their heads as they went forward. After some twenty yards, the passage made a sharp turn to the right, and there, on the floor, stood a small lantern, its faint light revealing a short flight of stone steps going downward.

Neil whispered, "Someone's here, all right."

When she reached the foot of the stairs, Claire could see the faint outline of the crypt, so dark at first that only the glow of a tiny lantern on the far wall was visible.

As Adrian flashed the torch over the interior, Claire

saw something on the floor by the wall and ran, hearing her own voice crying, "Sally!" Then she was crouched beside her daughter, her arms lifting her head.

"Sally! It's mother! Can you hear me?"

A moan.

"She's alive! Neil, she's alive!"

The two men had followed her, and there was a crashing sound as someone tripped over the glass of liquid Sally had drunk from.

Neil shouted, "Adrian, call 999!"

"Yes, sir. Thank God she's safe!" and Adrian ran.

By the time the ambulance came, Sally had opened her eyes and recognized her mother but had been unable to make any coherent statement. Neil had gathered her up, wrapped in the quilt, and carried her back to the drawing room, laying her gently on a sofa. Claire sat beside her, holding her hand, while Adrian knelt on the floor at her feet, smoothing the soft fabric of the comforter.

Looking up at Claire, he whispered, "It's Mummy's."

"What is, Adrian?"

"The duvet. It's Jasper, isn't it? He still uses her things."

Claire nodded.

At the hospital in Exeter, the doctor reported to Claire that Sally had suffered no physical injuries, nor was there any sign of sexual attack.

Staring into the doctor's eyes, Claire said, "She is really all right?"

"Yes, Mrs. Camden. I am happy to say there is no evidence of bodily harm."

Claire gave a long, shuddering sigh, and the tears, so long repressed, ran straight down her face. There were no sobs, no words. Like the snow pack that breaks up in the spring, sending streams down the mountainsides, her tears poured steadily from some limitless reservoir.

An hour later, sitting by Sally's bed, she saw her daughter's eyes open and heard her say, "Don't cry, Mums, I'm all right."

Once the barbiturates had worn off, Sally was able to speak clearly but with only confused recollections of what had happened to her. Her first question—"Is the baby all right?"—baffled Claire, and it was not until later that Sally was able to tell the story of her abduction.

By eight o'clock, the doctor was willing to release Sally to go home with her mother. Adrian hovered in the wings, waiting to drive them back to the cottage, where Claire had left her car.

Smiling at her attire, Sally emerged wearing a borrowed hospital gown and slippers, and a pair of nurse's trousers. Adrian gave her his anorak, saying, "My jersey will be enough for me. I'll turn up the car heater."

They spoke little on the short drive, neither Claire nor Adrian dwelling on the manhunt for Jasper Martinelli. Time enough later on to talk to Sally about her ordeal.

Adrian dropped them at the cottage, murmuring for the tenth time, "Thank God you're all right, Sally. I'll ring you tomorrow."

Sally changed into warm clothes while Claire packed a small bag for her, and a quarter of an hour later they were back at Bea's house.

Still dizzy and disoriented, Sally agreed to go straight to bed. They had both been given hot soup, bread, and tea at the hospital and wanted nothing more.

Claire's tears started again as she sat beside Sally, holding her in her arms. None of it was real—the terror, the utter despair, the sudden release. She would have to deal with the memories for a long time.

Sally's eyes were heavy. "It was Jasper, wasn't it, Mums?"

Claire nodded. "Yes, darling. It seems so. We'll talk tomorrow."

Hearing the phone, she went into her bedroom and picked up the receiver.

Neil.

"Claire, are you all right? And Sally?"

She tried to formulate words, but nothing came.

"Claire? Are you there?"

"Yes. We're all right. Sally is in bed."

"Good. We're combing the countryside for Martinelli."

A pause. Then Claire said, "I can't talk now. Good night."

Lying in her bed, she tried to focus on what had happened, but none of it was real to her. She only knew that she had believed Sally was dead and now she was alive. She lay with eyes wide open until exhaustion swept over her and at last she slept.

It was Sally who brought Claire out of her deep sleep. At her bedside the next morning, seeing that her mother was awake, she said, "I'll bring up our morning tea." Claire was ready, her pillows propped, when Sally arrived with the tray.

"Okay, Mums, let's talk about it!"

"Are you sure you want to do this, darling?"

"Of course! I took some aspirin for my head, but otherwise I'm fine. First, I want to know if they've found Jasper."

"Not that I've heard."

"Do they think he's the one who killed Cheryl?"

"Yes. Her clothes were found in the straw stack in the Priory garden."

"It's so strange, isn't it? Jasper was sort of eccentric

but he didn't seem like a madman. Maybe they never do."

"So it seems. Reading about serial killers, I've noticed that those who knew them invariably describe them as quite ordinary people and find it hard to believe what they have done."

Sally frowned. "Now, I want to know what happened to the baby?"

And Sally described the woman who had rung the bell of the cottage and laid an infant on the porch. "She dashed off around the corner of the house. I *had* to open the door, Mums. I couldn't leave the baby lying there in the cold, could I?"

"No, darling, of course you couldn't. But we know nothing about a baby."

"That's strange. Jasper must have used the woman as an accomplice. But where did she go?"

Claire mused. "Maybe there was no woman."

"But I saw her!"

"What if Jasper put on a skirt and wrapped up something—maybe a pillow—to look like a baby? You didn't see the person's face?"

"No. A scarf covered all but the eyes. Yes, it could have been a disguise. You know how dim that porch light is. Anyhow, I don't remember much after that horrid ether knocked me out. The next things I remember are so vague, they're like dreams."

And she told her mother about the hands caressing her body and the voice whispering, "Later."

"I woke up once and drank some more of whatever was in the glass. It tasted like sweet lemonade, only bitter at the same time. Must have been laced with something pretty strong, because most of the time, I was out of it."

Claire pressed her hand. "I'm so glad you weren't lying there in fear."

"Actually, I was too far gone to know what was

happening. I remember now, of course, that when he came at me on the porch, I was absolutely terrified. I tried to kick and struggle, but it was no use. The rest of it was simply unreal."

At the sound of the doorbell, Sally said, "I'll go," and started down the stairs, still in her gown and a robe borrowed from her mother.

Claire leaped out of bed and followed her. "Don't open the door!"

"I won't."

But she did, for it was Neil.

He held Sally in a long hug, then turned to Claire, his eyes searching her face.

"Are you all right, Claire?"

"I'm better this morning."

"I'm glad. Sally, we need a statement from you, but only when you're ready."

"No problem. I'm ready!"

At six o'clock that evening, a sergeant from the Morbridge police station was driving out on the moor, following a route prescribed on the map. On his tour of duty from four o'clock until midnight, he was part of a network combing the region in the search for Jasper Martinelli. His route took him some twelve to fifteen miles northwest of the town and covered three small villages, several farms, and large tracts of wild moorland, at least those portions accessible by road.

Not likely to be this close to home, the sergeant thought, but you never can tell with these weirdos. He may not know we're after him as yet, the bastard. Killing young women is the worst crime in the book. Good thing they found this last one before he finished her off.

At the tiny village of Lower Ashton, the sergeant pulled into the car park of the local inn and got out. Too bad he couldn't have a pint. Sometimes he bent the rules, along with others, but not on a case like this one.

The pub revealed no dark-haired, bearded chaps in their thirties. At the bar, he produced the police flyer with Jasper's picture. "Seen anyone like this?"

Half a dozen customers crowded around, but all shook their heads.

"If you see him, call in."

The sergeant went back to his car and had backed out onto the road when a car passed him going in the opposite direction. Wasn't that a Vauxhall? Hard to tell in the dark, but the lines looked right.

Backing and turning, he shot off in pursuit. Up a sharp incline, the road at the edge of the village forked. No car in sight. Then, on the right, a glimpse of headlamps beyond a curve.

Speeding along the narrow road, between a high stone wall on the left and hedgerows on the right, the sergeant gained on the car ahead of him, seeing the bulky lines that could be a Vauxhall. Around one more curve and he pulled close enough to see the number plate.

Yes! It was Martinelli, all right.

He turned on his siren, just as a car coming toward him passed the Vauxhall with inches to spare. As the car approached, the lane narrowed so that one of them must stop and give way, backing to a wider spot. Hearing the siren, the other driver backed up to let the police car pass, but time was lost in the maneuver.

Now the sergeant hurtled along the lane, at the same time calling in on his radio to give his location and to report that he had spotted Martinelli's car.

Minutes later, following the twisting road, he came up to the Vauxhall again, siren sounding. He saw the driver turn and stare. Looked like a beard, all right. This must be the man himself, not someone else driving his car.

Heart pounding, the sergeant tried to pull up beside the Vauxhall but was frustrated by another oncoming car. Pulling back until it had passed, he muttered, "Everybody and his bloody dog are out tonight."

A crossroad with a stop sign loomed ahead, and the Vauxhall came to a stop.

The sergeant leaped out and ran to the driver's window. "Are you Jasper Martinelli?"

"Yes."

"Please step out of the car."

Jasper stared at the officer. "What's this all about?"

"Just step out please."

Jerking the man's hands behind him, the sergeant fastened the handcuffs. "You have the right to remain silent. . . ."

He was still reciting the rights when another police car arrived, and the two officers exchanged looks of grim triumph.

"We've got him!"

Chapter

33

WHEN CLAIRE LEARNED that Jasper Martinelli had been captured, it was the final step in bringing her back to some semblance of normality. Well-being washed over her in healing waves. Sally was alive, and the world was swinging back into focus.

Sally stayed with her another night, but by Sunday morning, she was ready to go back to the cottage, and Claire agreed.

That afternoon, Sam Crane, Frieda's brother, took Claire out for a meal.

"I'm so glad your daughter's all right, Claire. What an ordeal for both of you."

They talked affectionately about Frieda, not so fondly of Barry Nolan. Barry had called Claire to tell her the lab results had confirmed that Frieda did have hypercholesterol. Claire had already read Barry off about his lying to her and his deceiving the police about Frieda's death, but it was like scolding a not-very-attentive child, and she decided it wasn't worth the effort.

She and Sam came back to her place for brandy, Sam sparkling with the special brand of charm that evoked bittersweet memories of Frieda. He had been divorced for two years and was obviously on the lookout, but decently so. He was going back to New York the next day, and when he said good-bye, he made it clear that he hoped to see her again, somehow, somewhere. She had told him about Neil, whom Sam had met the day before, when reporting his story of the cholesterol.

"He's a nice guy, Claire, but I can see the problems of a long-distance relationship."

She laughed. "From California to New York is not much better, Sam."

He kissed her lightly. "Keep me on the list, anyhow."

As he started out the door, Neil was coming up the walk, and the two shook hands.

"A pleasant chap," Neil said, as he settled by the fire. "I can't say the same for his brother-in-law. Barry and his lies have fouled things up between you and me. His solicitor told me yesterday the whole sordid tale of Mr. Bloody Nolan and his finding out about the 'C' mark on Cheryl's body. So he nicely carves one on his wife, puts her body out on the moor, and leads the constabulary on a merry chase."

"Barry says Nora McBain told him about the mark. Have you found out who told her?"

Neil gave a disgusted snort. "I sent a lad to ask her that question, and she looks at him with her innocent blue eyes and says, 'It was Bert Crofts.' One of my own constables. My God, Claire, I can't believe it. The little bastard came into my office—*my* office—one day to deliver a message and saw my DCI making a sketch of the mark, showing its placement between the breasts. He heard him say something that made it clear to Crofts what the mark was. So he gets little

Nora into the sack and babbles to her about it. Shows he's a big man, in the know, I suppose."

"What will happen to the constable?"

"If I have my way, he'll be out on his bum. He admits to having done it but he can't see what the bother is all about."

Silence.

"I know what you're thinking, Claire. That's what I want to talk about. This proves that someone else could—and did—know about the mark. I was wrong about that, and I am sorrier than I can say. Even if I'd known it was Crofts, I would not have seen a connection between him and Nolan. It was your friendship with Barry that misled me. I do apologize."

More silence.

"That's not really the point, Neil. If you had suspected such a thing and not asked me about it, I can see how you might make a wrong guess. But you did ask me, and I told you absolutely that I did not tell Barry, nor anyone. I know you tried to believe me but you couldn't be sure. What troubles me is that you were in doubt. Have I ever given you cause to believe you can't trust my word?"

"No, never."

"Then—?"

"This may sound odd, Claire, but I had begun to think of you as my wife, and that can cause all sort of short circuits in the brain."

"I don't understand."

"You see, Janice was an inveterate liar. She lied about everything, from trivia to matters of real import tance. It was so habitual with her that I came to won der if she knew the difference between truth and falsehood. At first, I didn't comprehend. I thought had misunderstood, or that there was some underlying reason for her to do what she did. Then I learned that it was a sort of compulsion."

"You've never told me this, Neil."

"No, I didn't like to remember it. In the beginning, I tried to change her, but it was no good. I grew accustomed to being unable to sort out the truth from the fiction, and in the end, I simply gave up."

"I see."

It was beginning to make sense. For sixteen years, Neil had lived with a woman who lied. He was conditioned to the proposition that wives are people who lie. It wasn't logical to extend that belief to Claire herself, but emotions don't usually follow the rules.

She put out her hand, and he took it in his. It might take her a while, but understanding was a major step toward healing.

The next afternoon, Claire had a phone call from a London art dealer. In her efforts to track down the missing Turner portrait, she had phoned the major auction houses in the city, asking for references to dealers who might be likely to have information for her, and sending letters to each.

"Dr. Camden? I have your letter concerning the possibility of unknown Turners. We are in the process of acquiring from a private collector a picture that appears to be a genuine Turner that has not been on the market for many years. Would you like to have a look at it?"

"What is the subject of the painting?"

"It's a small landscape. May be along the Thames at Twickenham. Looks to be from that period."

"No figures?"

"No."

"Unfortunately, that won't be of help to me. It's a portrait of a woman I'm looking for."

"Turner didn't do many portraits, you know."

Patiently, Claire said, "Yes, I am aware of that, but I should like to ask you a question, if I may?"

"Yes, of course."

The rather lengthy answer she received set her thinking once again about the missing Turner.

When she had seen Jasper Martinelli sitting with Rodney Simms at the Magistrate's Court, Claire had wondered if there could be a connection with the Turner in that apparent friendship. If Rodney knew, as she was sure he did, would he not have talked to his artist friend about it? Might they have conspired together to find the picture? Or would Jasper have pursued the search on his own?

If it were Jasper alone, it was possible that he was the one who attacked Mary Vickers and Claire herself that night in Sudbury. Had the two men been in collusion, Rodney would have left the cinema the moment he knew Mary Vickers was on her way home, to warn his friend. Since he did not do that, the intruder must have been acting alone. Rodney may have mentioned their plans to go to the film, and Jasper decided to take advantage of their absence.

Earlier, Claire would never have picked Jasper as her assailant, but now that he was known to be capable of murderous violence, it all made sense.

Talking with Neil about her suspicion, he had said he'd like to have some concrete evidence, if they could find any, and Claire had reminded him of the day she had gone up to London with Frieda. "At the Witt Library, someone had been there a few days before that, asking for Turner portraits. I had to sign in and out. Would you be able to find out who it was?"

And Neil had smiled. "The powers of the CID should easily cover a little matter of that kind."

Now the phone rang again.

"Hello, darling. I've just heard from London. Would you like to know whose name was given in at the Witt Library in London? None other than friend Jasper."

"Ah-hah. He certainly didn't learn anything there, but it does show that he knew about the painting."

Claire decided it was time for a little chat with Rodney. Phoning the Vickers household, she got Toby.

"I wonder if you can give me your neighbor Rodney's telephone number?"

"Rodney? I can, yes, but he's here. Shall I put him on?"

"Yes, please."

"Rodney here."

"If I come in to Sudbury around five o'clock today, may I see you?"

"Yes, of course. Shall I meet you here at The Laurels?"

"That would be fine. See you then."

Toby opened the door to Claire, put her in the parlor, and offered tea.

"Thank you, Toby, but I've had my tea."

Then Rodney Simms arrived, his round face looking anxious. "Something wrong, Dr. Camden?"

"No, not really. I think it's time we talked openly about the missing Turner. Do you agree?"

"Yes."

Toby stared. "The *what?*"

Then Claire told him the story of Prudence Halley's letters.

Toby looked at Rodney. "You knew about this, Rodney, and you didn't tell Mum and me?"

Rodney turned slightly pink but held his ground. "It's like this, Tobe. I thought I might find the painting and surprise your mother with it. It should fetch a very good price, if it's genuine."

Claire said, "And Mrs. Vickers would no doubt insist on a nice commission for the finder?"

Rodney nodded innocently. "Nothing wrong with that, is there?"

Ignoring this, Claire went on. "Rodney, I want to ask about your friendship with Jasper Martinelli."

Woebegone, Rodney shook his head. "The police have already questioned me about Jasper. I was horrified when I learned he had been arrested for murdering that girl, and now they say he abducted your daughter as well. I'm very glad she is safe, Dr. Camden. I can't believe it of Jasper, but I expect everyone says that when this sort of thing happens."

"Yes, I'm afraid so. Now, Rodney, did you tell Jasper about the painting?"

"Yes, I did. I thought, as he's an artist himself, he might have some ideas about how to find it."

"Did he tell you he had gone to the Courtauld in London to check on sources?"

"No, he never mentioned it."

"His name was on their check slips at the Witt Library several weeks ago."

"He must have been operating on his own, then."

"Yes, it would seem so. Now, Rodney, did you tell Jasper about going to the cinema with Toby and his mother the night she and I were attacked?"

Rodney's eyes rounded. "Why, yes. He was to join us there, but he never came. He told me next day he'd been ill the evening before. You don't mean—?"

"It's possible, isn't it? He believed the house would be empty for at least two hours, giving him a chance to search for the picture."

"That's daft, though, Dr. Camden. I told him—"

Rodney stopped, the pink flooding his face again.

"You told him you'd already searched pretty thoroughly yourself?" asked Claire.

"Well, I did have a look round, especially in the attic."

"It all seems rather silly to me, anyhow, Rodney. Surely, if Mrs. Vickers had found such a portrait, she would have told you about it."

"Yes, but I wondered if, instead of being on a stretcher, it might be rolled up or hidden in some other way. Perhaps that was Jasper's idea too, if he came to look for it. I found a bolt of fabric that might have served, but when I unrolled it, there was nothing there."

Presently, Mary Vickers came in and was told, at last, the story of the Turner. Claire half expected an explosion when the lady learned that Rodney had kept the information from her, but Mary looked at Rodney with a smile. "I never did read all those letters with the spidery handwriting. It was good of you, Rodney, to try to find the painting for me."

See no evil, thought Claire. Better this way.

Claire had been staring from time to time at the Prudence Halley painting in its gold frame over the mantel. A theory had been forming in her mind all day, ever since her talk with the London art dealer. She remembered the scene in the novel *Eleanor* when the painter, dissatisfied with his first effort at his lady's portrait, decided to begin again and capture the radiance of her face once they had declared their love.

If she, Claire, had been Prudence Halley, in terrible fear that her nephew's friend might rob her of her most precious possession, what would she have done?

She told her trio of listeners what she suspected, and secured Mary Vickers' permission to have the matter investigated.

Then Mary went to a cabinet in the desk and drew out a small packet, handing it to Claire. "I received these yesterday from a Halley cousin near Clovelly. I haven't looked at them as yet, but you are welcome to take them and return them if you like."

No objection from Toby this time.

When Claire took her leave, she drove into Sudbury and stopped at a small cafe for a coffee, opening the letters Mrs. Vickers had given her.

There were three letters, written by Eustace Halley to his wife while she was away on a visit to their daughter. The letters were dated 1908, by which time Eustace would have been in his sixties, an age which almost a century ago was regarded as nearing the end of one's life. Two gave accounts of the trivia of daily routine, adding personal expressions of affection. In the third letter, Eustace wrote that he had long wanted to tell her of an episode in his youth which troubled him deeply, but of which he had been unable to speak.

"As you know," he wrote, "I was a wayward youth, causing much pain to my family. When I was sent to stay with my dear Aunt Prudence, I behaved very badly to her, taking up with a man named Spicer who was disreputable in every way."

The letter then went on to recount the tragedy of his aunt's death, his terrible belief that Spicer was the culprit, and his fear that if he named the man, he would be implicated himself. The letter mentioned the Turner painting only in passing, Eustace evidently being more concerned with his own moral dilemma than with a piece of art.

"I truly loved my dear aunt," he wrote, "and after her death my whole way of life changed. I tried to become a person worthy of her memory, and only you, my dear wife, can tell me if I have succeeded."

Claire folded the letters and put them in her bag. Eustace's confession would appear in a few lines in her biography, as a wrap-up to the whole Halley episode. She only wished that Prudence might have seen the letter.

Chapter

34

DRIVING BACK TO MORBRIDGE, Claire checked her watch. Neil was due at seven, bringing takeaway from the Tandoori. With luck, she would make it just in time. It was good to be reconciled with Neil again. The night before, he had stayed over, the first time they had made love since the episode that had estranged them. When she had had a nightmare about Sally, it had been wonderful to have him there, holding her. Still, she had no intention of becoming dependent on his presence. Better to keep a balance, if she could.

Neil was waiting when she arrived at Bea's house, and they exchanged a warm kiss the moment they were inside the door. He put the food in the kitchen and went to the drinks trolley. "Do you mind if I have a whiskey?"

Claire said, "Of course not. Give me one, too."

She lit the fire and they took their drinks to the sofa.

"Something's come up, Claire, and I don't know what to make of it."

Glad he could talk to her again, she asked, "What is it?"

"I heard from the laboratory this afternoon. They've run DNA checks. You remember there was seminal fluid found in the bodies of both Cheryl Bailey and Frieda Nolan. We had cross-checked earlier and found they did not match, meaning it was probably not the same killer. When Barry Nolan was arrested, he was tested, and *there was no semen!* That's when the doctor guessed he had had a vasectomy, and Barry admitted that he had."

Claire felt a twinge of guilt at her assumption at the hearing that Neil had relied on his own knowledge for that fact.

Neil went on. "Since the semen in Cheryl's body could not have come from Barry, we didn't seriously suspect him of that crime. Furthermore, he's too old to fit the usual type in these cases—young men in their twenties or thirties. We'd never have let him out on bail except for that, believe me.

"We were puzzled about the semen in his wife's body, but knowing she had a lover cleared up that problem. Now you see why I believed someone had told him about the C mark."

"Of course. If he hadn't killed Cheryl, he could only have learned about it from someone else."

"Exactly. But now we come to the shocker. Jasper Martinelli's DNA matches that of the semen in *Frieda's* body but not in that of *Cheryl!*"

"Then Jasper must have been Frieda's lover?"

"Yes, he freely admits that he was but says he knows nothing about her death."

Claire pondered. "But if there is no match with Cheryl, Jasper could not be the killer?"

"Unless Cheryl had sexual relations with someone else that day, and the killer—Jasper or whoever—did not in fact attack her sexually. Not a very likely scenario."

"If Cheryl was actually having an affair with the professor, George Foley, that could account for it, I suppose. Or Foley himself could be the killer."

Neil nodded gloomily.

Claire asked, "Where does Jasper say he went after he left the Priory last Thursday?"

"He says he drove across the moor to Yelverton to look up a friend but found him gone, so he turned back to Twin Bridges, where he had dinner and spent the night at a pub. The people there confirmed that he came in quite late, close to nine o'clock, so he might have taken Sally, left her in the crypt, and driven anywhere at all, ending at the Bridges and intending to go back for her later, as that's not many miles from Morbridge."

Neil took a double swallow of his drink. "I feel as if the case is breaking apart, Claire. The truth is, I've been troubled about Martinelli from the day he came into the station. He looked like a startled rabbit when he was accused of the crimes, and he repeats quietly that he knows nothing about any of it. That in itself is nothing new for an accused person, but sex offenders often have a different pattern. They seem to be perfectly ordinary men, but under extensive questioning, they show a good deal of twitching and nervousness. Jasper looks baffled but quite tranquil. In itself, it means nothing, but it troubles me."

"What did he say about the diamond brooch with the initial C?"

"He says it isn't diamonds, just faux stones, and he gave it to Cynthia himself."

"And the doodles?"

"He says he's always doodled with her initial since they were married. He was extremely fond of her."

Claire said, "By the way, darling, I went to Sudbury

today." She gave him an account of her visit there, ending with the theory that Jasper had been Mary Vickers' and her attacker at The Laurels. "But just now I remembered something that should have been obvious before. I'm sure that the man who attacked me *did not have a beard.* His face was very close to mine, and I'd surely have felt it."

"Yes, I believe you would."

"Which reminds me: Sally didn't mention her attacker having a beard, but she was so sedated, she may not have known one way or the other."

Neil frowned. "Exactly. I've been thinking about the professor, and there's a problem. Since he has always been on our subsidiary list of suspects, I had someone check his whereabouts at the time Sally was abducted. He was at his local, with at least three cronies to testify he had been there from five o'clock until after half-past six, at which time his wife came in to join him and they stayed until seven. Furthermore, Foley has been at Exeter for only two years, has no acquaintance with either Adrian or Jasper, and would have no knowledge of the location of the crypt under the Priory."

Now Claire looked into Neil's eyes, and her voice shook. "That is the real crux, isn't it?"

"Yes. If Jasper Martinelli is innocent, who else could have known about the crypt?"

"Oh, my God! *Adrian!*"

They had agreed upon their plan. Claire rang up Sally to say she was coming to the cottage with a warm robe for her. "You forgot to take it with you yesterday, dear. Are you alone?"

"No, Adrian's here. We're having dinner."

"Good. I'll be there soon."

Claire took her own car, and Neil was to follow

after picking up a constable from the Morbridge station to accompany him.

Doing her best to behave naturally, Claire arrived at the cottage, handing Sally the warm robe she had brought for her and answering Adrian's greeting with a friendly smile.

"We've just finished our meal, Mums. Want some coffee?"

"Yes, sounds good."

Adrian began to clear the table, and Claire stood in the kitchen doorway watching as Sally made the coffee and Adrian put the dinner dishes in the sink to soak. Such a comfortable companionship. Impossible, what she and Neil had been thinking.

Hearing a car in the drive, Sally looked out the window. "It's Neil. And he has an officer with him. I thought I'd answered everything, but I suppose they always think of more questions."

Claire saw Adrian's face. Puzzled. Watchful.

As Sally opened the front door for Neil, Adrian looked at Claire. "I really must be going, Mrs. Camden. Will you tell Sally I'll see her later on?"

He turned and opened the service door at the back of the cottage, jumping back as he saw the uniformed constable on the stoop.

Neil stepped into the kitchen. "Adrian Abbott, we wish to question you in connection with the death of Cheryl Bailey and the abduction of Sally Camden. You may remain silent, but anything you say will be taken down and may be used in evidence."

At Neil's first words, Adrian's face was distorted with fury, and with the words of the caution hanging in the air, he burst out. "What are you saying? It's *Jasper* who did it! You said it was Jasper! You've arrested him because he's guilty! Mummy's name was Cynthia, and he desecrated her name. He carved her

267

initial on that girl's body, and he would have done it on Sally here, if we hadn't found her first!"

His eyes wild, he shouted, "Who but Jasper would put the girl's clothes in the compost heap? He was always mucking about in the garden. He drew Mummy's initial over everything he touched. He's nobody. His father was a common farm laborer, and he dared to make love to Mummy."

Now his voice dropped to a whisper. "It wasn't her fault, you see, he mesmerized her. She really loved me best all along, she told me so. I knew he was worthless, and now it's proved he's a murderer. Poor Mummy. She was so lovely, so lovely."

When Adrian had been taken away to the station, sobbing but still protesting, Claire held Sally close to her, expecting shocked incredulity. Instead, Sally said, "There's been something wrong with Adrian for the last week or so. Of course I had no idea it could be anything like this, but he's been extremely jumpy and nervous at times, and talked more than usual about his mother, as if he couldn't help himself. And ever since Jasper was arrested, Adrian's been jubilant. I began to see that he really hated Jasper and that all his tolerance had been a cover-up."

Claire bristled. "But Sally, I can't believe he would attack *you*. He seemed so genuinely fond of you."

Sally shook her head, and now the tears came. "I think he was—very fond of me, but obviously he's mentally disturbed."

Claire swallowed. "I've never asked you, darling, but were you in love with Adrian?"

"No, never. It was wonderful, in a way, to have him as a friend, because he never asked for more. I did think it was odd that he never tried to make love. For a while, I thought he might be—well, like Daddy. Then I decided he had some kind of hangup, and I suppose, if all this is true, that's what it was. But Mums, what's all this about the initial C?"

"I believe it's all right to tell you now, darling."

When she had finished, Sally said, "But how do we know it's really Adrian who did this? He may be insane, but maybe Jasper really did do the crimes?"

"I'm afraid Adrian gave himself away, dear. He spoke of Jasper carving the initial on Cheryl's body, but you see, no one but the killer knew about that."

Chapter

35

IT WAS FEBRUARY, and Claire, back in her London flat, was still haunted by the events of two months earlier, still trying to convince herself that Sally was safe. There had been no doubt about Adrian's guilt, confirmed by his DNA match to the semen in Cheryl Bailey's body. Although he had admitted to that crime, he claimed from the first that he never intended to kill Sally, that the whole episode was set up to incriminate Jasper. The idea came to him, he said, when Jasper told him he was going away for a few days and would stop at the house after the court hearing to pick up his things.

Adrian had taken a skirt and shawls from his mother's wardrobe and lured Sally out of the house. His plan was to reveal her whereabouts in the crypt, and when Sally described her abduction, Jasper would be suspected. What terrified Claire now was that the psychiatrists who examined Adrian were not sure this would have been the outcome.

To begin with, the doctors began to suspect that

Cheryl had not been Adrian's first victim. During the year or so after his mother's death, he had lived here and there on the Continent, and when his bank disclosed various addresses to which his quarterly stipend had been sent, investigation revealed other victims of unsolved crimes near the locations where he had lived. The bodies of two young women—one in France and one in Italy—had been marked with the telltale C, and Adrian, when confronted, had eventually confessed to both killings. Unable to have normal sexual relations with young women, he succeeded only when his victims became surrogates for his mother.

The doctors described Adrian's case as characteristic: he appeared in speech and behavior to be quite rational, but he showed no remorse for his actions, explaining that when he was seized with the desire to kill, it was beyond his control for the brief time it lasted. Asked if he would kill again if he were released, he had said quite calmly that he supposed he would if "the craving" returned. At this point, it seemed only too probable that if the madness had seized him while Sally was in the crypt, he would have ignored his plan about Jasper, and her death would have been inevitable.

Claire had said nothing to Sally but had confided in Neil her terrible fear that some day Adrian might get out of prison and come looking for Sally.

It was an early morning in the third week of February when the phone rang in her London flat as she was pouring her first cup of coffee. It was Neil, at his office in Kings Abbey. "Hello, darling. Something's happened. It will be in the news any minute, and I want you to hear it from me."

"Yes, what is it?"

"It's Adrian. He somehow managed to fashion a noose from his clothing and he hanged himself in his cell. He was found this morning."

Claire gripped the phone, her heart pounding. "Oh, Neil, I have to be glad. It's a terrible tragedy, but—"

"Yes, but what was there in store for him? A life behind bars, or worse, a release, only to kill another innocent victim."

Sally, when she was told, reacted as Neil had done. "It's for the best in the end, isn't it?"

Sally had rebounded with remarkable strength from the whole experience. Claire had worried that her daughter would be haunted by distrust, that each new friendship would bring an automatic fear that this person might prove to be false. On the contrary, Sally's response, after the initial shock had subsided, was the sensible one that this event was so bizarre, so utterly rare, that it couldn't happen to her again. She'd been mildly fond of Adrian, she told her mother, but had always found him a bit odd, not someone she could have cared for seriously, and she didn't intend to spend the rest of her life suspecting everybody she met.

As for Jasper, he had taken the whole episode with his customary tranquility. On his release, he had expressed little surprise on hearing of Adrian's attempt to frame him. "I always knew he disliked me, poor sod, but so long as he behaved decently, I stayed on at the Priory."

When asked about the Turner painting, he said he had told Adrian, in one of their rare conversations, the story as he heard it from Rodney Simms. "He was terribly keen about it. He was mad for money, you see. He hated living on what he regarded as a pittance from Cynthia, whereas my share is plenty for me."

Jasper said he had visited the Courtauld in London some time ago, but not the Witt Library, nor had he ever thought of searching for the painting. It must have been Adrian who signed his name at the Witt. Yes, he had been ill one evening and asked Adrian for some aspirins, saying he was due to meet Rodney and the Vickers family at the cinema in Sudbury but was unable to go. So, clearly, it had been Adrian who attacked Mary Vickers and Claire herself that night in Sudbury.

And now the missing Turner had been found, and Claire took modest pride in her part in the affair. On her last visit to Sudbury, the idea had formed in her mind after her conversation with the London art dealer, together with remembering the scene from the novel *Eleanor*. Then, as she sat in the Vickers parlor, staring at the Prudence Halley painting over the mantel, her theory began to take shape.

Putting herself into the mind of Prudence Halley on that long-ago day, alone, with no one to help her, afraid the man Spicer would steal her beloved portrait, what would she have done? Claire thought she knew.

Prudence took the portrait down from the wall in her bedroom, carried it to her studio, locked the door, and went to work. First she removed the frame, mounted the painting on a stretcher, and placed it on her easel. Over the next two days, she accomplished her purpose. First, a heavy coat of varnish, to preserve the finish of the original. When that was thoroughly dry, she covered the canvas with a white ground. Then the final step: a painting of her own, with the title *Sunrise at Sea* and her initials in the corner. Dried and back into the frame, she took it downstairs and hung it over the mantel in the parlor. Some day in the future, when the danger was past, she would carefully remove the outer layers and have her portrait back. The best guess was that the man Spicer had arrived at The Laurels with the intention of stealing the portrait, finding instead the wall empty and the painting gone. When Prudence came back unexpectedly, he must have tried to force her to tell him what she had done with the Turner, and struck her in his fury and frustration.

Claire had read about paintings being discovered under other ones, but what she did not know, and what the London art dealer had told her in answer to her question, was that under the right circumstances, the surface may be removed and the original completely restored. Prudence undoubtedly knew that too, perhaps from reading about such discoveries.

With Mary Vickers' cooperation, the Halley painting had been X-rayed and Claire's guess had been confirmed. It was painstaking work for the experts, but the heavy varnish over the original had made it possible to remove the outer layers and reveal the portrait underneath.

Now, in the last week of February, the work was to be ready to view. On the appointed day, Mary and Toby Vickers came up to London with the ubiquitous Rodney, and Claire joined them at the studio of the restorer.

"There are still bits and pieces to be done," the young woman explained, "but most of the original is intact."

She drew the cover from the canvas and there, at last, was Prudence. Certainly no beauty, but far more attractive than she had believed herself to be. Straight, level brows, a firm chin, eyes neither large nor luminous, but with a forthright expression a twist of humor in the mouth, warm but ironic, that added a touch of charm.

"Not much to look at, was she?" said Toby irreverently. "But I expect she was a nice lady all the same."

The portrait was to be auctioned, Claire firmly declining Mary's offer of a share in the proceeds, and asking only for permission to reproduce the painting in her biography.

Before she left Morbridge in January, Claire had seen little of Barry Nolan. Barry had landed on his feet, so to speak, and was back at the university. The charge of manslaughter had eventually been dropped and he pleaded to the lesser charge of interfering with a police investigation. Severely chastised by the judge and given a hefty fine, he apologized to the court, but the apology cut no ice with Neil Padgett, who said Claire could baby Nolan if she wanted to, but he washed his hands of him. Claire was inclined to agree, and Barry, sincerely mourning Frieda's death, kept his distance.

Recently, however, she had had a friendly note from Barry telling her that Nora McBain was engaged to be married and that he had been asked to give the bride away when the happy day came. Her friend Hubert Hart had finally made the break from his mother, taken a place of his own in Morbridge, and helped Nora obtain her divorce through the solicitor's office where he was a clerk. Nora was radiant, Barry wrote. It seems she had been "ever so taken" with Hubert from the first, and looked forward to a secure home for little Willie as well as a happy life for herself.

Barry also reported that he had met the wife of Maurice Webb, his solicitor, a sweet-faced woman who had told him they looked forward with pleasure to the arrival of their first grandchild, as "Maurice is so fond of babies." I was right, Claire thought. Webb was indeed a true Wemmick.

As for Neil, things were pretty much back to normal

between them. Who was she to expect a rose garden? As Shakespeare so aptly said:

> Roses have thorns and silver fountains mud,
> Clouds and eclipses stain both moon and sun,
> And loathsome canker lives in sweetest bud.

Thorns or not, she would certainly rather have Neil in her life right now than out of it.